Beth Ann didn't want to think about James Thomas going away and never coming back.

"Is Montana so very different from Nebraska?" she asked.

"Very different," James Thomas replied. "There are tall mountains topped with snow, even in the summer. And there are trees reaching to the heavens. The air is so fresh and clear you can taste it, and when you walk across the ground the dust does not swirl up and choke you."

His voice held a touch of wistfulness he had thought never to feel again. His dream of living in the beautiful country he had chosen was blighted by the knowledge that Beth Ann would not be there to share it with him. By the time he would be able to return to Fort Kearney, she would most likely have no thought for him other than a distant memory....

Dear Reader,

This month, we are happy to bring you the next installment in Margaret Moore's Warrior series. *A Warrior's Quest* follows the path of the disillusioned Urien Fitzroy, a mercenary soldier who is no longer content to live his life by the sword.

Julie Keane has no use for an indentured servant more suited to be the lord of the manor than a common laborer, but Zachariah Hale soon proves his mettle in *Bound by Love,* from the writing team of Erin Yorke.

Web of Loving Lies by Barbara Leigh is a heartwarming tale of two sisters whose lives become inescapably intertwined with a man who falls in love with one sister, but is forced into marrying the other.

From author Beverlee Ross comes the story of a weary gunslinger, Clint Strand, who finds himself amazingly willing to be saddled with *Annabelle,* a feisty young woman who isn't afraid of anything.

Next month marks the release of our Western historical short story collection—UNTAMED. With authors Heather Graham Pozzessere, Joan Johnston and Patricia Potter contributing, this is one collection you won't want to miss!

Sincerely,

Tracy Farrell
Senior Editor

Web of Loving Lies

BARBARA LEIGH

Harlequin Books

TORONTO • NEW YORK • LONDON
AMSTERDAM • PARIS • SYDNEY • HAMBURG
STOCKHOLM • ATHENS • TOKYO • MILAN
MADRID • WARSAW • BUDAPEST • AUCKLAND

Harlequin Historicals first edition June 1993

ISBN 0-373-28777-1

WEB OF LOVING LIES

BARBARA LEIGH

discovered romance at the tender age of five, when she got chills listening to Snow White sing about Prince Charming. It was then that she realized "there was life after Dick and Jane." Unable to find the kind of stories she sought, Barbara began making up her own and never stopped.

Barbara, who has five children and six grandchildren, lives in Southern California with her husband, a large doll collection, two dogs and a cat. Located high above the family room, the loft where she writes is affectionately known as "fairyland."

For my mother, Dorothy Young, who believes

Chapter One

While it had been said that all men were created equal, such was obviously not the case with women, for although Melisue Cadwalder was round and curvaceous, her younger sister, Beth Ann, was small, with a body as straight and flat as a board.

No matter which way she turned as she rotated before the mirror in her mother's stateroom on the *Louisiana Queen*, Beth Ann could not find an angle that gave her a more mature appearance. If she looked older, perhaps James Thomas, the handsome frontiersman her father had sent to escort them on their journey, would have taken some notice of her. It certainly wasn't Beth Ann's fault if she had fallen ill with the plague that ravaged New Orleans before the war. And it was a miracle she had survived.

She crossed herself quickly, hoping the good Lord didn't think her ungrateful that her life had been spared. But it did seem unfair that Beth Ann's health had been impaired, leaving her subject to spells of unwelcome weakness, while Melisue had come through unscathed, fairly bursting with beauty and life.

James Thomas certainly noticed Melisue, but then, everyone noticed Melisue. It was impossible to ignore her shining black hair and dancing blue eyes. While Beth Ann carried the same coloring, she lacked the sparkling effect of

Melisue's radiance. She felt like a faded copy of her beautiful sister, unable to appreciate the fragile loveliness that was her own.

She pinched her cheeks, which seemed paler than usual, and she looked closely in the wavering mirror, hoping she would not be seasick during the trip. She did not want to be cooped up in a cabin with Melisue. And Melisue had already decided to be indisposed for the whole journey. In a way it seemed only right that Melisue would not enjoy their trip, for had it not been for Melisue's wayward ways and ultimate indiscretion, there would have been no need for the Cadwalder Family to leave their lovely home in New Orleans.

But, as their mother had pointed out, it was too late to cry over spilt milk, and the journey on which they were about to embark would enable their family to be together again.

Beth Ann drew herself up to her full height. No, she wouldn't be sick, not Beth Ann Cadwalder. Not while James Thomas was aboard the same boat and she was free to keep him company. Somehow she must make him realize that she was, indeed, a young woman, hardly more than a year younger than her voluptuous sister.

Beth Ann had never given a thought to the contrast between her own appearance and that of her sister until the handsome frontiersman had come into their lives. Dismissing the problem of her development, or lack thereof, Beth Ann slipped through the door to the deck, almost colliding with a portly matron.

Her attempt at an apology was met with an effusive "Why, if it isn't little Beth Ann Cadwalder! What a surprise to see you here. I heard you folks were on your way to Boston after that unfortunate incident with Melisue." The woman's voice carried across the deck, and several heads turned in their direction.

"It seems you were misinformed," Beth Ann replied, with all the dignity she could muster.

"But I heard your house was all shut up and boarded over." The woman's eyes narrowed as she considered what she knew of the situation. The disgrace of the older daughter. The duel that had left a man dead and a warrant out for Brandt Cadwalder's arrest. The burning of the little shop near the cathedral, and the disappearance of the proprietor. The appearance of a tall, handsome young man who had insisted on wearing buckskins in one of the most prestigious areas of New Orleans as he accompanied Suzanna Cadwalder on her rounds. "Don't tell me you are movin' to St. Louis."

"Very well, Mrs. Bouchard, I won't tell you anything, except goodbye." Beth Ann turned on her heel and left the woman standing openmouthed in astonishment.

Cheeks burning with indignation, Beth Ann made her way to the rail, where she took deep breaths and watched the river churn by.

"You handled that very nicely," James Thomas said as he leaned casually against the rail beside her.

Somewhat taken aback by his sudden appearance and still trying to recover from the confrontation with the Bouchard woman, Beth Ann blurted out, "She's a nosy old busybody gloating over the misfortunes of others."

He put his arm around her shoulder. "It's all right. You handled the situation with dignity. I doubt if Melisue could have done better at putting the woman in her place."

"If it weren't for Melisue, this never would have happened." Beth Ann's voice caught in her throat. Then she amended, "But it wasn't all Melisue's fault. I should have found a better way to tell Mama and Papa."

He patted her shoulder. She seemed such a fragile girl to try to assume the burdens of her family. "Surely it wasn't your place to tell your parents of the situation."

"But I was the only one who knew, other than Melisue. When she came running into the house, she hardly had time to tell me what had happened before Mama and Papa came home. 'You tell them, Beth Ann,' she begged. 'They never get mad at you.' But gossip travels quickly in New Orleans, and I knew it was already too late when I heard Mama tell Papa she had heard that one of the young ladies from the convent school was seen in the company of a Madame Miggons, who ran a small shop near the cathedral."

As she poured out the story to James Thomas, Beth Ann agonized over the day her world had been turned upside down by Melisue's indiscretion. Everything had happened so quickly. It was as if a floodtide had raced through their lives and swept the Cadwalder Family away.

"They say the woman is a procurer for the houses of ill repute off Canal Street," she had heard her mother tell her father. "The old woman had actually sold the child's virginity to one of her customers, and was about to deliver her to the man when the girl saw something amiss and ran."

"She must have known the woman for some time to have become friendly enough to ride out with her," her father had said. "The girl's morals may have been a bit loose to begin with."

"It hardly matters now," Suzanna replied. "As soon as names are named, the poor thing will be ruined. I daresay it's doubtful that any of a family of that caliber would continue to be received in our circle." Suzanna Cadwalder was very proud of the social circle of which she was a leader. Her family was one of the oldest in Virginia, while her husband came from the Cadwalders of Boston. "There is no blight worse than a social blight," Suzanna intoned righteously. "As you say, the young woman must be lax morally, or quite a fool."

Her mother's words sent tremors of distress through Beth Ann's thin body. "That's not true," Beth Ann cried as she emerged from her hiding place and ran down the stairs. "She didn't have any idea the old woman was so wicked."

The look of astonishment on her mother's face told Beth Ann she had once again acted without thinking, but it was too late now.

"What do you know about this?" her father demanded.

"I heard ... that is, I was told ..." Her words trailed off into sobs.

"Merciful God, tell me it wasn't you!" her mother cried.

Beth Ann shook her head. "It wasn't me, Mama. It was Melisue!"

Her mother's hands fell to her side as the color drained from her face. "Where is your sister?" she managed, and Beth Ann motioned reluctantly to the second floor. Her mother raced up the stairs, and her father followed closely behind.

Brandt Cadwalder confronted his older daughter. "How did you get into this situation?" He tried to be calm, but his hands opened and closed spasmodically as he fought to hold his temper. "How does this woman know you?"

Melisue gave a little sob. "Madame Miggons had tippets of lace, and flowers crafted of satin ... and cakes, and biscuits with jam. Besides, it was no more than a few steps from the church. I would tell the nuns I was going with the other girls to pray, but instead I would go to Madame Miggons's shop. Then, this afternoon, Madame asked me if I would ride with her to make a delivery. She said she needed help, but after we got into the coach I realized she hadn't brought any of her goods. When I asked, she said I was not to be afraid. But I *was* afraid, and when the coach slowed down I jumped out and ran back to the school. The priest and two of the nuns brought me home."

Seeing the shock on her mother's face, and the almost insane anger on her father's, Melisue continued quickly, "Nothing happened, though, I swear it. And I've been punished enough. I thought my lungs would explode when I tried to run, my corset was laced so tightly."

"We will all bear the punishment for this day," her father said. "Now, who was the man? Think, Melissa. You must have some idea who he was."

"I don't remember anyone in particular. There have been a lot of men in Madame's shop lately. It could have been any one of them. I didn't pay any attention. Most of them were Yankees."

Brandt Cadwalder's face turned so red that his wife forgot her concern over her daughter and rushed after him as he bolted down the stairs, shouting for the butler.

"Get the men together. I want every able-bodied man on this place out here now," he ordered.

Caleb, the butler, had been born on Suzanna's parents' plantation outside Richmond, Virginia. Freed when Suzanna had married, he had served as valet and then taken over as butler for the Cadwalders. He was no less outraged than his employer. "The men are already waiting out back," he assured them.

"What are you going to do?" Suzanna asked as she grabbed her husband's cloak. "You can't take an army of men into the French Quarter. The Yankees won't allow it. The Yankees will kill you. Please, Brandt, don't go."

"Our daughter's reputation is ruined. Our family name will be on every vicious tongue in New Orleans by morning. I will have restitution, and have it now, by God!"

"They may never know," Suzanna fired back. "The priest and nuns wouldn't dare tell. It reflects on their ability to watch their students."

"And what of the people who must have seen her racing down the street like a madwoman? What of them? Do you believe they will not remember, or did not recognize Melisue?''

Suzanna hid her face in her hands and sobbed quietly. Brandt put his arms around his wife and held her close, stroking her soft, dark hair.

His eyes met those of Beth Ann, and he held out his hand to her. She looked up at him with the same guileless blue eyes her mother possessed. How proud he had always been of his daughters, who were the very image of his darkhaired, blue-eyed wife. Now, that vanity had proven to be his undoing.

''I will do what must be done.'' He released them both and walked through the door without looking back.

''The next morning our father was gone,'' Beth Ann said in sad summation, ''and I had not heard from him until you arrived to take us away.''

She looked up at James Thomas, her eyes filled with gratitude and awash with tears. It had been such a relief to pour her heart out to him. To feel the solid pressure of his hand on her shoulder, encouraging, protecting, and understanding the sorrow in her heart. She had no words with which to express the full extent of her gratitude, so she said instead, ''It was ever so nice of you to escort us to our destination, Mister James Thomas.''

He smiled at her habit of calling him by both names. ''I am honored to have the opportunity to escort such lovely ladies, but my real job will not begin until we reach St. Louis.''

''What is your real job?'' She looked up at him speculatively, squinting her eyes against the sun.

''I'm a scout. I ride with the wagon trains that take people across the prairie.''

''But isn't that dangerous and lonely?''

''There is danger everywhere, and loneliness is only a state of mind. You can be lonely right here on this boat full of people, and you can be completely happy alone in the wilderness."

Beth Ann considered his words. "I'm certainly not lonely with all these people around, but Melisue has had a perfectly terrible time. She hasn't seen anyone but Mama and myself, and, of course, our servants."

The frown that crossed James Thomas's face was not lost on the girl. He hadn't approved of their taking a full complement of servants, but Suzanna had insisted that any of their people who did not want to return to the plantation in Virginia be allowed to come along. Five of them, including Caleb, the butler, and Rachael Bright, were making the trip.

"One can't be without one's servants," Suzanna had protested. They were part of the Cadwalder entourage; where the Cadwalder family went, their servants went, also.

There was no sense in arguing the point with Beth Ann, James Thomas decided. The family would have to cope with the opinions of the people who would be their neighbors. People who had fought on both sides in the War between the States and who were very opinionated in their ideas of what was right and wrong. There was no way to bring a group of darkies into the area without causing consternation.

Though free, the servants must either work and live within the house with the family without noticeable remuneration, which would be viewed by some as an extension of a form of slavery, or be given land and help to build houses of their own, which would place them as equals to their neighbors, some of whom were Southerners and would not appreciate the situation.

"Your sister decided long before we boarded the boat that she would not leave her bed until we reached our destination," James Thomas said. "Any discomfort she suffered was brought on by her own inclination."

Beth Ann giggled. "I didn't think you knew."

He reached out to ruffle her hair as he would with a child on a wagon train, but he stopped before completing his action. There was a dignity about her, despite her size. Just as there was trust in the wide blue eyes that gazed up at him, eyes filled with merriment at the secret they shared. He laughed aloud, as much at himself for being in awe of the girl as at anything that had been said.

"We are even, Miss Beth. I hadn't realized you were aware of your sister's wiles."

Beth Ann paused for a few moments. "My sister has many wiles," she said in a small voice. "Please remember that when she decides to use them on you."

This time his laughter rang out over the deck. He leaned forward. "And would you be jealous, little one, if I were to succumb to her wiles?"

Beth Ann turned away, her hoops swishing in female indignation. "I would be very disappointed to find you were fool enough to be taken in after you've been warned."

She tripped off down the deck and disappeared around the corner while James Thomas hooted with laughter.

Once out of his sight, Beth Ann leaned weakly against the rail. She had made a fool of herself in front of a man she liked, and she had most probably led him to believe she was jealous and vindictive regarding Melisue. Would she never learn not to speak on impulse? Why did her tongue act before her brain censored her words? Melisue never had such problems, but then, Melisue never said anything to a man except "How handsome you look" and "My, aren't you just too intelligent." There had to be more to conversation than that.

It didn't matter that James Thomas had laughed at her. Beth Ann could bear that, but she worried that he would hate her for her unkind words regarding her sister. While they were true, she was afraid they had sounded mean and cruel, and that was the last thing in the world she wanted James Thomas to think of her.

Beth Ann had never met anyone like him before. The moment he had arrived at their home in New Orleans, everything had changed.

Her mother had just finished marking the last of a number of boxes with Boston printed prominently on each one when the butler had announced a visitor.

"James Thomas, at your service. Your husband sent me." The man bowed over Suzanna Cadwalder's hand, his movements strangely graceful for a man wearing the garb of a frontiersman. "This letter will explain everything."

He placed the letter in Suzanna's outstretched hand and stepped back to give her some privacy while she read it.

"What is it, Mama?" Melisue asked as she swayed forward. Her words were for her mother, but her eyes never left the man.

Suzanna's eyes scanned the missive. "It's a letter from your father. He's well. He has a place for us to live. Mr. Thomas will escort us to him."

"All the way to Boston?" Melisue batted her eyes furiously as she strove to enchant the man. "How lovely. I'm sure we'll become fast friends by the time we reach our destination. However, I cannot comprehend what Papa must be thinking, for I vow we do not need an escort to ride the train to Boston."

Beth Ann watched the smile play at the corners of the man's mouth. His mouth was large and mobile. His chin was strong and square. His eyes were widely set and a deep velvet-brown, and his hair was thick and blond and fell in waves about his well-shaped head.

James Thomas clearly sensed her interest, and he rewarded her curiosity with an engaging smile. Then he seemed to block out Melisue and her words and did noth-

ing either to agree or to argue as Suzanna finished reading
the letter and turned back to the room. Suzanna's blue eyes
glowed with a happiness not seen since the fateful day Melisue had committed her indiscretion.

"It is, indeed, as you have said." Suzanna gave James
Thomas the full benefit of her Southern drawl. "And we
thank you for bringing us this welcome news." She motioned her daughters forward. "Girls, this is James Thomas,
who will serve as our escort until we reach your father." Her
blue gaze returned to the tall man. "These are my daughters, Melissa Suzanne and Elizabeth Ann."

He bowed over their hands in turn, and once again Beth
Ann noted that despite his mode of dress, he seemed quite
at ease as they escorted him into the drawing room while
their mother ordered tea.

As soon as Suzanna returned, she sat down and motioned James Thomas to a chair. "Now, tell me of my husband," she urged.

"When I left Mr. Cadwalder, he was busy overseeing the
men working on your new home." He balanced his teacup
with an expertise that was not lost on Beth Ann. Her own
darling Papa could have done no better.

"The house—" Suzanna stopped in midsentence. "I have
no idea what to expect."

"I believe you will find it comfortable and quite impressive. Your husband was able to keep a great deal of money
invested through his family in Boston, so your fortunes are
not as dire as some of your neighbors'."

"When may we leave?" Suzanna asked.

"The first phase of the journey begins next week. We will
take the boat to St. Louis."

"Boat? Boat!" Melisue cried. "I can't travel on a boat. I
get sick. Mama, tell him he must make other arrangements! Why can't we take the train to Boston?"

"We aren't going to Boston," her mother said quietly.

"But of course we are," Melisue objected. "I saw the name on the trunks."

"I sent some things to be cared for by the Cadwalders, but we are not going with them."

"But I expected to have my season in Boston," Melisue protested. "If we aren't going there, why did you order so many new clothes for Beth Ann and me?"

"Because I have no idea what the situation will be when we reach our destination. New, fashionable gowns may be few and far between."

"But, Mama," Beth Ann said as she touched her mother's sleeve in an effort to get her attention, "where is it we are going? St. Louis? Will Papa meet us in St. Louis?"

Suzanna's eyes met those of James Thomas. He nodded his head acquiescently. "You're father isn't in St. Louis. We are to meet him at our new home, near Fort Kearney."

"Fort Kearney!" Melisue gasped. "You can't mean to make me live at a fort out in the middle of the prairie!"

"If your father sets foot in Louisiana, he will be hanged for murder. Even the Cadwalder connections are not great enough to save him here in the South. Our only hope is to begin a new life where the laws are less vengeful and the people more forgiving."

"I won't go!" Melisue jumped to her feet, upsetting her tea. "I'll stay here. Some of my friends will take me in. Ellen's parents would have me if you'd just ask."

"Are you referring to the same Ellen who hasn't spoken to you since the day you took your ill-fated carriage ride?" her mother asked. "Are you talking about the girl whose parents won't receive me, although they swore to be our best and most loyal friends?"

Beth Ann sipped her tea. Looking at James Thomas, she realized he knew the full situation. In the dark depths of his eyes she caught a twinkle of amusement at her sister's tantrum.

"There are some fine folks at Fort Kearney," he assured them. "Many Southern people like yourselves who left at the end of the war."

Melisue sniffed and tossed her head.

"I'm sure you'll find girls your own age—both of you."

"What do the people there do for entertainment?" Melisue ventured, not really caring, for she surely wouldn't participate.

"They have dances and soirées much the same as you have here," he told them. "They go on picnics in the summer and have quilting bees and . . ."

Melisue's eyes rolled back in her head as though she could stand to hear no more. "It sounds uncouth, boring, uncivilized. I won't go! I can't live that kind of life." She sobbed out the words.

"Think of the dances, Melisue," her mother said consolingly. Beth Ann realized for the first time that Melisue was echoing their mother's own doubts. "Think of the picnics and the soirées," Suzanna continued.

"Think of all the young men at the fort," Beth Ann interspersed, moving aside a split second before Melisue's saucer sped past her ear.

As the memory of that first meeting faded, Beth Ann retraced her steps, relieved to find the formidable Mrs. Bouchard no longer around. But any relief she might have felt was banished by a glimpse of her sister's tear-stained face in the doorway of the cabin they shared, and she slowed her steps, unwilling to endure another tearful confrontation.

Beth Ann chided herself for her reluctance. After all, Melisue had been through some terrible disappointments. Not being allowed a season in which to formally "come out" was bad enough. But believing they were moving to Boston—where "coming out" was tantamount to being

launched into the best society—and having to trade that for
Fort Kearney was possibly Melisue's worst nightmare.

"I'll show those girls," Melisue had gloated. "They'll
wish they'd never snubbed a Cadwalder. I'll come back here
with a wealthy, socially prominent Northern husband who
hasn't lost all his money in that silly old war. I'll have furs
and fine Paris gowns while they're still scrimping to put food
on the table and turning the collars of their clothes. Just
wait and see." Hurt to the quick that her friends had abandoned her for an indiscretion that might well have happened to any of them, Melisue snubbed even the girls who
defied their parents and offered friendship.

Try as she might, Beth Ann had not been able to convince her sister that the move to Boston was nothing but a
fantasy.

"After my season in Boston, I can't see myself associat-
ing with people who have lost all their money while losing a
war," Melisue had babbled. "Besides, poor Southerners
have very little social standing in the North."

Her words had been heard and repeated, and what little
compassion there had been for her had disappeared. Melisue's mother and sister had been classified as having the
same opinions, and the few friends they might have held had
drifted away. Suzanna had lost the friends she had thought
loyal throughout her married life. She was a Southerner
through and through and had no intention of spending the
rest of her life in Boston. As a Southerner, she was too
proud to beg and plead for friendship, which should have
been hers without question.

Beth Ann, too, was disappointed, but she had discovered
a heretofore-untapped inner strength of her own that had,
so far, carried her through. An inner strength, and the
friendship of a man named James Thomas.

Chapter Two

During the long days, as the paddle wheeler slipped through the muddy waters, Melisue lay abed, demanding cool cloths for her head, while Beth Ann roamed the boat, watching the towns slide past and amusing herself by conversing with the passengers.

Beth Ann's greatest disappointment was that James Thomas was seldom to be found in the areas to which a young lady had access. The disappointment was eased somewhat by the fact that Melisue remained in their cabin, leaving the company of James Thomas exclusively to Beth Ann.

It wasn't until the last day of the journey that Melisue was enough recovered to don her finery and take the air on deck.

"I will be forever grateful to be off this thing and back on solid ground," she remarked as she twirled her little parasol.

The air was warm and humid on the river and would be even warmer when they left the paddle wheeler, yet Melisue, like her mother and sister, wore long sleeves and a high neckline to protect white skin from the sun's rays.

Although Melisue had professed to be anxious to leave the boat, she lingered, hoping James Thomas would comment on her appearance. She was well aware of the glances of the men who had made the journey without the benefit of her presence and now all but ogled the lovely young woman who had appeared suddenly in their midst.

It occurred to her that she might have made a miscalculation in allowing her illness to take precedence over what could have been a very entertaining trip.

Although the men cast glances in her direction, Melisue knew the women were watching James Thomas with equal interest.

"I don't know what they see in him," she complained to her sister. "He's an Indian scout, a frontiersman, not a gentleman like our papa."

Beth Ann's eyes never left James Thomas. "I think he's more of a gentlemen than any other man on the boat," she replied.

"Just because he is kind and talks to you, you think he's wonderful," Melisue teased. "Look at him. He doesn't even know how to dress properly."

"He dresses like what he is," Beth Ann replied, though she knew he needed no defending. James Thomas was a free spirit. She wouldn't want him to be any other way. It was that spirit that she most admired about him, and it was that spirit that she felt caused the attraction of the other passengers, both male and female. Of course, Melisue could not see that, for she had been abed for the duration of the journey and only now realized how much she had missed. The company of James Thomas being paramount, Beth Ann surmised. She wasn't about to admit that even she had seldom seen him during the journey. "And he has been most considerate of Mama and myself."

Melisue glanced at her little sister. Could it be the girl was smitten by the scout? No! Beth Ann's illness, and being shut away from society for so long, had made her see things out of perspective. She was hardly more than a child, and by the time she was of an age to be any competition Melisue would be married wealthily and have a home and fine things of her own. And, she thought, narrowing her eyes in calculation, married to a man who wore something more elegant than buckskins, no matter how intriguing buckskins looked on James Thomas's muscular body.

Their mother's call to leave the boat was welcomed by Melisue, especially when, after helping Suzanna onto the dock, James Thomas offered the same consideration to her. Her hand lingered in his as her eyes held his dark gaze.

"Right over here, Miz Suzanna." Caleb stood beside an open carriage a few feet away, and Melisue reluctantly moved on.

To her disgust, James Thomas turned and lifted Beth Ann from the gangplank and carried her to the carriage on his arm. Melisue's protests were silenced when she realized how childlike her sister looked against the big man. Melisue smiled. No one could take the friendship between her sister and the frontiersman seriously, especially when she was available.

The Embassy Hotel stood in the center of town, far enough from the docks to avoid the roughhousing of the sailors, but near enough to catch the breeze that blew in from the river. It was a formidable building, and it housed an assortment of people from all walks of life.

Beth Ann found it enchanting from the moment she stepped into the dark but bustling lobby. Melisue hung back, complaining of feeling faint, in the hope that James Thomas would offer to carry her into the hotel as he had carried Beth Ann from the boat. He ignored her pleas and unloaded their luggage while she sat beneath her parasol, complaining of the vapors. James Thomas was taking the Cadwalders belongings into the hotel when Suzanna noticed the absence of her eldest daughter and sent Beth Ann to fetch her.

It was Caleb who helped Melisue from the carriage. She shook his hand away when he offered to escort her into the hotel lobby. Beth Ann made a face and raised her eyebrows in mock exasperation before following Melisue into the building. The smile on James Thomas's face was her reward, as well as the sound of his deep chuckle, which followed her through the door.

Melisue was delighted to be staying at a hotel that was renowned as the hub of travel going east or west. But as the time for dinner approached, it became apparent that Suzanna was not disposed to leave their suite of rooms and go down to dine.

"But, Mama, you must eat something," Melisue argued sweetly. "The food in the dining room is known as the best in this area."

"I'm exhausted, Melisue. I'll have something sent up here."

"But I've been shut up for the whole journey!" Melisue wailed. "You can't expect me to eat in here with you and Beth Ann."

"That's exactly what I expect you to do," her mother said firmly.

"I could take Beth Ann and go down to the dining room. We're guests here, so it would be acceptable."

"It's never acceptable for young ladies to appear in public alone."

"Perhaps Mr. Thomas would accompany us," Melisue persisted. "After all, that is his job, is it not?"

"Mr. Thomas agreed to see that we reached our destination safely. He is not here to dance attendance on childish whims. We will dine in our rooms. I'll hear no more about this matter." Suzanna went into her room and closed the door. Rachael Bright, the only one of the servants to stay in the hotel with them, pulled over a straight-backed chair and sat with her arms crossed next to the door. The dour expression on her face left no doubt that Suzanna's privacy would be protected.

Melisue stamped her foot and went in search of her sister. Beth Ann sat in the window of the room they shared, watching the parade of people on the street below.

"I've just been told the most terrible thing," Melisue said in a most melancholy tone. But Beth Ann paid little attention, keeping her mind centered on the street. "Mama said Mr. Thomas has finished his job for us and won't be coming back. Why, we never even gave him proper thanks for his efforts in our behalf."

The mention of the scout's name pulled Beth Ann's attention back into the room. "I thought he was to see us to our destination." She swung her legs off the window seat and looked at her sister's flushed face.

"So did I," Melisue said. "This is just too terrible. I did so want to thank him for being so kind."

While it was unclear in what capacity the man had been kind to Melisue, Beth Ann shared her sister's desire to thank him.

"Did he mention to you where he would be staying?" Melisue was flitting nervously about the room and Beth Ann began to wonder why she should be so anxious.

"I have no idea where he might be, but I suppose if you really wanted to thank him you might leave a message at the front desk. If he came here he'd be sure to receive it."

Melisue's face brightened. "Of course!" She gave her sister a hug. "What a smart girl you are to think of such a thing. I declare it never would have occurred to me."

Melisue scribbled a few words on a piece of paper, folding it carefully before slipping it in her reticule. "I'll be back in a moment," she announced, loudly enough for Rachael Bright to hear. "Don't you worry about me."

She had gathered up her skirts and was reaching for the latch when her mother's door opened with such force that it almost upset Rachael Bright, who was leaning against the doorjamb.

"Where are you going?" Suzanna demanded, disheveled and heavy eyed from lack of sleep.

"Why, only down the hall to the powder room." Melisue lied gracefully, ignoring her sister's gasp.

"Why are you carrying your reticule?" her mother asked firmly. Hearing no reply, she came across the floor, stopped before her daughter, took the purse from the girl's hand, extracted the note and read it aloud: "Dear Mr. Thomas, As much as I hate to prevail upon your good nature, I must venture to ask you to escort my daughter Melissa Suzanne to dinner in the hotel dining room this evening. Thank you for considering my request."

Suzanna's hand shook as she crumpled the note and threw it into the corner. "And it's signed 'Mrs. Brandt Cadwalder.' Now who do you think would do a thing like that?"

Melisue hesitated for only a moment. "Beth Ann did so want to go down to dinner tonight," she explained breathlessly. "I had no idea what she said in the note, Mama. I only agreed to leave it at the desk. It was her idea. Why, I would never have thought of leaving a note for a man at the front desk of a hotel." Melisue knew her mother didn't believe her, and she groped for confirmation. She knew she wouldn't get it from her sister, who stood openmouthed from shock. She turned instead to Rachael Bright, who had returned to her post beside the bedroom door. "Rachael Bright can tell you. She heard what Beth Ann said about leaving a note."

Rachael Bright's eyes narrowed. Melisue was setting her up to corroborate a lie to avoid her mother's wrath. "I didn't hear a thing," she said. "I was almost asleep."

"You always hear everything, Rachael Bright," Melisue complimented. "You must have heard our conversation."

"Go ahead, Rachael," Suzanna urged. "Tell me what happened."

"I just didn't want the girls to disturb your rest, Miss Suzanna," the woman explained. "They were talking about that young man who escorted us here, and Melisue was saying how we wouldn't be seeing him again, because he was going off on his scouting business."

Melisue tried to interrupt. Rachael Bright had heard far too much. In a moment she would be in worse trouble than if she had left the woman out of the conversation.

"Go on, Rachael," Suzanna urged, putting a restraining hand on her daughter's wrist.

"Then Melisue said there ought to be some way to thank the man for being so kind, and Beth Ann suggested they leave a note at the front desk."

A smile of satisfaction lit Melisue's face. "See, Mama! I told you it was Beth Ann's idea."

Suzanna retrieved the note from where it lay on the floor and reread the contents. "That's a very good story, Melisue, but I'm afraid you've forgotten two things."

Melisue batted her eyes in bewildered innocence.

"First, the note only refers to Mr. Thomas escorting *you* to dinner, and secondly, the note is written in beautiful script. Beth Ann doesn't write that precisely."

"I only wanted to go out and have a little fun. What's so wrong with having dinner in a big dining room rather than being stuffed in this little hotel room?" Tears poured pitifully down Melisue cheeks as she tried to soften her mother's heart.

"No lady would have considered writing a note like that, and I resent that you signed my name to it," Suzanna told her. "Now go to your bedroom and put on your nightgown." She turned to Rachael Bright and ordered, "Get Miss Melisue's trunk and bring it into my room."

Melisue let out a gasp of anger laced liberally with despair. "How can you punish me like this? I haven't done anything wrong. Just because you're tired doesn't mean the rest of us have to suffer!''

Suzanna's hand shot out and caught the girl across the face. The slap had the velocity of a gunshot and a sound so resonant that even the noises of the street outside were silenced for a moment.

''Your foolish indiscretion caused me to have to leave my home, to lose my friends…to pack away all the things I love and cherish and go and live like poor white trash in the middle of some godforsaken prairie. It won't happen again. This time, by the grace of God, your father was spared. I refuse to take any more chances with my life or the lives of the rest of my family. You will cease your foolish headstrong ways if I have to keep you in your shimmy and chained to the foot of the bed until you're forty! You'll not take any more of my life away with your loose morals and headstrong ways.''

Both girls were rendered speechless by their mother's outburst. Melisue meekly crept into the room she shared with her sister and allowed Rachael Bright to help her out of her clothing. Properly garbed in her nightclothes, she crawled onto the bed and curled up into a little ball while Rachael moved her trunk to her mother's room.

Beth Ann returned to her post at the window, relieved that she hadn't received the same punishment for her part—no matter how innocent—in writing the note. As the afternoon faded to dusk, she mulled over her mother's words and wondered if perhaps she had not completely understood the full story of her sister's indiscretion in New Orleans. Had Melisue not been as innocent as she had been given to believe?

She glanced over her shoulder to where Melisue lay curled up on the bed and was instantly ashamed of her suspicions. No one could be more innocently beautiful than Melisue. And yet Melisue would have gladly seen Beth Ann punished in her place for a mischief she had not committed. Even Rachael Bright had been careful with her words out of fear of having Melisue twist them to her own purposes.

The meal was served by the hotel staff under Rachael's watchful eye, but even with the sustenance of the food, Suzanna's face was still drawn, and the dark circles beneath her eyes had not lessened with sleep.

Beth Ann longed for her old room above the garden in New Orleans, with the night birds singing in the vines and the smell of jasmine so thick and sweet you could almost taste it. She found herself listening for the sound of her father's voice among those on the street, and she prayed Melisue had been wrong about James Thomas going away. He was her link between the familiarity of the past and the uncertainty of the future, and she needed the solidity of his presence to assure her that her world could be rebuilt, no matter how badly it was shattered.

After everyone had retired, she again crept to the window. The scene on the street below had become rough and rowdy. She dozed while sitting there, and when she awakened, the street was all but deserted.

Beth Ann was about to go back to her bed when she saw a man step from the shadows. He stood in the moonlight, looking up at the windows. He raised his hand in silent salute, but she could not decide whether it was a salute of farewell or an acknowledgment of her presence in the window, or whether in fact he saw her at all, for James Thomas walked away without looking back.

It was impossible to imagine a mode of transportation not available to travelers in St. Louis. Everything from stagecoaches to trains, from steamboats to covered wagons found their way from the town to far destinations. The promise of this excitement made Melisue forget her defiance of the previous day. Morning found her spirits recovered and the tongue-lashing her mother had given her all but forgotten. She sat at the little vanity and directed Rachael Bright, who was arranging her dark curls. "Not there," she said as she jerked the woman's hand away. "Over here, on the side. The way Mother wears hers."

"Miz Suzanna only wears her hair like that when she's goin' to a fancy party. You're too young to fancy up so much."

"If I were back in New Orleans, I'd be getting ready for my coming-out season," she reminded the older woman. "I assume my hair would be suitable if we were there?"

"Only for evening parties," Rachael Bright replied. "You wear your hair like a proper young lady should or I'll tie it up in rags and make you go around with it like that."

Beth Ann, who had been ignoring the argument, spied a gingham dress placed neatly across the foot of her bed. She held it up against her body. It looked to be a perfect fit. "Who does this dress belong to, Rachael Bright?" she asked.

Melisue's eyes darted past her sister to the garment at the foot of the bed in which she had slept.

Melisue gasped. "Don't tell me we're so poor we can't pay our bill and have to clean the rooms instead!"

Beth Ann would have been the first to agree that the dresses looked like the ones worn by their house servants. The browns and reds did little to enhance the feminine wearer, and the brown canvas apron could hardly be called becoming.

"Your mama said you should wear them to travel in."

Melisue placed her wrist against her forehead and closed her eyes. "Merciful heavens," she lamented, "what have we come to?"

Beth Ann made no comment, but silently echoed Melisue's question before her usual spontaneous spirit prevailed. "Travel is very dirty. You wouldn't want to ruin one of your good gowns, would you?"

"I would rather take the chance of ruining one of my gowns than look like a drab old peahen," Melisue replied, sniffing indignantly. Turning to Rachael Bright, she pointed to the door. "Go tell Mama I will wear my blue muslin."

"Your mama isn't in her room just now," Rachael Bright answered. "And when she gets back to her room you'd best be dressed and ready to leave."

Melisue tossed her head defiantly. "We'll just see about that," she said as she picked up the dress and marched out of the room.

Beth Ann was at the window when James Thomas drove a buggy up before the hotel and began loading their luggage. Her heart skipped several beats when she realized he was indeed accompanying them on the remainder of their journey. She was about to inform her sister of this wonderful circumstance when their mother entered the room.

Although she noted the excitement on Beth Ann's face, Suzanna was forced to turn her attention to her older daughter."Melisue! Why aren't you ready?" she demanded.

"I can't wear that horrible old dress, Mama," Melisue cried. "I'd look like poor white trash. What will people think?"

"You'll look like a fool rigged out the way you are," her mother said, eyeing her blue dress trimmed with ribbons and tiny white rosebuds. "How did you find that dress?"

"Why, you were out when I went to ask you what I should wear, so I took it from the trunk. I knew you wouldn't want me to wear a dress identical to Beth Ann's." Her eyes shifted guiltily as she remembered the tongue-lashing she had received the night before.

"There's no time to bring the trunk back in so that you can change. You'll just have to make the best of it." Suzanna moved through the suite to make sure nothing was left behind before ushering her daughters out the door.

James Thomas smiled when he heard Beth Ann call his name and run to join him beside the wagon. Melisue kept her distance, twirling her parasol as she stood framed in the double doors of the hotel. It was hard to believe Suzanna Cadwalder would allow her daughter to begin her journey in such a costume. The girl would be dirty and uncomfortable before the day was out. He loaded the last of the trunks into the wagon and lifted Beth Ann onto one of the double seats.

"I'm glad you didn't leave us, Mr. James Thomas," Beth said.

The sincerity in her voice touched him. "I told you I wouldn't leave you," he reminded her.

"Until your job was done," she said.

"And my job isn't done until you and your mother and sister are safely in your new home."

"And that can't be soon enough for me," Melisue said, sashaying up behind them. "You can't expect me to ride in this farm wagon!" One thought followed the other so quickly that neither James Thomas nor Beth Ann could respond before she surged on. "Why can't we catch the stage right here? Or go to the train in a buggy instead of this—" She gestured disparagingly toward the wagon.

"I'm sorry it took me longer than I'd planned," Suzanna said as she allowed herself to be helped into the buggy. She wore a brown paisley dress with blue and gold accents and leg-o'-mutton sleeves. She looked more rested and ready for travel than she had the day before.

By the time they reached the edge of town, James Thomas was relatively certain that Melisue had no idea as to the mode of transportation that would take them to their destination.

At first she talked of the merits of stagecoach travel. Then, upon realizing they had passed the stage stop, she began expounding on how the train was her favorite means of transportation, although she should never have chosen the white parasol, for it would become full of cinders.

Suzanna ignored her words. Beth Ann knew little more than did her sister, and James Thomas refused to try to tell the girl anything.

He pulled the horse to a stop at the edge of an encampment. Several people hurried over to greet him.

"Is this your wagon train?" Beth Ann asked as soon as the introductions were over.

"I'm the scout for this wagon train," he responded, pleased that she should remember their conversation about his occupation.

Melisue allowed him to lift her from the wagon, but, for once, her eyes and mind were on something other than the close proximity of a man. They roved over the nearby wagons. Prairie schooners, she'd heard them called. Suddenly her face went white and she uttered a little gasp.

"There's Caleb, and his wife, Lucy." She forgot all semblance of etiquette and pointed to a nearby wagon. "And Rachael Bright is with them." She turned to her mother, her eyes wide with emotion. "You can't let them go off on this wagon train. Who will 'do' for us in our new home?"

"They're not 'going off,'" her mother replied. "We're going with them."

"In a wagon train?" Excitement danced in Beth Ann's eyes and rang out in her voice.

"In a wagon train?" Melisue choked on the words, as well as the dust that rose around her with each movement.

"In a wagon train." Suzanna managed to hide the nervousness in her voice. In her wildest dreams she had never thought she would be traveling in a covered wagon.

"I can't go!" Melisue wailed. "The rough wood will snag my gown, and the sun will make me red as an Indian! My skin will be ruined forever! How can you even think of traveling that way?" She turned on her mother, ignoring the anger in the woman's eyes. "I shall stay right here until James Thomas brings an enclosed carriage."

"Then you'd better prepare to wait a very long time alone," her mother said quietly, "because Beth Ann and I are leaving with the wagon train, and I have neither the time, the money nor the inclination to give in to your whims."

"Welcome." A booming voice greeted them as a burly man in buckskins came striding up. "You must be the Cadwalder ladies. I'm Jed Burtram, the wagon master. Welcome to our family."

"Family?" Melisue hung on the word.

"Why, yes, Miss Cadwalder. Until we get you to your new home, we're going to all be like one big family, sharing hardships and happiness together."

He took off his hat and bowed over her hand. Melisue's eyes opened in shock. Her fingers trembled as her eyes went from her mother to the covered wagon. "Oh . . . no . . ." she managed, before fluttering to the ground like a fallen butterfly as both men jumped forward to catch her.

Chapter Three

Beth Ann sat beside her sister as the covered wagon lumbered across the prairie. She had tried sitting on a low stool, but that had been a failure. Each bump had knocked her onto the floor of the wagon. She had also tried sitting on the bunk built into the side of the wagon on which her sister lay. The ridge made to hold in mattress and occupant alike was uncomfortable, to say the least. "Debilitating" might have been a more precise description. She finally sat on a cushion on the floor, which was little better than on the bare boards themselves, and wondered how Melisue could remain unconscious for such a long time.

One of the women had come running with smelling salts. They had burned feathers under Melisue's nose, a sure remedy for the vapors, but to no avail. Her eyes had opened once but then rolled back into her head. She had remained unconscious from that time on.

Now, as the wagon jogged over the ruts and bumps, Melisue again opened her eyes. Beth Ann began to struggle to her feet to tell her mother, but Melisue's hand closed on her arm.

"Where are we?" she whispered, her eyes surprisingly clear for someone who had been unconscious for several hours.

"We're riding in a covered wagon on our way to Fort Kearney," Beth Ann told her.

"Are we alone?"

"Mama is with Mr. James Thomas."

"Mama is out there in the sun?" Melisue gasped. "She'll ruin her complexion."

Beth Ann nodded. "She's wearing a Poke Bonnet."

"Our mama?"

Beth Ann nodded in the affirmative. "And she says as soon as she learns to handle the reins she's going to drive the wagon."

"Then there's no chance she's going to turn around and go back?"

Beth Ann shook her head, and Melisue burst into tears. Stunned by her sister's sudden emotion, Beth Ann slid to the side of the bunk and put her arms around Melisue.

"Don't worry, Melisue," she said comfortingly. "Mama won't ruin her complexion."

Melisue sniffled quietly. "That's not the problem, Beth. It's...well, it's the wagon master."

"Mr. Burtram? What about him?" The man had seemed jovial and jocular.

"Beth Ann, I recognize him. I saw him in Madame Miggons's shop. I know I did. He must have seen me there, too. He might be the man Madame Miggons was...taking me to see."

"Oh, Melisue, how you do run on! He didn't seem to recognize you," Beth Ann pointed out.

"That doesn't matter. I saw him, I tell you. And the terrible part about the whole situation is... Don't you see, Beth Ann? Our papa may have killed the wrong man. And if Mr. Burtram really is the guilty party, we are both in terrible danger."

"Both? You mean me?" Beth Ann squeaked. "Why would I be in trouble? The man never even saw me until to-day."

"I'm in trouble because he paid a lot of money for my virginity and didn't get anything for his money. And you are in trouble," she explained, "simply because you are still a virgin too."

Beth Ann looked at her sister, who lay back on the pillow, tears squeezing from beneath her lashes and leaving little streams against her cheeks. "I do believe you may have a fever, Melisue." Beth Ann put a tentative hand on her sister's forehead. "I'll bet Mama will think you'd be better off staying right here in this wagon for most of the trip."

Melisue looked at her little sister and managed a smile. "I knew you'd think of something. You're such a clever girl." She settled herself against the pillow. "Now, could you get me a cup of water—or, better yet, some tea?" A smile touched her lips. "And, as soon as we stop, perhaps Mr. Thomas will come in and join us."

Beth Ann watched her sister speculatively. There was no denying that the girl looked beautiful. Her face was framed by a cloud of dark hair that looked like a shadow on the whiteness of the linen pillowcase her mother had insisted on bringing. Beth didn't want Mr. James Thomas to see Melisue in this condition. She knew without being told that if he was to join the sisters now, the wagon master wouldn't be the only man they had to worry about in protecting Melisue's virginity.

"I think you'd better rest," she said. "You don't want anyone coming back here when you are so pale and have dark circles under your eyes."

Melisue blinked and sat up. "Where is my looking glass?" she demanded.

Caught in her own lie, Beth Ann improvised and prayed for forgiveness. "I have no idea. It must be packed. Maybe

Mama knows. I'll go ask her. She'll be so happy to see you've awakened.''

"Beth Ann!" Melisue's wail was ignored as Beth Ann went to the front of the wagon and climbed onto the seat beside James Thomas while their mother came to minister to Melisue.

"Have you been scouting for wagon trains for a long time?" Beth Ann launched into conversation, though her mind was in a turmoil as to how to ask James Thomas about the wagon master and the probability of Melisue's story.

"A considerable time," he replied, and clucked to the team as they plodded along. For all her fragility, Beth Ann was precocious and forward, but now he sensed something beneath the question, and he turned his attention to the little girl at his side. It was strange that her eyes, though innocent and, for the most part, carefree, held an awareness usually credited to a much older woman. "How is your sister?"

"She's much better," Beth Ann said seriously. "Mama told her she should have worn a bonnet instead of carrying that silly parasol, but she would have her own way."

"The sun is hot, and that's no lie," he agreed. "I had the feeling she was upset over the fact that she would reach her destination by wagon train."

Beth Ann squirmed, not wanting him to think her family was casting aspersions on his chosen profession. "She... That is . . . she was just surprised."

James Thomas laughed. "That she was! And it will be fun to tease Jed about women fainting at his feet when he so much as bows over their hands."

Beth Ann watched the prairie grass ripple in the wind, wishing it would carry off the problem of approaching James Thomas with Melisue's assumption about the wagon master.

"Melisue thought she had seen Mr. Burtram in New Orleans."

James Thomas gave her a sharp look. "I can hardly believe a young woman as lovely as your sister would remember an older, balding wagon master after a chance meeting. Were they formally introduced?"

Beth Ann swallowed. "It never quite came to that," she hedged. "Has Mr. Burtram been to New Orleans in the past year or so?"

Now James Thomas turned his full attention to the girl on the seat beside him. "Is there something more that you want to tell me about?" he asked.

"No... That is, yes, but—"

Before she could come up with a substantial excuse to keep from telling him, the wagon master gave the order to pull the wagons into a circle for the night. All thoughts of conversation and confidences were forgotten with the activity of the evening.

Although the other travelers looked on with a mixture of envy and scorn, the servants cooked and waited on the Cadwalder women on the prairie just as they had at home.

Melisue deigned to leave the wagon and grace the circle around their campfire. Rachael Bright clucked over the girl, but watched the mother; her concern was so obvious that Beth Ann could not help but notice. The description she had given of her sister earlier in the day came back to her as she looked into her mother's face. The dark circles beneath the eyes, the drawn look around the mouth, were all there, while Melisue blossomed with life.

James Thomas noticed, too, and stopped to talk to Rachael Bright and Caleb while the family ate.

"Rachael, do you know how to drive a wagon?" he inquired, feeling his question to be nothing more than a courtesy as Rachael Bright looked as though there were very few things she couldn't do and do well.

"I most surely can," she told him. "I can drive as well as Caleb, maybe better."

Caleb sniffed at her boast, but didn't argue.

"That's fine." The relief in James Thomas's voice was obvious." Tomorrow I ride point. I want you to take turns driving Mrs. Cadwalder's wagon."

Caleb harrumphed. "There was never any question but that we would," he said defensively.

"That's why we're here," Rachael Bright told him. "To take care of Miss Suzanna at a time like this."

James Thomas nodded. "I'm glad you see it that way. She's going to need all the help you can give her."

"Amen to that," Rachael said. "This whole thing couldn't have happened at a worse time as far as Miss Suzanna is concerned."

"You've known her for a long time, haven't you?" It wasn't truly a question, but Rachael responded with an expansive answer. "Miss Suzanna's grandfather visited New Orleans on business and went to the Quadroon Ball. His family was grown and he had buried two wives when he saw my mama and fell in love with her. Instead of setting her up with a little house of her own, he bought the house we just left and brought Mama into it, living with her openly. They were very happy for several years, but then my mother became pregnant with me and died shortly after I was born. He took me to the plantation in Virginia and insisted I be raised right alongside his granddaughter, Miss Suzanna. When he died, Miss Suzanna's papa felt that I must have some way to support myself, and he sent me to France to study. I came back about the time Miss Suzanna got married to Mr. Cadwalder, and he asked me if I would come to work for them."

"But if you were accepted by Suzanna's family, how come your name is Rachael Bright?"

"My mother was darker than I am, and when she saw how light my skin was, she called me Rachael Bright. I use those two names, and most people don't know I have another. But my name is Rachael Bright Delancey."

"As you were speaking, I noticed a change in your... choice of words. You said you were raised with Mrs. Cadwalder, yet the pattern of your speech is more like Caleb's."

She smiled broadly, knowing that he knew the answer. She was more than willing to verify his suspicions. "Southern people don't like their servants to be too eloquent. They find it reassuring if we are grammatically incorrect—at least part of the time. I find it to my advantage to oblige them."

"Surely you can't include the Cadwalders." He watched her closely, testing her loyalty.

"Sometimes I can let down and talk to Miss Suzanna, but I work for them, and they don't want to feel I am superior to them in any way."

James Thomas accepted her explanation without further question, his eyes suddenly opened to facts he had never before given more than perfunctory thought. With the new revelations occupying his mind, he moved back toward the cooking fire, where the Cadwalder women sat.

"You should be in the wagon getting ready for bed, little one," he admonished Beth Ann good-naturedly. "We start very early tomorrow. You'll be up before the sun rises."

Melisue made a face. "You can't really expect me to get up and eat at dawn. I can't possibly be ready to travel before noon."

"You will travel, ready or not. We must take advantage of every minute of daylight." He wondered vaguely if their mother would indeed be able to travel, for the flush of the morning had gone and she looked bone-weary.

"This is a terrible way to travel," Melisue complained. "I don't see why we couldn't have taken the train, or even a stagecoach."

"Hush," Suzanna warned. "What's done is done. This is the way your father and I have chosen to move our belongings and our daughters."

Melisue flounced off and James Thomas turned his attention to Suzanna. "I've made arrangements for Caleb and Rachael Bright to drive your wagon tomorrow."

Suzanna nodded in agreement. "Thank you, Mr. Thomas. I knew this afternoon I wouldn't be able to handle the team for any great length of time."

"Why can't you drive our wagon tomorrow?" Beth Ann asked.

"Because tomorrow I must start working for the wagon train. I ride out on point and make sure everything is safe for the rest of you."

"Safe?" Beth Ann's eyes widened. "You mean like from wild Indians?"

"Most of the Indians around here are friendly, but there is a greater danger, and that is from the bushwhackers."

"What are bushwhackers?" Melisue rejoined the conversation, her curiosity piqued.

"Bushwhackers are men from the South who have come west to rob and pillage and get revenge on the world, in general, because the South didn't win the war." He took off his hat and wiped his forehead with his arm. "They are the real threat, not the Indians."

"I'd just as soon not meet any of them." Suzanna allowed James Thomas to help her to her feet as Rachael Bright hurried over to assist the women in readying themselves for bed.

Their soft voices could be heard for nearly an hour before fading into the stillness of night.

Because of the uncertainty of Suzanna's condition and the fact that Melisue preferred to play the invalid rather than assist or participate in the wagon train's activities, Rachael Bright took it upon herself to drive the horses. Beth Ann chose to sit on the wagon seat beside her rather than join the ailing women inside the wagon.

From their vantage point, they watched a tiny cloud of dust grow larger against the horizon.

"Look, Rachael! Mr. James Thomas is coming back."

Rachael Bright clucked to the horses. "He's coming too fast for any good use. You get back in the wagon and tell your mama."

The wagon master shouted an order, and the wagons began to form the circle used for protection. Beth Ann could see a huge cloud of dust following the little puff made by James Thomas's horse.

"We're being attacked by Indians. They'll kill us all," Melisue lamented. She was on the verge of hysterics. "They'll scalp me. I know it."

But the men who galloped headlong down either side of the wagons were not Indians. They were white men. Dirty and unshaven, but white nonetheless.

"Who are they?" Melisue whispered. As she crouched in the back of the wagon she was more frightened than she would have been by an Indian attack.

"James Thomas said he was worried about bushwhackers," Beth Ann told her. "I guess that's what they are."

"You mean Southerners?" Melisue jerked upright, disregarding her sister's anxious tugs to keep her head down, as gunshots rang out.

The bushwackers swarmed around the wagons like flies. They crisscrossed in front of the horses, and the drivers were forced to rein in to avoid flipping the swaying wagons.

Rachael Bright fought to control the frightened animals as the wagon rocked precariously from side to side. Before she could come to a halt one of the men grabbed the halter on the lead horses, effectively blocking any hope of escape, while the leader rode the length of the train, assessing the booty he would collect.

"Get down off that wagon," he ordered as he pulled his horse to a halt. "Everybody out."

Rachael Bright jumped down and hurried around to help Suzanna, who was having some difficulty alighting. The men laughed and hooted as Suzanna's skirt caught on a wheel, exposing a quantity of petticoat. The sound of their raucous laughter sent Beth Ann to her feet. Before anyone could stop her, the girl had jumped from the back of the wagon and stood before the astonished men, blue eyes flashing, hands on hips.

"How dare you treat a Southern lady in such a manner. And you would have us believe you are Southern gentlemen and the last champions of our glorious cause."

Her words took them unawares and they stopped their various occupations to turn to the furious girl.

"We have no fight with Southerners," one of the men said. "Who are you and where are you from?"

Seeing that her daughter had struck the right chord, Suzanna, now in full control of her clothing, turned to the man. "I am Suzanna Delancey Cadwalder, of the Delanceys of Virginia. These are my daughters, and these are our sl—servants." She corrected herself trying to make the men believe her reference to slaves had been a mere slip of the tongue. "We are going to join my husband in the West."

"What is your husband doing in the West?"

"Papa would have been arrested had he stayed in the South. He killed a Yankee after the war and was forced to leave," Beth Ann volunteered.

"Why have you chosen to travel with a wagon train instead of on the railroad?" the leader asked suspiciously.

Beth Ann blinked her eyes in what she hoped mimicked Melisue's most pathetic style. "My mother and I are terrified of Indians. The only thing worse is Yankees. The wagon train seemed our only safe mode of transportation."

Some of the men pulled their horses off to the side and talked, while others held their guns on the people from the wagons. When the apparent leader came back, it was to Beth Ann that he spoke.

"We've decided to let you go with a fine for passing through the territory. Jed Burtram is from Kentucky. Some of us know that for a fact, and he swears by your story. He'll collect the bounty and we'll be on our way. You won't be bothered again." His horse danced dangerously close to the women. "And, ma'am, if your husband wants to come ride with us, you send him out. We'll be glad to have his company."

Suzanna swallowed her disgust and gave a nod of assent. Brandt Cadwalder would rather die than ride with the likes of these men. Aloud she said, "I'll give him the message, but it's been many months since I've seen him, so don't look for him too soon."

Several of the men whooped loudly as they came out holding bags with the bounty they had collected.

"These people are Southerners, like us." The leader rubbed the scar that ran from his mouth through his beard and out of sight beneath the collar of his shirt. "We take nothing but the specified offering. Is that understood?"

The men were silent. A horse whinnied. The wind blew through the grass. "Any man found with these people's possessions will be shot."

Several of the men reluctantly reached into their pockets
and unceremoniously dumped jewelry and silver onto the
dirt. No one moved to pick it up until they had ridden out
of sight.

"That was a mighty brave thing you ladies did," Jed
Burtram said as he helped Beth Ann and her mother back
up onto the wagon.

Suzanna smiled proudly at Beth Ann. "I couldn't be less
brave than my daughter."

"You probably saved the lives of most of the men on this
wagon train," he told them. "Those bushwhackers are
ruthless. As it is, our worst casualty is our guide."

"James Thomas?" Beth Ann gasped. "Where is he?
What happened?"

"They shot him when he tried to warn us. He rode in
anyway, though I have no idea how he managed to stay in
the saddle. He's over yonder." He gestured toward the front
of the train. "I scarce know how I'm going to manage a sick
man, a wagon train and riding point all at the same time."

"Show me where he is," Suzanna directed, her eyes
meeting those of Rachael Bright. "Perhaps it's our turn to
take care of him."

With Jed leading the way, they hurried toward the fallen
man. Before anyone realized what was happening, Beth Ann
rushed ahead and knelt at James Thomas's side.

His eyes were closed, and his face was gray with pain.
There was blood on his shirt. Beth Ann hesitated for a moment as she bent over him, fearing her light touch might
cause him more pain.

"You promised you wouldn't leave us, James Thomas,"
she whispered. "You promised you'd see us to our destination. You can't go back on your word."

His eyes opened and, despite his pain, he tried to smile. "I won't go back on my word, little one. You won't let me."

Once again, his eyes closed, but Beth Ann knew he would be all right. A man like James Thomas would keep his word. It was a matter of honor.

Chapter Four

Beth Ann was not allowed to do any of the nursing of James Thomas. For the most part, that task was left to Rachael Bright and Suzanna, but once the man was on his way to recovery, permission was given for the girl to sit with him.

She begged or borrowed every available book on the wagon train to read to him. She spent a good deal of her evenings gleaning stories from the other members of the wagon train about the events of the day, and she related them to James Thomas during the tedious hours of travel.

He called her "little one" as he always had, and welcomed her company. It amazed him that a child could be so entertaining, and so compassionate. Due to her diminutive size, it never occurred to him that she was anything more than the little girl she looked to be, but Beth Ann felt the first stirrings of a woman's heart, and her devotion to James Thomas was absolute.

One night when she returned to the wagon with her mother, she asked, "How old were you when you married Papa?"

"I was but fifteen," Suzanna replied.

"Why, that's younger than I am!" Beth Ann said wonderingly.

Melisue, who could only relate to a conversation about herself, immediately spoke up. "You mean you were already married when you were my age? And I will never even get the opportunity to come out! There's not a man we know who is eligible to court me, much less ask for my hand in marriage. I can't believe you and Papa would allow such a thing to happen to me. Surely you could have arranged a marriage before we left New Orleans.''

"We thought you would want to chose your own husband, a man you could fall in love with, as I did with Papa.''

"Most certainly I do,'' Melisue declared. "But I don't believe I'll find anyone suitable where we're going. There's surely no one on this wagon train who could be considered eligible—and these are the people who will be our neighbors!''

"You don't know many of the people on the wagon train,'' Beth Ann reminded her. "You sit in the wagon and sulk day after day, and at night you don't join in with the group around the big campfire.''

"I don't wish to be party to their wild shenanigans,'' Melisue said, lifting her nose in the air. "Besides, I don't trust the wagon master. Sometimes he watches me in a strange way. I still think he was the man who wanted me back in New Orleans.'' A faint touch of color tinged her cheeks, and she turned away from her sister, unwilling to confide more of her private thoughts and suspicions.

In the long days of self-imposed exile, Melisue had taken to wondering what it would have been like to have had her virginity taken. The revelation that her own mother had been a bride when she was younger than Melisue herself had given her pause. Was she indeed doomed to be an old maid and never know the surgings of a woman's body? Where would she find a man worthy of her in this godforsaken country? Yet, for all that, she couldn't help but wonder how it would feel to know the touch of a man's lips against hers in something more than a kiss of courtesy, of his hands against her body. The thoughts made shivers of excitement course through her.

She wondered if Papa would ever find a man he deemed worthy of courting her now that they were so far from their own kind of people. There was certainly no one of that caliber on the wagon train. The only man with any breeding was James Thomas, and it was likely that he only aped his betters with his bowing and kissing of hands.

No, she would have to look elsewhere, and her eyes roamed the barren prairie as she sat on the back of the wagon and wondered vaguely about the lives the bush-whackers had lived in the South before turning to a life of lawlessness. What would it be like to feel the ruthless kisses of a gentleman turned outlaw? Of—

"Here." Beth Ann dropped a shawl in her sister's lap as the wagon slowed to a halt.

Melisue stared at the unwanted garment in surprise. "What's this for?"

"There are goose bumps all over your arms," Beth Ann told her. "You don't want to catch cold." She swung from the wagon to the ground. "I'm going to sit with Mr. James Thomas this afternoon. I'll see you at supper."

Without waiting for an answer, Beth Ann hurried toward the wagon where James Thomas waited. She had borrowed a book from one of the families of the wagon train, having exhausted the Bible, as well as any other material that came to hand. She read well, and she wasn't frustrated when she realized that her audience of one had drifted off to sleep. Today, despite the new reading material, Beth Ann had no intention of reading. Today she wanted to talk.

"Tell me about Fort Kearney," she urged as soon as she had settled herself in the wagon.

"Do you know what a fort looks like?" he asked, and she nodded her head in affirmation. "Well then, imagine a fort anyplace out there and you'll know what it's like."

"Will all the people from this wagon train settle there?" came the next question.

"As a matter of fact, most of them will go on, and I don't doubt there will be people waiting to join the train at that point."

"Are you going on?"

James Thomas stared out the back of the wagon. "I've been thinking about that," he said quietly. "Thinking about it a lot. I'm tired of being shot at by Indians and bushwhackers for trying to take settlers to their destinations. If I'm going to be shot, I'd rather it be for doing something for myself. As soon as I'm able, I'm planning on going as far west as I can and finding someplace to settle. Somewhere the bushwhackers haven't found and where the Indians live in peace."

"Is there such a place?" Beth Ann breathed the words in a voice filled with wonder. It seemed that her whole life had been filled with war and fear. She could not remember life without the sound of marching men and the loud strains of patriotic music. The life of which her parents spoke was as unreal to her as was the dream of the man across from her.

"If there is such a place, I'll find it," he assured her.

"I wish you luck." She reached over and gently touched his sleeve in silent communion.

He placed his hand over hers, patting it in a paternal gesture. Someday, perhaps, he would have a lovely daughter like this. Yet, at this moment he knew a sudden surge of emotion that was anything but paternal. It was difficult for him to understand how this little girl could sometimes be so adult in her empathy.

"I will miss you, wherever I go. You've been very kind to me during the past days."

"And I will miss you," she said. "But surely you will come back to civilization at some point. For supplies, or just for camaraderie. Perhaps I will see you then." She blinked back the tears that threatened to expose the feelings locked in her heart.

How could she live a whole lifetime without ever seeing this man again? Next to her own father, she cared more for James Thomas than any man she had ever met. If only he would return when she was as old as Melisue was now. If only he would see her as something more than a child to be indulged and petted. Should she tell him she cared for him? Or would that revelation destroy the precious relationship they had built between them? She wanted to shout that she would follow him anywhere in the world just to be with him. To share his hardships and his happiness, as she had silently shared each moment of his pain during these days of recovery.

It was her desire to try to make his life more bearable during his convalescence, that sent her to his wagon at every opportunity; for, even if he did not return her love, at least he accepted her presence and sometimes confided in her. And he would miss her. He had said so, and she believed him, although she knew he would never miss her as much as she would miss him.

At the end of the second week, some of the women were beginning to lament the lack of civilization.

"There are no shops. When I lose a needle or run out of thread I cannot replace it," one woman cried.

"Isn't there a trading post where we might replenish our supplies?" another asked.

"There's no trading post nearby," the wagon master told them, "but I have laid by a supply of sundry items which you might be able to use."

He smiled at Beth Ann who had left James Thomas's side to find out what the ruckus was about. "It happens during every trip. The ladies discover that there is more clothing to be mended than they could have dreamed of at home. They need supplies, as well as some trinkets and gewgaws to keep them happy. I load up on these things, as well as tools for the men, and when the time comes I'm a regular emporium unto myself."

"You must have been a wagon master for a long time," Beth Ann observed. Despite Melisue's warnings and distrust, she found it next to impossible to dislike Jed Burtram. He seemed open and kind—not at all the sort of man who would try to take advantage of a young girl.

He brought several chests from his wagon, and the women flocked around. Even Melisue couldn't resist the temptation to join the others in picking through his goods.

Most of the other women had made their purchases and had gone when Melisue lifted a satin rosette from the bottom of a chest and gave out a little cry. "I told you!" She thrust the item in her sister's face. "I told you he was not to be trusted. I did see him in New Orleans. And here's proof."

Beth Ann hadn't thought seriously about Melisue's accusations since the day she had tried, and failed, to tell James Thomas. Now she wished she had taken him into her confidence, for the confusion on the faces of both men was apparent. Plus, there was something in James Thomas's eyes that made her feel guilty about not having come to him with her concerns. Had she done so it needn't have come to this, and Melisue might not be sobbing noisily and cowering against the wheel of Jed Burtram's wagon.

"Miss Melisue, whatever is the matter?" the man asked, helpless against the onslaught of her tears.

"You know what's the matter! You were in New Orleans! That's where you got these rosettes."

"Why, yes, that's right. But I don't see why it should upset you so terribly." The man's eyes shifted from the nearly hysterical girl to James Thomas and finally to Beth Ann, who looked as upset as he felt. "I believe I bought those rosettes at a little shop in the French Quarter, across from

the Saint Louis Cathedral." He snapped his fingers. "It was
you I saw as I left the shop." He stepped closer to Melisue,
who let out a little cry and covered her face with her hands.
He turned to James Thomas in explanation. "All this time
I've been trying to think how I could have met the mother
of these young ladies. It never occurred to me that it was the
daughter whom I almost bumped into as I left the shop." He
stepped near the sobbing girl and lifted her tear-stained face
with his hand. "I'm sorry if I've brought back memories of
the home you've left behind. Had I remembered I had the
little rosettes in my chest, I would have taken them out
rather than cause you so much distress."

Having heard that her daughter was on the verge of hys-
teria, Suzanna came running toward them, with Rachael
Bright close on her heels.

Before Melisue could speak, the wagon master stepped
forward. "Your daughter is suffering from a spell of home-
sickness, and I'm afraid it's all my fault," he explained. "I
was in New Orleans several months ago, and, as I'm always
on the lookout for items I can offer to the ladies in my
wagon train, I was pleased when I was able to purchase
some items in a little shop near the Cathedral. I'm afraid
seeing them has reminded Miss Melisue of the loss of her
home."

Melisue was about to call him a liar when Beth Ann put a
restraining hand on her wrist. "Hush, Melisue," she said
soothingly. "Everything will be all right. Come along back
to our wagon." With Rachael Bright's help, she drew her
sister away from the gathering crowd.

Melisue bristled with indignation. "I won't go. That
man's a liar. I want these people to know what kind of a
man they've entrusted their lives with."

"He's explained his presence at the shop, Melisue," Beth
reminded her. "How can you explain yours?"

Melisue swallowed. "He's already told James Thomas. What makes you think he won't tell the rest of the members of the wagon train?"

"Because he didn't even tell our mother he had seen you. If you tell everyone that you think he was the man who tried to buy you from that Miggons woman, you'll shame us again, before the whole wagon train."

"What do I care?" Melisue struggled against the arms that kept moving her toward the privacy of their wagon. "I'll never see them again once we get to Fort Kearney and our papa."

"But you *will* see them again, Miz Melisue," Rachael Bright said. "They will be your neighbors, and they are decent, God-fearing people, just like the ones you called your friends in New Orleans. A story like the one you want to spread would send your family running to the ends of the earth to escape the shame associated with your experience."

"They are farmers! Settlers! I don't care what they think or what they say."

"But your mama and papa care, and your sister Beth Ann cares. They're tired of runnin' away to save your reputation. You stayed in the wagon for the first part of the trip due to your own bad disposition and of your own choice. You'll stay in the wagon until we reach Fort Kearney because of your bad disposition and of *my* choice." Rachael Bright shoved the girl into the wagon none too gently.

"You can't keep me here if I don't want to stay. I'll tell Mama. You have no right to order me around."

"If you accuse an innocent man of something simply because he happened to be in a place where he had business, and where you had no place being, I, or any decent person, have the right to keep you silent."

"If I'm right—"

"If you're right, the man will be especially careful to protect his reputation, and you have nothing to worry about," Rachael Bright pointed out. "And if you're wrong, and you expose your own impropriety, you will make a fool of yourself before the whole territory."

Melisue jerked away from Rachael Bright's restraining hand and flounced over to the bunk, where she pouted. "Wait until I tell Papa. He'll have you whipped."

Beth Ann opened her mouth in surprise. She had never seen a servant whipped, and she doubted her father had, either, much less given the order to have such punishment meted out.

"Unless you change your ways, Melisue Cadwalder, it's you who will get the whippin' and don't you ever think otherwise."

Melisue's head snapped up in challenge. "Are you threatening me?"

"I'm telling you that there's no place for people who walk all over others in order to get their own way in this part of the country."

"Then they'd better make a place," Melisue said as she narrowed her eyes and glared at the older woman, "because I'm here, and I intend to have my way."

"Hush, Melisue," Beth Ann admonished her. "I won't have you upsetting Mother. And if you make accusations against Mr. Burtram, we will be forced to take our wagons and set out alone to try to reach Father."

"James Thomas would have to come with us," Melisue said. "It's his job to see that we reach our destination. I've heard him say so."

"James Thomas is in no condition to ride, or to take care of a group of people, most of whom are women. I believe Mr. Burtram."

"How can you believe that evil man rather than me?" Melisue gasped at the injustice of it all as her mother came into the wagon, turned away and slumped onto her own bunk, exhausted by the rigors of the journey.

"You can't cast suspicion on every man who was in the city of New Orleans the day you got into the carriage with Madame Miggons," her mother told her. "Your father found the man who would have dishonored you, burned Madame Miggons's shop and drove her out of town. The situation has been handled with honor and dispatch. I will hear no more about it." She turned her back on her daughter. The subject was closed.

"I'll help you get ready for bed," Rachael Bright offered.

Suzanna gratefully accepted her help in removing the dress and petticoats.

"Whatever I've done it can't be too terrible," Melisue said self-righteously. "I do believe Mama's gaining weight, so it can't have disturbed her appetite."

Beth Ann looked at her mother's wan face and saw hollow cheeks and dark circles beneath the eyes that belied the rounded figure. Something was terribly wrong. Tomorrow she would go talk to James Thomas. Perhaps he would have the answer.

Although Beth Ann broached the subject of her mother's health to James Thomas, he was unable, or unwilling, to throw any light on the subject.

"Your mother is sad because she has been uprooted from her home. She's been away from your father a long time and has had the full brunt of the responsibility for moving your family's belongings and closing up the business and the house in New Orleans. She has a right to be tired."

Beth Ann recognized the truth in his words, but they did little to answer her questions or reassure her feeling that something was amiss.

Rachael Bright was even more vague. "I'm sure your mama will be just fine once she sees your papa again," she told the worried girl. "You don't see your sister frettin', now, do you? And well she should be worried, because if there is anything wrong with your mama, it would be made worse by Miss Melisue's defiance."

"I'm not being defiant, Rachael Bright," Beth Ann said. "I'm worried about my mama. Something isn't right, and no one will tell me what it is."

Rachael Bright put her arm around the girl's shoulder. "Trust me, honey. Everything's goin' be just fine. I promise." But though her words were reassuring, her eyes were troubled. "We'll take good care of your mama, you and I."

The first of the settlers left the wagon train several days later. It was late in the afternoon when the wagons drew to a halt to bid farewell to one of their own.

The land was flat and covered with prairie grass that rolled like waves in the constant breeze. Far in the distance, a small structure could be seen.

"Oh, Herman," the woman said, and threw her arms around the neck of her husband in an unwonted display of affection. "A log cabin. Just as you promised. Isn't it beautiful?"

Melisue sniffed from her vantage point on the seat of the wagon next to Rachael Bright. "I thought it was an outhouse," she said dryly. "How could anyone be thrilled at having to live in something like that?"

The look on Suzanna's face left no doubt that she reflected her daughter's feelings, though she had enough manners to hold her tongue.

"It's a good solid house." James Thomas sat easily on his horse, riding slowly beside them. "Far more impressive than the soddies some of them will be living in."

"What's a soddy?" Beth Ann asked.

"A house made out of mud." James Thomas laughed. "Most of the time they cut them into the side of a hill, if there's one available. Then they only have to make one wall out of sod bricks. It stays cool in the summer and relatively warm in the winter. Works fine until they are able to build something proper."

"Like a log cabin." Melisue's voice oozed distaste. "Well, I certainly couldn't live like that. Why, our livestock had better quarters than that in New Orleans."

"We didn't have any livestock other than a few chickens and horses," Beth Ann reminded her.

"Nevertheless, we wouldn't have expected them to live in a cave in the side of a hill."

Several of the people moved away, their heads bowed, to return to their wagons. The girl's scorn had cut them to the quick, for they knew they would be lucky to build soddies before winter set in. Like Melisue, they had left homes far superior to what they would live in now. It was difficult to raise the gumption to refute the girl's words, no matter how unkind they might be, when in their hearts they felt them to be true.

"It's absolutely degrading for a Southerner to have to live like that," Melisue declared.

"The war was degrading. The way the Yankees have taken over the South is degrading," James Thomas said quietly. "But there's nothing degrading about trying to survive in any possible way. Even if it means living in a soddy or a one-room log cabin in the middle of the plains."

Feeling herself chastised, Melisue was silent. She always seemed to say the wrong thing in James Thomas's presence. Unlike Beth Ann, who managed to earn compliments on her understanding and her outlook on any given situation.

"She's just a child," Melisue grumbled to herself. "She has no worries. She doesn't have to worry about being an old maid. Why, I'll be eighteen on my next birthday, and I don't even know a man I would think of marrying."

"Even if one was foolish enough to ask you," Rachael Bright said in an equally quiet voice as she clucked to the horses and guided the wagon behind the rest.

Melisue jerked her shoulders impatiently. "It's not polite to listen to other people's conversations," she said, reprimanding the woman.

Rachael Bright glanced past the girl to the vacant boards that comprised the rest of the seat. "And it's not normal for people to talk to themselves," she replied.

Melisue moved as far from Rachael Bright as the seat would allow, leaving plenty of room for Beth Ann's lithe body to fit in between them when James Thomas handed her from his saddle, where she had been riding, to the wagon.

"Thank you, Mr. James Thomas," she said as she settled herself between Rachael Bright and her sister.

James Thomas touched the rim of his hat in departure, but before he could ride off, Melisue spoke up.

"Why don't you ever take me for a ride, James Thomas?" she asked innocently.

He looked at the wide-eyed mock innocence so prevalent among Southern girls, willing his eyes not to move to the girl's sister and compare them. "Maybe when I feel strong enough I'll do that," he replied as he put spurs to his horse and rode off, a good deal faster than was either comfortable or wise in his condition. But Melisue Cadwalder meant trouble, and trouble was the last thing James Thomas needed at this point in his life.

"Beth Ann says you're going out into the wilderness after you deliver us to our father," Melisue remarked one evening after James Thomas had joined them for supper. It wasn't that she cared where he went or what he did; she was simply amused at her sister's obvious infatuation with the man. The best part, in Melisue's mind, was that he was just as obvious in thinking of Beth Ann as a child because of her diminutive size. Melisue enjoyed watching her little sister squirm with apprehension when he talked of going into the wilderness and never coming back.

"I'm committed to taking one more wagon train across, and then it's very possible I will go farther west and settle down." He watched the girl with interest, knowing she didn't care if he went or stayed, and wondered about her sudden curiosity.

"Are you going alone?" she asked, "or do you have a wife waiting somewhere?"

Beth Ann had never thought that James Thomas might have a wife, and she almost choked on the last of her food upon hearing her sister's question. Eyes watering, she took a drink of water and tried to keep from choking so that she could follow the conversation.

"I have no wife. It would take a very special kind of woman to be happy in the area I intend to settle."

"I'm sure you'll find somebody." Melisue gave a satisfied smile at the wistful expression on her sister's face. "Perhaps some Indian woman would be happy in your sort of life?"

"Perhaps," he agreed, wishing the girl would have done with it and go on about her own business. He knew she was needling him, but had no idea for what purpose. He caught the smug expression on her face in the firelight and was unable to keep silent any longer. "Have you seen many of the Indians?" he asked her.

Melisue shook her head. "No, nor do I wish to. They are all dirty savages as far as I'm concerned."

"Believe me, that's not true," he assured her. "Many of them are far cleaner than most white people, and some of the tribes produce very handsome people who, in their own ways, have high ideals and intelligence. I've known several women who have been captured by Indians and have chosen to stay with their captors rather than return to the so-called *civilized* world."

Melisue threw back her head and laughed. The false, hollow sound echoed across the campsite. "I can't believe any woman would really choose to stay with an Indian," she admonished. "I think someone has been telling you tales and you've been believing them." She got to her feet and moved gracefully toward the wagon, fully aware of the picture she presented against the last rays of the setting sun. "I know I could never do a such a thing."

"Circumstances change people," James Thomas said quietly.

"Then maybe you'll change your mind, Mr. James Thomas, and decide life in the wilderness isn't really what you want at all."

Beth Ann's eyes moved from her sister's receding figure to that of the man sitting across the fire. Why had Melisue baited him like that? She had never bothered to hide her contempt for James Thomas, the wagon train, and the whole move in general. Now she almost seemed to be flirting with him. Beth Ann rubbed her head. As much as she enjoyed James Thomas's company, she wished Rachael Bright would call her into the wagon so that she could unbraid her hair and brush it out.

As though in answer to her thought, Rachael Bright called out, and Beth Ann bid her friend good night and watched as he disappeared into the shadows.

But sleep did not come, and she lay awake, listening to the sound of the camp settling down for the night. She was on the edge of sleep when she heard her mother's voice, and that of the wagon master.

"Thank you for escorting me back to my wagon," Suzanna said graciously.

"It's the least I could do for your help in occupying the children of the other settlers during the evening." His voice was warm and friendly. "You and your daughter Beth Ann have been the mainstay of the wagon train. I wish I had someone like you every time I made the passage."

Suzanna laughed. "Surely not. There are so many things I cannot do. I find myself depending more and more on Beth Ann to carry out my duties for me, and she is so young and very frail herself—"

"Your daughter is to be commended for her willingness to try. Many times I bring Southern ladies to the prairie and, by the time they reach their new home, I know there is no way they can possibly survive. With you folks it's just the opposite. You'll survive, and your family will prosper."

"It's kind of you to say so, but we are nothing without Mr. Cadwalder's love and support."

"But that's so in every family. It's those who must try to survive alone that I feel for," he told her, not realizing how his words must sound.

"Are you one of those people?" she asked.

A smile passed over his face before he could contain himself. He was becoming a gabby old man. Before he knew it, he would be confiding to this Southern lady that he had a wife waiting for him in St. Louis, as well as a little Indian bride expecting him to stay with her for a few months after he dropped off the last of the settlers.

"I have the best of both worlds," he said honestly. "I have chosen to live in two different worlds and enjoy both of them. Some people don't want to juggle two different lives. Take James Thomas, for instance. He scouts for the wagon trains, but his heart isn't in it. He wants to go off into the wilderness and build himself a little trading post out in the middle of nowhere. What makes a man like that? I admit I don't know! He's from one of the most influential families in Virginia, and—"

Suzanna interrupted, her natural curiosity about their guide overcoming her natural courtesy. "My family is from Virginia, but I never heard of a family by the name of Thomas," she mused, hoping he would take up the explanation.

"His family name isn't Thomas. It's Montgomery."

"Of the Carlton Montgomery family?" Suzanna's voice lifted with excitement.

"The same," the man assured her.

"But our families have been friends for generations," she exclaimed. "Why didn't he tell me?"

"His home is in shambles, and his family scattered. He says he'll go back for one last farewell and then disappear. That's one of the reasons he's agreed to take one last train across. To say goodbye."

"How sad." Suzanna bowed her head. "But I know how he feels. There is very little left of the home and the gracious way of life I remember from when I was a girl. Sometimes I'm almost glad we decided to make this move. It may be easier in the long run to learn a new way of life than to see the demise of the old."

"Don't grieve for the old," he said, placing a hand on her shoulder. "Look forward to the challenge of the new. That's where the future lies. Only those people whose souls are dead live in the past."

"I shan't be one of those," she told him. "I promise."

"Now get a good night's rest. We've a long day ahead of us tomorrow." He tipped his hat as she disappeared into the wagon.

The sound of deep, even breathing met her as she entered and readied herself for sleep. She slept quickly and deeply, feeling that all was right with the world as they came closer to their destination. But sleep did not come so easily to her daughters.

Melisue lay awake pondering what she had heard. Perhaps she *had* found a man worthy of marriage. Of course, she would have to convince him that they must move back to Virginia, but surely that wouldn't be too difficult. Her eyelids drooped as she thought how sweet she would be to James Thomas Montgomery and how surprised and pleased he would be over her change of heart.

A few feet away, Beth Ann watched the narrow slits of her sister's eyes glistening in the shadows and thought how the light of the moon made them look like the eyes of a cat lying in wait to strike an unsuspecting victim.

Chapter Five

The sun hung just above the horizon, waiting to slide out of sight as the wagon train pulled up within the confines of Fort Kearney.

Suzanna paid little attention to the fort, so happy was she to be with her husband again and place her burdens in his capable hands.

He helped her from the wagon and took her in his arms, to the cheers of the entire company. She swayed against him as he released her and turned to pluck his daughters from the wagon.

Beth Ann had eyes only for her father, but Melisue, though she hugged her papa, was quickly assessing the men stationed at the fort. In her eyes, they came up short. The grimy uniforms did nothing to enhance their appearance. Her eyes sought out James Thomas, only to find that he was watching her little sister with an indulgent smile on his lips. The man obviously liked children. Perhaps she could make the most of his wanting a family. Perhaps she and James Thomas would have a child who looked like Beth Ann. She would concentrate on his weakness for the girl and see if she could pique his interest.

In the weeks that followed, Melisue seemed to be thwarted at every turn. When she asked James Thomas to go on a picnic, or a buggy ride, or even just out for an evening walk, the man insisted on including Beth Ann, and the girl happily complied.

Not that it made any difference to Melisue. She had plenty of beaux. "For the most part they're hardly a step above white trash," she complained to Beth Ann as they took tea with their mother in their quarters at the fort where they awaited the completion of their new house. Despite her joy at rejoining her husband, Suzanna's health remained delicate. Beth Ann had assumed the household duties, allowing her mother the luxury of complete rest.

The one thing Suzanna delighted in doing was taking her tea each afternoon, and sometimes, when the fancy struck her, she invited some of the wives of the officers at the fort. The women were hungry for a bit of culture and vied for Suzanna's favor, each bringing tidbits to be served on the delicate china dishes.

"And where do you live, Mrs. Wexler?" Suzanna was asking as she poured a second cup of tea.

"Oh, just a few miles from here to the west, and north a bit."

"Do you have one of those places in the side of a hill?" Melisue asked.

"Actually, we have a rather large home," the woman said. "And, while it is sod, it's freestanding. We keep having to add on because of the size of our family."

"How many children do you have?" Beth Ann asked politely.

"I have nine, the baby being less than three months."

"Congratulations." Suzanna took a sip of scalding tea, silently thanking the Almighty that the nine children were Mrs. Wexler's and not her own. "It sounds like a lovely family."

"I don't know how lovely it is," Mrs. Wexler fussed, "but we do need the extra hands to help with the land. And that's gospel." She glanced about the room in deference. "Of course, I suppose you might not agree . . ."

"I agree completely," Suzanna assured her. "Everyone does their best to care for what is theirs. I know I can hardly wait for Mr. Cadwalder to tell us our home is ready, and neither can the girls. Isn't that right?" She beamed at her daughters, silently willing them to agree.

They nodded obediently. Beth Ann's gesture was spontaneous and completely honest, but Melisue had reservations regarding their home. Papa had been adamant about its being a surprise. He wouldn't even let them see it before they were to take up residence there.

"Well," Melisue said, sipping her tea daintily, "I just don't believe I could ever get used to living in a clay house in the side of the hill."

"Oh, but our house isn't in the side of a hill. It sits right out in the middle of the prairie. My man says we need something the size of the prairie to hold a growing family like ours." She laughed nervously.

"I don't see why you don't use wood." Melisue inspected her fingernails. "It sounds so much more civilized than living in a sod house."

"There isn't a great deal of wood out here, Miss Cadwalder," the woman said. "And we are very careful how we use it."

"Of course," Melisue agreed. "Why, the women on the wagon train even burned buffalo chips for warmth."

Stunned by the girl's perception of everything they had discovered in order to survive, Mrs. Wexler decided it was time to make a hasty retreat. She got to her feet and made her excuses. "I do hope someday I will have the honor of returning your hospitality," she told them.

"Not likely," Melisue mumbled under the clatter of the cup and saucer that she placed on the table.

"I'll look forward to it," Suzanna said graciously.

"Could I come and see your baby?" Beth Ann's bright eyes shone with sincerity.

"Of course, you can come anytime," Mrs. Wexler said. "But you must ask your papa to bring you. It wouldn't do for you to come all that way alone."

Beth Ann knew her father was a busy man and would have no time for social calls. She welcomed the touch of her mother's hand on her shoulder.

"We'll see what we can do," Suzanna promised.

Melisue lifted the little bell next to her mother's chair and rang for the maid to clear the tea table.

"Perhaps your sister could bring you," the woman suggested, unable to hold her silence in face of the overpowering urge to see the look on the older girl's face. "Or perhaps that nice Mr. Thomas would take the time. We are all surprised that he's still here. Ordinarily he doesn't stay around more than a few days, and this time he's been here... why, I believe it's almost a month." The woman's eyes swept over Melisue. If he were smitten with any of the local girls it would undoubtedly be that little minx instead of some strong, good-hearted young woman who would make him a good, God-fearing wife, she thought. Surely it couldn't be the younger child—unless, of course, he wanted to adopt her. She laughed at her own silent joke as she climbed ponderously into her carriage, waving goodbye with her free hand and guiding the horses with the other.

"Do you think I'll ever be able to drive my own carriage like that?" Beth Ann asked.

"Why would you want to?" Melisue replied. "That's why God created servants, so people like us wouldn't have to ruin our hands on the reins of a carriage."

"God didn't create servants, Melisue," their mother corrected. "Some people find fulfillment in helping others, and they choose to serve."

"Well, I'm not one of them," Melisue shot back. "I choose to be served. Now where is that girl? I rang the bell to have her clean up after our tea."

"Perhaps she's gone with Caleb and Lucy to see our new house," Beth Ann suggested.

"Perhaps she's just lazy. Besides, why does everyone get to see our new house before we do? I don't think Papa is being fair."

"He wants to surprise us," Suzanna said, "and I, for one, want to be surprised."

Her declaration should have ended the conversation, but it did not. Beth Ann waited patiently until Melisue left the room. "I thought our house was to be ready for us to move into when we arrived," she said watching her mother closely.

"He decided to add another room." Suzanna picked up her sewing basket and began embroidering tiny garlands that could be recognized from either side of the material, so perfect was her work.

The fact that James Thomas did not go on with the wagon train caused little comment. When he refused the opportunity to accompany the people returning from the Oregon Territory, however, speculation ran high as to his motives for staying so long in one place.

Bolstered by Melisue's blatant hints that the man was interested in courting her and that she alone was holding him at the fort, gossip abounded throughout the feminine population. Although Beth Ann did her best to thwart the rumors, her very denials seemed to spur them on. She wondered if she dared tell James Thomas what people were saying, but she cast the thought away, certain in her own mind that he was not the sort of man who would care about idle gossip. It was enough to know that the rumors were untrue, for he never sought out Melisue's company, and he paid her little attention when she was present.

His business and his attention, to the distress of both girls, were centered on Brandt Cadwalder. The men would isolate themselves for hours without giving anyone a hint about their topic of discussion.

It was only by accident that Beth Ann received an inkling that they were discussing a treaty with the Indians. Her father had stopped to tell her mother that he would be away for a few hours. James Thomas had stood just outside the door.

"But Mama," Beth Ann had persisted, "we promised Mrs. Wexler ever so long ago that we would visit her. The baby will be grown by the time we pay our respects."

Suzanna sighed. The girl's argument held a great deal of truth. She had been putting off the visit to preserve her strength for the rigors of the move, which her husband promised would take place in the near future. Despite her weariness, however, she did not want to neglect the people who would be her neighbors.

"Very well, Beth Ann, I'll take you tomorrow afternoon, providing, of course, Mrs. Wexler will be at home."

"I'll be going out that way," Brandt said, interrupting their conversation. "I'll stop and give her your message."

The loving smile Suzanna always saved for her husband lit her face. "Thank you," she murmured as the men left the room.

Mrs. Wexler was looking forward to their visit, Brandt assured them when he returned. Melisue argued that she had other things to do and would be unable to go, while Beth Ann practically danced with excitement.

Unfortunately, the next morning dawned to find Suzanna ill and unable to meet her commitment. Beth Ann was sitting on the step outside their living quarters—her face the very picture of disappointment—when James Thomas stopped before her.

"What seems to be the trouble, little one?"

"Mama isn't feeling well, so we can't go to Mrs. Wexler's and see the baby," she told him.

"There's always another day," he reminded her.

"I know, but I've made a bonnet for the baby, and if I don't take it soon it will be too small." She showed him the finely stitched bonnet embroidered with tiny flowers.

Without thinking, he turned it over and looked at the back, remembering how his mother had always said the proof of the stitching in embroidery was if the back was as neatly done as the front.

"You embroider very well," he said, placing the little bonnet in her lap.

"Not nearly as well as my mother," she told him. "And not nearly as fast. Mother made several little garments while I worked on this one."

For the first time, he was aware of her hands. Her long, tapering fingers and neatly cut nails were so unlike the rough, work-worn hands of the women of the plains. How would this transplanted flower survive the rough life into which she had been thrust? The determined set of her chin sent a smile to his lips. Beth Ann would most likely survive very well. If anything, it was the mother and sister who would be unable to adapt.

"Perhaps your mother would allow me to accompany you on your visit," he offered, somewhat surprised at his own words.

"Oh, but—" Thoughts of the impropriety of traveling alone with a man popped into Beth Ann's mind before she could control her words.

Born and bred to the same code of ethics, James Thomas understood without being told. "Perhaps Rachael Bright could spare the time to accompany us." He smiled at the relief on the girl's face as she ran from the room to ask her mother.

Rachael Bright sat in the back seat of the buggy as Beth Ann kissed her mother goodbye. Before James Thomas could lift her to the seat, Melisue came running toward them, her hoops swaying precariously across the dusty path.

"Wait for me!" she called, waving her lacy little parasol. She stopped beside the buggy, her breasts heaving from the combination of the effort of running and a tightly laced corset. "I thought for a moment you were going to leave without me." She gasped out her words, smiling breathlessly at James Thomas.

"I thought you were too busy to visit the Wexlers," Rachael Bright said.

"I managed to get all my errands taken care of just so I could go," she explained sweetly. "I declare, a nice ride in the country will be just like a tonic. It's too bad Mama can't come, too. I'm sure it would do her good." Her smile encompassed both her mother and her little sister. "You don't need to come, Bethy" she cooed. "I know how you worry about Mama. I'll give your regards to Mrs. Wexler and—"

"Beth Ann is going," Suzanna said, in a tone of voice that allowed no argument.

"Oh, well, how nice..." Melisue batted her eyes in innocent confusion. "I just thought she would rather stay with you, since Rachael Bright is going along. Are you sure you should be alone when you're not feeling well?"

Beth Ann looked from her sister to her mother, indecision and guilt at leaving her mother alone when she was ill written on her face.

"I'll be fine," Suzanna assured them. "You run along." Kissing her mother again, Beth Ann started toward the wagon, waiting her turn as James Thomas prepared to help Melisue into the seat next to Rachael Bright.

"Oh, but I couldn't possibly sit next to Rachael Bright," Melisue protested. "The seat is too narrow, especially with the hamper Mama is sending to Mrs. Wexler. My dress will be crushed. Do you mind terribly if I sit on the front seat with you?" Again she batted her eyes in what she thought was a gesture of irresistible seduction.

"As a matter of fact, I do mind." James Thomas placed the hamper behind the seat. "There." He lifted her as he spoke. "The back seat is much wider than the front. I'm sure you'll be more comfortable here."

Leaving no room for argument, he held out his hand to Beth Ann and placed her in the front seat before climbing up beside her.

Thwarted in her attempt to sit next to James Thomas, Melisue pouted and complained all the way to their destination.

The house was larger by far than any sod house the girls had yet seen. Beth Ann was impressed by every aspect of it. She could not hide her delight as she played with the baby, and she was even more delighted when she found there were two more children under the age of four years, which, in her mind, put them in the baby category also.

"The house doesn't look like much now," Mrs. Wexler was saying, "but in the spring the sod flowers bloom all over the walls, not to mention the roof."

"How . . . quaint." Melisue smiled through stiff lips. She thought this whole way of life was just short of barbaric. Surely even the Indians must live better.

Beth Ann was oblivious to her sister's lack of enthusiasm. The Wexler babies climbed onto her lap and begged her to tell them stories while Rachael Bright and Mrs. Wexler chatted politely and James Thomas walked the fields with one of the older boys. Unwilling to allow the children near her for fear of soiling her gown, Melisue stood apart in bored dejection.

"I'll send over some slips of my flowers as soon as you're settled," Mrs. Wexler promised uneasily as she escorted them to the wagon. Seeing her home through Melisue's eyes had diminished its grandeur, and she hid her disappointment in her environment with great effort. "You know, we haven't always lived like this. Before the war we had a lovely home in Tennessee."

"I'm sure coming from Tennessee has made the transition much easier for you." Something in the tone of Melisue's voice imparted the notion that everything in Tennessee was inferior.

There was a look of confusion on Mrs. Wexler's face. It was difficult for her to believe that Melisue, who obviously came from a good family, could be so unthinking in her choice of words.

Without hesitation, James Thomas entered the conversation. "I think it's time we were on our way." He noticed the expression of relief on Beth Ann's face as he escorted the women toward the buggy. "I wanted to show the girls their new home."

Melisue gave his arm a little squeeze. "Why, in that case we'll just have to forgive you cutting our visit short. Thank you for letting us come." The words were gracious, but Melisue was so anxious to leave that she fairly ran to the buggy.

Beth Ann lagged behind, promising the children she would come back and bring some storybooks to read to them. She spent another moment tucking the light blanket around the sleeping baby. "I hope you'll let me come back after we move into our new house." She watched the woman's face, aware of the pain caused by her sister's thoughtless words.

"You are welcome anytime." Mrs. Wexler gave her a little hug.

When Beth Ann reached the wagon, she saw that Melisue had taken the front seat. "You'll just have to sit in the back with Rachael Bright. That's what you get for lagging behind." She smiled rapturously at James Thomas, who helped Beth Ann into the rear seat before jumping into the front of the buggy and dropping unceremoniously onto Melisue's skirt, which covered both sides of the narrow seat.

He snapped the reins at the same time the hoops beneath Melisue's petticoats broke beneath his weight. He raised up just enough to allow her to pull her skirts around her, well aware that the damage had already been done.

He winked at Beth Ann as he set the horse to trotting down the road.

It seemed only minutes before he pulled the horses to a halt.

"Well, there it is!" He motioned expansively. "What do you think?"

Beth Ann stared in disbelief. Melisue gave a little gasp and put her hand to her heart as though she might faint, while Rachael Bright did her best to stifle her laughter.

The house was a smaller replica of the one they had just left. Little tufts of grass popped from its walls. The ground nearby was scarred and bare where the sod bricks had been cut.

Melisue allowed James Thomas to help her from the buggy, then started toward the house as though walking in a dream. The rest of them followed a short distance behind. James Thomas held Beth Ann's hand. His firm grip, combined with a little squeeze now and again, warned her to keep silent. Although she guessed this was his way of making Melisue pay for her behavior at the Wexlers, Beth Ann found it difficult to remain silent when they entered the house.

It was obvious that their father had lived here. His heavy coat hung on a peg on the wall. A pair of his boots stood in a corner. There was a gun she had often seen him carry hanging on the wall and a picture of their mother on the table.

"See," James Thomas said expansively, "everything's here and ready for you. All you have to do is move in."

"But... there's only one room here." Melisue stared at each wall in turn. "There's only one bed."

"Oh, no, there's another bed behind that blanket against the far wall," he assured her. He went over and lifted a corner of the blanket, allowing her a glimpse of a rough-hewn bed sandwiched against the wall. "That'll be for your mama and papa, I imagine," he explained. "The one out here you'll share with your sister."

He grinned at Beth Ann and put his hand on her shoulder. She exhaled slowly, aware that he hadn't finished with his joke.

Rachael Bright rushed around the room. "Oh, look at this stove," she gushed. "A real stove, too. I thought we'd have to cook on the hearth."

"You must be wrong, James Thomas," Melisue managed. "There's no place for our servants to sleep."

"Why, they'll just roll out their blankets along the wall over there, I imagine," he answered, undaunted.

"And just look at that," Rachael Bright said as she hurried from one side of the room to the other. "There are two windows besides the door."

"There must be some mistake." Tears filled Melisue's eyes. "Our father would never expect Mama to live in a place like this. Why, the floor is made of dirt! The floor in our house in New Orleans was fine heart of pine. This is an insult to the women of our family. Just look at this place. This is all a terrible mistake. And—" Her voice stopped, and her eyes widened. "That's our rug."

Rachael Bright swooped it from the floor and went to the door, where she shook the dust into the still air. The snap of the material accentuated Melisue's moans as she sank onto one of the rough wooden chairs, looking delightfully pathetic.

"We'd better be on our way," James Thomas said. "I told your father I'd meet him down the road a bit."

"I don't ever want to see him again. How could he do this to me?"

Beth Ann looked at the man with questioning eyes. At any moment she expected him to tell Melisue it was all a joke, but he kept his silence, enjoying Rachael Bright's excitement.

Melisue was so unnerved that she didn't even argue when he lifted her into the seat beside Rachael Bright. "Don't you think you should tell her?" Beth Ann whispered.

He looked at her for a moment before asking just as quietly, "Tell her what?"

"That we're not going to live there."

"What makes you think that?"

"Rachael Bright was so excited ... I think that's going to be her house."

"You don't say," he mused. "Then how do you explain your father's clothes? It's obvious he's been staying there."

Having no good answer to that, Beth Ann dropped the subject and began talking about the Wexler babies.

Melisue sniffled all the way home, but James Thomas did nothing to comfort her. As he assisted her from the buggy, he paused. She looked up at him, tears sparkling on her lashes.

"I just don't see how Papa can be so mean," she sobbed, hoping he would offer his shoulder for her to cry on.

"Your papa is doing a fine job of finding you a place to live," James Thomas assured her. "And I don't want to ruin his surprise, so don't you say a thing to anyone about our little trip today. It'll be our secret."

"Don't you worry," Melisue assured him. "I don't even want to think about that place until I absolutely must!" Her hoops swung dejectedly as she walked toward her living quarters.

"I think that was rather harsh," Beth Ann said righteously.

"Do you, really?" he asked, reading her answer in her eyes even before she could reply.

She giggled, unable to hide from him her hidden thoughts, save one. "No. I don't, really. She deserved every bit after the way she treated Mrs. Wexler. I was ashamed for her."

"Don't be. Melisue wasn't ashamed. She thought she was being clever."

"But she should have been ashamed," Beth Ann concluded.

"Perhaps she will learn some sort of humility if she spends a few days believing she will be forced to live in a house somewhat less than that of her neighbor."

"Then I was right," Beth Ann said exuberantly. "The house is for Rachael Bright."

"To the best of my knowledge, those are your father's plans."

Beth Ann waltzed about the room in sheer ecstasy. "Oh, I'm so happy for her. She deserves a place of her own." She paused in midstep. "But what about Caleb and Lucy?"

"They will have their own house some distance away. Rachael Bright's house is the one your father built when he arrived and lived in while he built a home for your mother."

Beth Ann threw her arms around his neck, and he swung her around the room. "I think that's the most wonderful news I've ever heard," Beth Ann shouted as she clung to him breathlessly.

He swung her around again, reluctant to let her go. Her happiness and her spontaneity seeped into his heart and soul until he longed to keep her with him. He wanted to hold this moment of happiness within himself and never let it go.

When he set her back on the floor, he discovered an utter, irrevocable loss. His hands lingered for a few seconds before releasing hers.

"Thank you for understanding my motives," he said solemnly.

"And thank you for sharing them with me," she answered.

The gulf between them returned like the waters of the Red Sea. It flooded the chasm between them and shut them out, one from the other, and they turned and retreated into the worlds they had chosen for themselves, without saying goodbye. Knowing that "Goodbye" was too harsh and "Farewell" too soft, neither even dared so much as whisper the phrase their souls cried: "Till we meet again."

Beth Ann hurried back and forth between the rooms in which they'd been staying at the fort and the wagon that held their belongings. Her excitement over moving into their new home was not shared by her sister, who sat in a corner of the carriage and sulked.

"I'd rather stay here at the fort than live in a mud hut," she complained as Beth Ann brought the last of their belongings and climbed in beside her.

"You wouldn't feel that way if you'd come with us when Papa gave us the grand tour of our new house," Beth Ann told her.

"I saw all I needed to see when Mr. Montgomery took us out there. I know I'm going to hate the place, and I want to go home!"

Beth Ann restrained herself from reminding Melisue that it was her own indiscretion that had forced them to leave their home in the first place. She, too, missed their lovely house in New Orleans, as well as the company of her friends. She remembered with longing the lush greenery and the sound of soft Southern voices, so in contrast to the dust, the never-ceasing noise, and the raucous tones of the people at the fort.

But wishing couldn't take them back—except in memory—and Beth Ann followed the example of her mother and accepted what she could not change.

Melisue stared at the floor of the carriage, refusing to look outside as they approached their destination. She turned her head away when they stopped in front of the house and would not so much as glance at the structure until it was absolutely necessary.

"Come along, dear," her mother urged, and Melisue reluctantly followed her sister from the carriage.

She lifted her head and stopped. Her jaw dropped open in surprise.

Before her stood a two-story wooden structure with whitewashed boards, a bright contrast to the fields of flax stretching out behind it as far as the eye could see.

A veranda extended across the front of the building before curving around the side, softening the stark, square lines. Above the veranda was a balcony with a door open to catch the breeze.

"This isn't the house I saw," Melisue declared in astonishment.

"You saw Rachael Bright's house," Beth Ann said. "It's over there." She pointed to a squat structure almost hidden by the trees.

Melisue hardly acknowledged her sister's words. "I like this much better," she said as she started toward the house.

An open staircase graced the entry hall, and a small hallway led to the rooms above. After a quick inspection of the living area, the girls reached the upper regions of the house.

"This is our room," Beth Ann said opening the door to a large, bright room extending along one side of the house.

Melisue glanced at the two beds, the vanity and the matching armoires. Not even the lace curtains at the windows warranted comment. She turned her back on the room and continued her inspection.

"But, Mama, why can't Beth Ann have the little bedroom next to yours?" Melisue argued. "Surely we won't have that many overnight guests. Besides, when we have company I'll gladly share my room."

Brandt Cadwalder put his arm around his wife's shoulder. "I think it's time we told the girls our news," he beamed.

At his call, Beth Ann came from the doorway of the room Melisue coveted and stood near her sister.

"The reason we were unable to move into the house when you arrived was due to the addition of the small room we've been discussing. That room is for the youngest member of our family."

"Oh, thank you, Papa," Melisue said, dancing with happiness. "I'll help Beth Ann move her things out of my room right away."

She was almost to the door when Suzanna's soft voice stopped her. "You don't understand, Melisue," she said. "What your father is trying to tell you is that I'm going to have a baby."

Beth Ann hugged her mother in delight, but Melisue didn't move, even when her parents held out their arms, expecting her congratulations.

"A baby?" She repeated the words, not bothering to hide her abject horror. "Mama is having a baby? At her age? Why—why, that's disgraceful! I'll never be able to hold my head up in public again."

Her chin quivered with self-pity. "Oh, Mama, Papa, how could you?"

She turned her back on her family, slamming behind her the door to the room she was destined to share with her sister.

Chapter Six

James Thomas knew he had to leave Fort Kearney. The more distance he put between himself and the Cadwalder family, the better it would be for all concerned. He vowed to himself that the minute he managed to finalize the treaty between the Pawnee Indians and the settlers he would be on his way.

Each day became more painful to him. He took to spending more time with the Indians. His friend, Black Hawk, watched him closely.

"You are troubled, Jim. Can I help?"

"It is nothing," James Thomas assured him.

"Then it is a woman."

"Worse than that." James Thomas tried to laugh. "It is two women."

"One woman is much the same as another. We have many women in our village. If one of them would please you . . ."

"Thank you, my friend—" James Thomas put his arm around the brave's shoulder "—but I'm afraid even the most beautiful of your women could not ease my heart."

"The woman you love does not love you?" Black Hawk asked.

"The woman I love is a girl, and I shame myself each time I dream she will someday find it in her heart to love me." He shook his head and wiped his hands over his eyes, as though to scrub away his problem.

"But you said there were two women," his friend prodded.

"The other is the sister of the girl I care for. She is older and very beautiful—as beautiful as she is vain and heartless. I see what she is and pray with each breath that her little sister will not grow to be like her. It breaks my heart to leave them together, but should I take the younger I would be accused, and rightly so, of robbing the cradle."

"How old is the girl that you love?"

"Probably no more than fifteen or sixteen summers." James Thomas fell easily into his friend's vernacular.

"That is not so young. The men of our tribe have been known to take a woman no older than what you mention."

"But the Indian women are not so gently raised. This girl is little more than a child. It is dishonorable on my part to even think so of her, and before God, I would not make her my wife for years to come, even if she and I were wed. It is wrong to even think on it," he said. "But it is a unique kind of hell to think of spending the rest of my life without her."

"Why do you not take her with you?"

"She is so young, so delicate. I doubt she could survive the rigors of the journey, much less the life we would be destined to endure so far from civilization." He sighed. "There are no doctors. There are no other women for that matter, and it could be many years before the area is settled."

"Perhaps, for you, she would be willing to wait many years," Black Hawk observed.

"And perhaps it's all a pipe dream," James Thomas returned. "She's young and should have the experience of being courted and cosseted by a man who will love and care for her in the comfort and luxury she deserves."

"You say she is a girl, but in your heart you see her as a woman—your woman."

"That is true," James Thomas agreed. "She is old beyond her years. Her humor, her understanding, her compassion and her enthusiasm are far beyond the years of her body. We will settle this pact between the tribe and the white men at the fort. After that I will return to Virginia and make peace with my family. Then I will go into the wilderness and try to forget."

"Do you believe that living without a woman will make you forget the one you love?"

"I believe that there is only unhappiness for both of us if I stay."

"I will miss you, my friend," Black Hawk said. "Be easy in your mind, knowing I will watch the girl and keep her from harm."

"And I will miss you, but I know my way is best for me."

"That is all a man can know. I wish you peace, whatever path you choose."

Without speaking again, they moved silently along the riverbank stalking their prey. Their thoughts, once again, were their own.

It was shortly after the Cadwalders moved into their new home that Melisue first saw Black Hawk.

He was watering his horse at a stream that bordered their property.

"You can't water your horse here," Melisue said imperiously. "Go away. Go someplace else." She turned to her sister. "Beth Ann, don't look! You shouldn't cast your eyes on a half-naked savage."

Beth Ann didn't challenge her sister, nor did she obey her. It was all too obvious, both to Beth Ann and to the Indian, that Melisue was doing more than casting her eyes on the man. She was feasting her eyes on him. Taking in every sinew, every curve and angle of the man's body.

"Melisue, I think the water on that side of the creek belongs to someone else. Maybe it's his. We'd better go."

The Indian gave Beth Ann a rudimentary glance before returning his impassive stare to her sister. It was impossible to tell what he was thinking, and Beth Ann was just as happy she didn't know. The air snapped with tension. The man didn't speak, but continued to water his horse, ignoring Melisue's words, but obviously very aware of her body.

"Go on, now." She shooed him with her fingers. "Get out of here. You have no business so near our home."

"It is *you* who have no business so near my home," he replied.

Melisue gasped, obviously startled at his use of the English language. "Who are you?" she asked, moving her horse closer to the water.

"I am called Black Hawk." His gaze never faltered as he held her blue eyes with his black ones.

"I'm Melisue," came the reply.

"I know who you are." He swung effortlessly onto his horse. "And you are everything I was told you would be."

A moment later he was gone.

"I wonder what he meant by that remark?" Melisue asked aloud as he disappeared over the nearest hill.

"Maybe he's coming back to offer Papa half a dozen horses and a few blankets for you." Beth Ann giggled, remembering some of the stories James Thomas had told of Indian bartering.

"And I suppose you think Papa should take them," she shot back.

"I don't think you should have looked at him the way you did," Beth Ann told her. "I think he took it as an invitation to return."

"How you do run on," Melisue said as she turned her horse and started back toward the house. "He probably didn't understand half of what was said, and if he did, he probably didn't like it."

"He understood the way you looked at him, and he liked that a great deal," Beth Ann commented, following her sister. She wished that James Thomas hadn't gone to visit his family and was there to counsel her on the possible ramifications of the meeting.

Beth Ann felt a certain amount of embarrassment at the grandeur of their new house. It was so obviously the largest and most ostentatious on the plains. Many acres of timber had been stripped to produce it, and some of the settlers seemed to resent the situation.

What they thought, or *why* they thought it, didn't bother Melisue in the least. She believed herself to be far above the local populace. The house only gave credence to her assumption that she was above the rest of the women in the area by right of birth.

Incapacitated by her advancing pregnancy, Suzanna gratefully allowed Beth Ann to take over the management of the house, which she did with the same gracious hospitality her mother had maintained in New Orleans.

Upon learning that Suzanna was incapacitated and somewhat of an invalid, the local women took time from their myriad duties and flocked to see her at home, anxious for the touch of elegance the house gave their lives and the memories it invoked, despite the pain those memories caused.

"My family could have bought and sold that girl before the war," one of the transplanted matrons confided to her neighbor as Melisue left the room.

"I worry for the younger girl," Mrs. Wexler told them. "She's such a sweet little thing. I hope the men won't think she's as fast as her sister."

"You live close by." The matron leaned toward Mrs. Wexler. "Have you heard something we should know?"

"Oh, heavens, no," Mrs. Wexler said, her teacup rattling into the saucer. "I simply meant Melisue is always flirting with the men from the fort. It may have been acceptable behavior in New Orleans, but I assure you that out here it means trouble."

The matron nodded. "Men in this part of the world have little time for flirting. Too much work to do. Any girl who teases may find herself in a peck of trouble." She jerked her chin to emphasize her words.

Beth Ann stood frozen behind them, allowing the air to escape her lungs only after they had gone on to another subject.

As she served the tea cakes, her mother entered the room from the veranda and all thoughts of conversation regarding Melisue were discontinued. Beth Ann couldn't help but be relieved that they didn't know of Melisue's meeting with Black Hawk at the creek, or of the meetings that had followed. But her relief was short-lived, as Mrs. Wexler soon launched into the subject.

"I tell you, I was absolutely terrified when they appeared at my door. I'd been baking bread all morning, and apparently the smell attracted them."

"Bears?" Suzanna inquired, thinking she had missed the beginning of the conversation.

"Raccoons?" the widow Howard speculated.

"Good heavens, no. Indians."

The look of astonishment on the faces of the other women brought a look of satisfaction to Mrs. Wexler's face.

"Where was your husband?" Suzanna asked.

"Gone off somewhere in the fields. Not near enough for me to call and have him hear me. I gave the Indian a loaf of bread, and he went on his way. Thought I was done with him, but a while later he came back and brought his friends with him. I gave them all the rest of the bread I'd baked. They took it and left. Now I'm almost afraid to bake for fear they'll come back again."

"They were probably just passing through," the widow assured her. "Most Indians keep pretty much to themselves. And with the treaty that Mr. Thomas is making with them, we shouldn't have to worry."

"Mr. Thomas isn't here," Mrs. Wexler reminded her.

"But his treaty is, and so is his Indian friend, Black Hawk. I've seen him around several times. Nice-looking young man—for an Indian. Probably has some white blood in him." The widow Howard sipped her tea and smiled at the other women.

"I'd just as soon they'd keep their distance," Mrs. Wexler fussed. "They make me nervous, no matter how good-looking they are. Besides, they smell . . . gamy." She sniffed the air dramatically as Melisue breezed into the room and settled herself on the settee next to the woman.

"What game are you talking about?" Melisue asked, helping herself to a tea cake. "I just love games myself, and heaven knows we have little enough to entertain us out here."

"Most of us are too busy to play games," the widow Howard said, puffed up with indignation.

Mrs. Wexler sniffed again, but this time a strange expression crossed her face, and she quickly hid in the depths of her teacup.

Beth's eyes shifted nervously from the woman to her sister.

Mrs. Wexler's nose twitched like a rabbit's, and her eyes widened by the second. Then the teacup slipped from her saucer onto Melisue's lap.

"Oh, my dear, I am so sorry. How clumsy of me." She leaned even closer to Melisue and brushed the drops of liquid from her skirt as Beth jumped to her feet to retrieve the cup and saucer and place herself between her sister and Mrs. Wexler.

Melisue shocked everyone by replying graciously. "It's all right. I didn't have time to change from my riding clothes. A drop or two of tea won't be noticed after the workout I gave that horse."

"Oh," Mrs. Wexler mumbled, unable to hide the hint of disappointment in her voice, "of course, it's the horse."

"The horse?" Suzanna repeated.

"The . . . scent . . ." Mrs. Wexler said weakly.

Melisue laughed aloud. "Well, certainly. You didn't think I was wearing the newest fragrance from France, did you?"

"Oh, no." Mrs. Wexler groped for a good excuse to explain her behavior. Unable to do so, she said bluntly, "We were talking about the Indians, and, well, not realizing you had just come in from riding, I thought I . . . sensed some nearby."

Beth put the cup and saucer on the sideboard, silently congratulating Mrs. Wexler on her choice of words. The explanation had pacified both Melisue, who had good reason for not wanting the whereabouts of her ride to be known, and their mother, who was upset with her daughter for coming to tea without changing from her riding habit, as well as being perturbed with Mrs. Wexler for thinking there were Indians in her drawing room.

"Would you care for another cup of tea?" Beth Ann offered.

Mrs. Wexler was already halfway to the door. "No, thank you. I didn't realize it was so late. We really must hurry along." She eyed her companion meaningfully. Reluctantly the woman followed her from the house.

"I thought that nosy Mrs. Wexler would swallow her tongue trying to find out where I'd been," Melisue said as she smoothed her dark curls into place and turned before the mirror.

"I thought Mother would collapse when you came in to tea smelling for all the world like you'd just come from the stable," Beth Ann told her.

"Now don't you start. Perhaps I was a bit late. I still put in my appearance in time for tea. That's really all that mattered, wasn't it?"

Beth Ann giggled. "Actually, it was your timing that caused all the trouble."

"Whatever are you talking about?" Melisue turned her full attention from her toilette to her sister.

"Mrs. Wexler had just said that Indians smelled gamy, and when you sat down beside her it was so obvious she included you in the same category that I could scarcely keep from laughing."

"She thought I smelled like an Indian?"

"Maybe she associates Indians with horses," Beth Ann explained.

"Maybe she knows more than she's telling." Melisue tapped her hairbrush against the palm of her hand.

"What could she know?" There was a hint of nervousness in Beth Ann's voice.

"I was with Black Hawk this afternoon." Melisue relished the shock in her younger sister's eyes. "You remember Black Hawk, that handsome man we met by the river the other day?"

The river Melisue spoke of was hardly more than a running stream, but Beth Ann didn't bother to correct her as her sister continued.

"I've seen him several times. I think he's in love with me."

Beth Ann blinked in astonishment. It was unthinkable for a young woman of Melisue's social standing to fall in love with an Indian, no matter how handsome. "Are you in love with him?" she managed.

"He is the most handsome, exciting, beautiful creature I've ever laid eyes on." Melisue's eyes gleamed with unnatural brilliance. "We go off and ride together and I sit behind him on his horse and wrap my hands around his chest and hang on for dear life."

When she saw that Beth Ann was too astonished to respond, Melisue went on. "Today he put me on the horse in front of him and held me close against him. I don't think he smells gamy. Maybe some Indians, but not Black Hawk. He smells like the grass in the meadow and the earth just after a light rain. He smells like the wind as the dark clouds appear on the horizon."

"Oh," Beth Ann mumbled.

"Oh? Is that all you have to say? You're always complaining because I never talk to you, and now here I am baring my very soul and all you can say is 'Oh.'" She moved closer, smiling. "Don't you want to know how it feels to be pressed against a man's naked body?"

Beth Ann shook her head, but Melisue took no notice.

"He feels like fine leather, soft and pliable, but with all the strength in the world just beneath my fingertips. And his skin is warmed by the sun. It radiates through him, and when I'm near him, it radiates right into me. I love to be near him like that and feel the muscles in his legs and arms and back and—"

"Never mind," Beth Ann choked out. "I understand."

"Oh, my poor little sister. I've embarrassed you." Melisue laughed. "But just imagine the thrill, the excitement of being his woman."

"Wha-what are you going to do? You aren't thinking of marrying Black Hawk, are you?" The thought was too outrageous to contemplate. Papa would have apoplexy, and Mama would die of embarrassment.

Melisue allayed her fears. "Good heavens, no! Can you see me wandering around the country picking nuts and berries with a bunch of squaws? But that doesn't mean I can't enjoy his company. I wouldn't think of marrying any man we know, unless, of course, it would be Mr. Montgomery."

"Does he know how you feel?" Beth Ann asked.

"Mr. Montgomery? Well, I hardly think so. You don't believe I'd throw myself at his head, do you?"

"I meant Black Hawk," Beth Ann explained lamely.

"Oh, Black Hawk most certainly does. He's 'felt' just about all of me there is, within certain proprieties, of course." Melisue wrapped a light shawl around her shoulders. "Now you'd better hurry and get ready for dinner. Papa doesn't like to wait." She waltzed out of the room as Beth Ann sank weakly onto the bed.

Her fingers automatically went to her hair, smoothing the strands and tucking her braids more securely on top of her head. Melisue's words echoed through her brain. She had never thought of a man in the way Melisue had described. She had never thought of the scent of his body, or the feeling of his skin. Once in a while, when her hand touched James Thomas's she felt her heart jump so hard she was sure he must have noticed, though he was too much of a gentlemen to let on.

She was aware of a certain scent about him. He smelled of rich leather and sometimes of shaving soap. His hands were big and warm and strong, and she felt safe when he lifted her into the wagon. Safe in his hands. She wondered if the touch of his lips would be as jolting as the touch of his hand, warm and gentle and so very, very wonderful.

She could feel his eyes as they sought her out when he came into a room, or when he made a little joke that he knew she would understand and share with him. She had never given thought to the fact that he had a body beneath the buckskins he wore, although she was certain it exceeded Black Hawk's, no matter how highly her sister praised the Indian.

Rachael Bright's voice calling her to dinner brought her from her reverie. She glanced in the mirror once more before running down the stairs. Breathless, she paused at the door of the dining room to compose herself. It was then that she saw Melisue seated at the table, the candlelight enhancing her soft white skin, her ebony hair and her shining blue eyes. Once again she heard her sister's words: "I wouldn't think of marrying any man we know unless, of course, it would be Mr. Montgomery." And Mr. Montgomery was Beth Ann's own James Thomas.

Chapter Seven

The day the treaty was formally accepted proved to be one of great excitement. The Indian chiefs rode past the Cadwalder home, followed by their entourage of braves, all carrying themselves with silent dignity.

"There he is!" Melisue waved her handkerchief from the balcony above the veranda. "There's Black Hawk. See him right behind the Indian with all the feathers on his head?"

She pointed and waved again. Some of the braves raised a hand in response, but for the most part her greeting was ignored.

Beth Ann had eyes only for James Thomas, whose shining hair was in direct contrast to the dark heads of the Indians. Like the sun in the midst of night, Beth Ann thought dreamily. He looked toward their house as he passed. She felt their eyes meet, as she always did when he looked her way.

Once more, Melisue tried to get Black Hawk's attention, waving furiously as she leaned over the balcony railing.

A hand closed on her waist and jerked her back so abruptly the handkerchief fell from her hand and fluttered to the ground.

"What do you think you're doing?" Rachael Bright demanded. "Well-bred young ladies don't hang over balcony railings trying to attract the attention of a bunch of Indians!''

"We thought it was like a parade," Melisue explained lamely. "We thought we were supposed to wave."

Beth Ann read the disbelief in Rachael Bright's eyes and said nothing.

"Get back inside," the woman ordered, shooing them before her. "And don't let me catch you waving at Indians again." She fired the words at Melisue, who gave her a haughty stare before flouncing through the door.

The voices in the sitting room brought Beth Ann to a halt at the foot of the stairs. She crept toward the door, very much aware that it was not polite to eavesdrop, but unable to resist when she identified the deep, resonant tones coming from the room as those of James Thomas. She slipped into a little alcove at the side of the door and prayed that Caleb or Rachael Bright wouldn't see her there.

"I appreciate your offer to stay here as your assistant," James Thomas was saying, "but I've already made plans to go on up toward Montana. It's too crowded here to suit me."

"I hope you aren't in a big hurry to leave us," Brandt Cadwalder said. "We've been planning a formal gala at the end of the week. The ladies are looking forward to it."

"I'm afraid I'll have to forgo that pleasure," he replied. "There's a wagon train coming through here on Friday morning. I've agreed to scout for them."

Brandt hesitated before asking, "Isn't there any way we can change your mind? You see, the gala is to be in your honor."

Before James Thomas could reply, Beth Ann heard the soft rustle of her mother's skirts and moved away from the door. "I was just looking for you," Beth Ann lied. "I heard voices and thought you might be with Papa."

"I'm just going to join him." Suzanna took her daughter's arm and drew her into the room. "Come along. There's someone here I'm sure you'll want to see."

Beth Ann wished that instead of eavesdropping she had gone back to her room and made herself more presentable. Here she was in a drab housedress, her hair in braids instead of the tight curls Rachael Bright was teaching her to make. She wondered if it would do any good to pinch her cheeks and bite her lips to give them color the way Melisue did.

The men rose to their feet as Beth Ann and her mother entered the room. Suzanna went to greet their guest, but Beth Ann hung back, memorizing every feature, every line and contour of James Thomas's face. If he left, she might never see him again, but she would remember him forever.

He bowed over her mother's hand before turning to Beth Ann. "Little one!" The joy in his voice was reflected in his face. Without further word, he broke every propriety of social decorum and held out his hands.

Ignoring the shocked expression on her mother's face, Beth Ann ran across the room and threw herself in his arms.

"You've grown." He held her at arm's length before hugging her again. "In the short time I've been gone you've grown taller and even prettier."

"Have I grown prettier, too?" Melisue stood framed in the doorway, the ultimate picture of a Southern belle. Then she skimmed across the room, hoops swaying, until she stood before James Thomas with an expectant smile on her face, waiting for his reply.

"You always manage to look very nice," he said, returning his attention to Beth Ann.

"Don't I get a hug?" Melisue persisted, punctuating her words with a pretty pout.

He bent over her hand, displaying all the formality befitting a Southern gentlemen.

"You're too old to be hugged like a child," Suzanna admonished.

"I've been trying to talk James into staying with us until after the gala," Brandt said, before either of his daughters could speak again. "Perhaps you girls can succeed where I have failed."

"Oh, please, do stay and be my escort," Melisue pleaded. "I've turned down ever so many offers waiting for you to return." She looked up at him through her lashes.

"You can't mean to leave right away." Beth Ann's voice echoed her sister's distress. "You've only just come back."

A gentle smile touched his eyes. "Are you going to the gala?" he asked.

Beth Ann floundered in confusion. She had given little thought to the gala. It was to be an all-day barbecue followed by a ball, and there was little chance she would be allowed to attend both functions.

Realizing that the presence of the guest of honor might depend on his younger daughter, Brandt Cadwalder announced, "Most certainly Beth Ann will be there. This is her first ball, and I'm certain she would consider it more memorable if she could be assured you would attend." He ignored the disapproval on his wife's face and beamed at their guest.

Seeing the excitement on Beth Ann's face, James Thomas gave up all thought of further protest. "In that case, I would be honored to escort both of your daughters to the gala."

Suzanna's obvious surprise kept Melisue from protesting aloud. Their mother had not planned on having Beth Ann attend the ball. With a few well-placed words, permission might well be denied, and Melisue would have James Thomas to herself, at least throughout the evening. Secure in her own mind that Suzanna did not plan to let Beth Ann go to the evening festivities, Melisue remained silent, attaching herself to the arm of their guest as Caleb announced dinner.

Suzanna hung back, waiting for the girls and their guest to leave the room before addressing her husband.

"Have you taken leave of your senses?" she demanded. "Beth Ann is hardly old enough to attend the ball. Such a thing wouldn't be contemplated if we were back home."

"You can ask anyone, Suzanna," Brandt said heatedly. "Other girls Beth Ann's age will be at the ball. Talk to Mrs. Wexler and see if I'm not correct. There is no impropriety."

Suzanna wrung her hands. "I'm sure you'd never do anything that might be misconstrued as inappropriate with regard to our daughters. I suppose it will be all right if she doesn't stay too late. Rachael Bright can come along and take her home when the time comes."

Brandt put his arm around his wife. "That sounds like a fine idea to me. I can't wait to show off all my lovely ladies to our neighbors."

Suzanna did not bother to mention that most of their neighbors had seen them already.

Tiny whirlwinds of dust punctuated the air as the barbecue got underway. For hours, wagons and carriages had been arriving at the fort carrying excited settlers to the affair.

Due to Suzanna's failing health and Melisue's total lack of interest, it fell to Beth Ann to arrange the fort building that would be used by the women when it was time for them to change into their ball gowns. She took special pride in showing her new acquaintances where they could leave their finery until needed.

The wagons kept arriving throughout the day, and it wasn't until James Thomas sought her out that she gave any thought to her own enjoyment of the barbecue.

"The food is almost ready," he told her. "Why don't you let one of the other women greet the newcomers while we find something to eat?"

She smiled in agreement as they walked together toward the shaded area. Most of the women were busy setting out the food or watching the antics of the excited children, but Melisue sat regally, surrounded by a bevy of young men.

"Oh, there you are, James," she called, waving prettily. "I've saved a place for you right here." She moved her voluminous hoops and patted the bench beside her.

James Thomas looked at the designated area and then at Beth Ann. "I'm afraid there's not enough room," he said.

"But of course there's room," Melisue told him, pouting prettily. "Beth can go along and help mind the children."

Beth Ann bit back an angry retort, but James Thomas saw the hurt in her eyes.

"Your sister has agreed to join me to eat barbecue," he said firmly. "We'll have to decline your offer."

He was rewarded by the smiles of the young men swarming around Melisue, and he turned a deaf ear to her protests as he led Beth Ann away.

"You didn't have to do that," she told him as she took the plate he gave her.

"I wanted to be with you," he replied. "I want to tell you about the country where I'm going to live."

Beth Ann didn't want to think about him going away and never coming back, but if he must go, she wanted to be able to visualize the land in which he would live. "Is it so very different from this?" she asked.

"Very different," he replied. "There are tall mountains topped with snow, even in the summer. And there are trees reaching to the heavens. Animals abound. There is no lack of rain or food or beauty. The air is so fresh and clear you can taste it, and when you walk across the ground the dust does not swirl up and choke you."

"Will you build a soddy?"

"I'll build a cabin, and perhaps a trading post. There are beaver in the many streams, and other fur-bearing animals for the taking."

"You want to run a trading post?" She had never thought of him as a trader, but the idea appealed to her.

"People are beginning to settle that area. Once there, they'll need supplies. I can work with the Indians, as well as the settlers."

"I know you'll be successful at whatever you do," she said. "But if you have a trading post, won't you have to come back for supplies?"

He understood her guileless query and found it almost impossible to tell her the truth. "I will be able to get my supplies much closer than Fort Kearney—but," he added, "I may come back just to visit you."

"You'll always be welcome," she managed, feeling as though her heart would break if she never saw him again. Then the words burst out, unbidden: "I wish my father would move on. He could run a trading post, too. Perhaps we could live closer together."

"I think your father has settled in. He doesn't want to move again."

His voice held a touch of wistfulness he had thought never to feel again. His dream of living in the beautiful country he had chosen was blighted by the knowledge that Beth Ann would not be there to share it with him. Even as he had said his farewells to his family, his mind had been on the girl. Her gentle beauty, her spirit and her generosity toward others made him want to claim her as his own.

By the time he would be able to return to Fort Kearney, she would most likely be besieged by beaux, as her sister was now. She would have no thought for him other than a distant memory of an older man she had befriended.

There was a noticeable bustle as the women began clearing away the remaining food, and the chatter took on a new cadence as they talked of getting ready for the evening's festivities.

Beth Ann shifted nervously, watching the others disappear. As much as she wanted to stay with James Thomas, she wanted even more to prepare for the ball.

He understood her anxiety and helped her to her feet. "I believe I saw your mother heading toward your carriage. Perhaps you should join her." He softened the words with a promise: "I'll see you in a few hours and take you to the ball."

A smile lit her face as she walked at his side across the yard.

"There you are!" Melisue's voice rang above the ceaseless chatter. "Hurry on now. I'll scarcely have time to make myself presentable before it's time for Mr. Montgomery to come for me." She smiled up at him through her lashes and was slightly confused when he took no notice of the flirtatious effort that had worked without fail on the young men that afternoon. "I swear, it will take hours to rid myself of this dust." She brushed ineffectually at her dress.

Pushing forward, she reached the carriage. It was only after she seated herself and looked for her sister that she realized that James Thomas was solicitously assisting the girl into the carriage.

"Well, I never," Melisue exploded as they left the Fort. "What was meant by that little display? Surely Caleb could have helped you into the carriage as he did the rest of us. You're going to ruin my reputation the way you carry on with that man."

"I don't think I need to worry about that," Beth Ann returned impassively.

"Mama, see how childish she is," Melisue complained. "She doesn't even see how ridiculous it looks for her to be chasing after that Indian scout all the time. She's too young and immature to go to the ball. She should stay home and go to bed like the other children her age."

"I saw nothing improper in Beth Ann's deportment today. She worked all morning helping the settlers find their quarters, and she took her barbecue in a crowd of people of all ages, not in a secluded alcove with a group of young men." Suzanna was already exhausted, and she dreaded the long hours before she could rest. Once again she thanked God that Beth Ann had taken on the duties that should have been her own.

Melisue pouted in annoyance.

"If you dance with each of the young men you favored with your smiles today you won't have time to dance with your escort," her father observed.

"Oh, I'll always find time for James Montgomery," Melisue said, tossing her head. "And when he sees me tonight, he won't so much as look at anyone else. And that's a fact!"

With one last meaningful look at her younger sister, Melisue let the others to talk of the happenings at the barbecue.

For three solid hours, the Cadwalder house rang with the sound of scurrying feet as the ladies prepared for the ball. Servants flew up and down the stairs carrying bathwater, while the sound of Rachael Bright's name echoed from every corner.

"Where's Rachael Bright?" Melisue raised her voice beyond what could be construed as ladylike. "I want her to wash my back. I think my nose is reddened from the sun. Tell her to bring some buttermilk. And hurry!"

Lucy entered the room with the buttermilk and was ready to apply it to Melisue's skin, but the girl brushed her hand away. "I said I wanted Rachael Bright. Where is she?"

"She's with your mama," Caleb's wife told her. "You'll just have to make do with me until the missus gets dressed."

Melisue sniffed indignantly. "This is an important night for me. My first ball at the fort. Mama should be able to get ready with your help. Go help her and send Rachael Bright to me."

The girl was immersed in a tub of water with her hair tied up on her head. Beth Ann sat across the room, smoothing the folds of the gown her mother had made over for her to wear that evening.

"Go on!" Melisue urged. "Tell Mama I need Rachael Bright."

Lucy put the pitcher of buttermilk on the wash stand and ambled out of the room.

"And hurry!" Melisue yelled after her.

"There's no rush," Beth Ann pointed out. "It's hours before we have to leave. You'll have plenty of time to get ready."

"You take all the time you want, but I intend to be ready when Mr. Montgomery arrives." Melisue leaned back in the cooling water and stared dreamily into space.

Her anxiety over getting ready was more than just nervousness about being on time. She had planned to be dressed before the rest of the family. Thus, when James Thomas came to the door, she would float down the stairs, a vision of loveliness in her ball gown, and win his heart and everlasting devotion.

How the rest of the community would gape when she arrived on his arm and made a grand entrance into the beautifully decorated hall where the ball would be held! If only she didn't have to share her moment of triumph with her little sister.

She sloshed water over her shoulders, wondering idly if he had anything to wear besides his buckskins. Anything less than formal attire would ruin her entrance. Besides, if she had to be escorted by a man in buckskins, she would rather it be Black Hawk. Her smile changed to a low laugh. Entering the ball with Black Hawk would certainly start the settlers to talking.

Of course, the whole idea was so outlandish it was hardly worth thinking of as more than a joke. Still, she wanted Black Hawk to see her in her ball gown. She had told him as much the last time they had met, and he had promised to try to fulfill her wishes.

Lucy came back into the room, dipped a soft cloth in the buttermilk, and began rubbing it on Melisue's face.

"What are you doing?" the girl sputtered. "I told you to get Rachael Bright. Where is she?"

"I told you she was with your mama, and there she stays. If you want to get ready in such an all-fired hurry, you'll have to make do with me."

Silently Melisue allowed Lucy to continue her ministrations. The bathwater was cold and floating with the remnants of buttermilk when the girl stood up and allowed the woman to rinse her with clear water and wrap her in a towel.

Then Lucy started toward the door.

"Where are you going?" Melisue demanded.

"I'm callin' Caleb to come get this bath emptied."

"He can't come in here until I'm dressed," Melisue said.

"But Miss Beth Ann needs her bath," Lucy explained patiently.

"She can use my water. Now you come over here and help me dress."

Beth Ann looked at the congealing buttermilk floating on the dirty water and made a face.

"Miss Melisue, you'd better cover yourself, because I said Caleb was comin' in to empty that bathwater, and comin' in he is!''

"You forget your place, Lucy." Melisue bristled with indignation. "My father will—"

"Mr. Cadwalder will nothin'," the woman replied. "I'm a free woman. I work for your family, and I get paid for workin'. I don't have to put up with somethin' I know is wrong. Now put on your dressin' gown, 'cause Caleb is on his way."

Melisue wrapped the gown around her body as the butler knocked on the door.

Melisue was dressed, coifed and ready before her sister had even put on her dress. Secure that her plans were going well, she placed herself in the upstairs hall, where she could see when James Thomas came to the door. She gave Rachael Bright a little smile as the woman went to fix Beth Ann's hair.

"I don't see why she needs to have you braid her hair," Melisue complained as Rachael Bright hurried down the hall. "After all, a braid is a braid. How much can you do with it?" She patted her own glistening curls and smoothed the hair piled high on her head and secured with jeweled clasps.

"Don't you worry about your sister, Melisue," Rachael Bright answered. "She's going to look just fine." The woman stopped at the door and looked back at the lovely creature preening herself at the top of the stairs. "Or was that what you were worried about?"

Melisue stamped her foot in agitation as Rachael Bright slipped through the door.

Beth Ann's ball gown was a soft blue with ruffles across the bodice—both outside and inside—giving her diminutive figure a more mature look. Her hair hung like an ebony shawl around her shoulders.

Rachael Bright motioned to a stool before the mirror. "Sit down here." As soon as the girl was seated, the woman began working the silken strands and pinning them up on her head.

"Aren't you going to braid it?" Beth Ann had been almost afraid to ask. Her mother would surely have objected to anything more than pinning the usual braids on top of her head, but Rachael Bright obviously had other ideas.

Her hair was drawn back off her face and coaxed into long, thick curls that fell from the back of her head, where they were secured by blue satin rosettes trimmed in lace. The transformation that took place in the mirror before Beth Ann's eyes was so dramatic that the girl could scarcely believe what she saw.

She had entered the room a girl, and now, thanks to the ruffles in the gown and the magic of Rachael Bright's hands, she would leave it a pretty young woman. Had she not seen how lovely her sister looked, she would have actually thought herself beautiful.

She jumped to her feet and hugged Rachael Bright in uninhibited enthusiasm. "Oh, thank you, thank you," she cried.

"Now, now, none of that," Rachael Bright admonished gently. "You don't want to streak your cheeks with tears." She patted some powder on the girl's face. "There! You don't need to pinch your cheeks. The sun has given you a little color, and you look good enough to eat."

The dogs barked as a carriage drew up in front of the house. Beth Ann stopped breathing. Would James Thomas like her this way? Would he think she was pretty? Or would she be diminished by Melisue's undeniable beauty?

"Do I look all right?" she asked Rachael Bright. "Did I forget anything?"

"You look just fine, honey," the woman assured her. "You're going to be the belle of the ball."

Beth Ann opened the bedroom door in time to see Melisue begin her descent down the stairs.

Melisue's voice floated through the house. "Why, Mr. Montgomery, aren't you just the handsomest thing?"

"I couldn't very well wear buckskins when I was escorting two lovely young ladies to a ball, now could I?"

Melisue's voice took on a note of regret. "I am so sorry, Mr. Montgomery, but Beth Ann got too much sun this afternoon. I'm afraid you'll just have to make do with my company tonight. Come now, let's do go. Mama and Papa will meet us there."

Beth Ann raced through the hall. She was halfway down the stairs when James Thomas found his voice.

"My God . . ." It was a prayer. He came toward her, his words for her ears alone. "You are so beautiful, you break my heart."

"And you are so beautiful you have stolen mine forever," she answered.

The young woman in her ball gown, with her hair curled like a fashionable young lady, and the man in his dress suit, complete with tie and white collar, stood frozen in time for the span of several seconds. They stood in unabashed awe of each other while Caleb grinned from the doorway and Rachael Bright beamed from the hall above.

Beth Ann placed her hand on his as he escorted her down the rest of the stairs.

"Thank you for getting dressed up to take us to the ball," Beth Ann managed. "I know you don't like to."

"You remembered that from when we were talking on the wagon train?" He laughed in delight. Then he sobered, and no one who heard them could doubt his words as he told her, "I consider it an honor to be allowed to escort a lady as lovely as yourself, and well worth dressing for."

Brandt Cadwalder stopped short at the sight of his younger daughter. He turned to his wife, scarcely able to hide the emotion in his voice. "That is exactly the way you wore your hair the first time I saw you. For a moment I thought time had stopped and I'd been transported back to my youth. It is like seeing you three times the girls look so identical to you—as a young woman, a bride, and my beautiful wife.''

''That's right, Papa. Make me feel badly because Mama was married before she was my age.'' Melisue's words brought everyone back to reality.

''The last thing I want is to have anyone feel badly this evening. After seeing your popularity at the barbecue, I'm sure you could marry any of the young men who were so enthralled with you this afternoon. Why, I wouldn't be surprised if at least one of them asked for your hand tonight.''

Without giving his eldest daughter a chance to object, Brandt escorted both Melisue and her mother out the door.

Chapter Eight

The carriage carrying Melisue and her parents arrived at the fort and stopped before the hall. Flowers and streamers climbed every post and rafter. Greenery abounded along the draped entry leading to the area where the ball was to be held. Suzanna and Brandt were anxious to enter the gaily decorated building, but Melisue hung back, waiting for her sister and James Thomas.

"I would simply die of embarrassment if I had to go into that room on the arm of my father," she said. "It's bad enough that I have to share my escort with my sister, and I want you to know that if he were anything less than the guest of honor I would never have considered such a thing."

A pained expression crossed Suzanna's face. Where had she failed with this headstrong but beautiful daughter? Why had she no control over the girl? And where in the world would she find the strength to correct the problem?

Before Melisue could be properly reprimanded, James Thomas was helping Beth Ann from his carriage as though she were made of fine porcelain and he feared that any sudden movement might cause her damage.

"Oh, there you are, Mr. Montgomery," Melisue called. "I swear, we thought you'd eloped with my baby sister. Papa was about to call out the cavalry to bring about your return, weren't you, Papa?'' Her forced laughter sounded above the music from inside the hall.

With one of the Cadwalder girls on each arm, James Thomas entered the ballroom. Even the music halted as all eyes turned to the new arrivals.

The young men stationed at the fort converged on them before they were able to so much as move. Unerringly James Thomas extricated himself and Beth Ann, leaving Melisue to cope with her admirers. Before she realized what was happening, the music had started again and James Thomas swung Beth Ann out onto the floor.

Seething with anger, Melisue accepted the offer of the nearest man and danced lightly across the room. She was a vision of cream-colored ruffles and pink roses, her hoops twice the width of those of any other woman in the hall.

Beth Ann glanced at her sister with a twinge of foreboding. How could James Thomas continue to pretend to prefer her company to that of Melisue when every other man at the ball found it impossible to hide his admiration? Determined to do her best not to embarrass her partner, Beth Ann concentrated on his steps, not realizing how unbelievably beautiful she looked as she followed him gracefully across the floor.

James Thomas saw Beth Ann's beauty and realized how their steps matched—just as their thoughts had matched so many times. Once the music stopped, he led her from the floor and brought her some punch.

Her eyes sparkled above her glass. ''This is the happiest night of my life,'' she told him.

''A girl's first ball should be just that.''

''Not because it is my first ball, but because I am here with you. Each moment I spend with you is the happiest of my life.'' Her eyes were a liquid blue, gleaming in the soft light.

Before he could speak, they saw Melisue bearing down on them.

"Can you believe it?" she challenged. "Everyone says it's going to rain. What a disaster! Imagine, rain on the night of our first ball. I wonder if it's a bad omen? Do you believe in omens, Mr. Montgomery?" She paused for breath, her breasts heaving from exertion.

"I believe in myself and my own instincts," James Thomas told her. "It won't rain until the ball is well under way, if it does at all. The soldiers are running a canopy from the front of the building just in case, so don't worry about ruining your gown."

"I'll never wear this gown again," Melisue told him, laughing. "It's Beth Ann who should worry about its being ruined. After all, when I'm done with it, most likely I'll give the gown to her."

"And I'm sure she will look as lovely in it as you do," James Thomas said gallantly.

"I doubt it," Melisue said dryly. "She hasn't the figure for it, but then, if I remember correctly, neither did I at her age. However, I believe I do the gown justice now, don't you, Mr. Montgomery?"

"You look lovely," he replied obediently, "as I'm sure you've been told by every young man here tonight."

"I believe I've missed a few." Melisue smiled up at him. "But the music is starting again, and, as my escort, it's your duty to dance with me. I'm sure you'll find dancing with me far more enjoyable than trying to teach poor little Beth Ann."

"I was delighted to discover that Beth Ann knew exactly what she was doing," James Thomas said as he left Beth Ann with her mother and escorted Melisue to the floor.

"You aren't really going away tomorrow, are you?" she asked, looking provocatively into his eyes.

"I must leave at the first light of dawn. I've pledged my services to the people on the wagon train that went through here the latter part of the week. I can't leave them on their own any longer.''

"When will you be back?"

"I am settling up near Montana," he explained. "I don't plan to return."

"You don't want to live out in the wild, do you?" she teased. "Why don't you take a wife and stay here? I know my father offered you a job. Would it be so bad to live here with a beautiful, devoted wife for a few years and then return to the loving arms of your family in Virginia? Think how happy they would be if you returned to take your rightful place. You'd never have to work again."

"The plantation is in shambles. I almost stayed just to try to help them get it back to rights, but they convinced me that I would only be another mouth to feed. Should I do as you suggest and marry, it would be not only myself, but my wife, and eventually my children, who would have to be fed, clothed and housed. I am better off making my own way and sending what I can spare back to my family until they are able to support themselves."

"How you do go on!" Melisue said, gliding along to the music. "Look at my family. You don't see us starving, do you?"

"Your father is from the North, and that's where his money was invested when the war broke out. Your mother's family is in almost as bad straits as my own. That's one of the reasons you were not sent to them, rather than coming out here."

Melisue digested the information. "I must say you do present a convincing case, Mr. Montgomery. You should have studied law."

"I did," he said as he swung her across the hall to the strains of the violins.

* * *

When the music stopped, James Thomas excused himself, leaving Melisue once again with her throngs of admirers. She tried to call him back, but was unable to attract his attention. Her face flushed when she saw him again seek out Beth Ann's company.

"I do believe I need some fresh air," Melisue said. "It's so close in here, I can hardly breathe."

Several of her admirers escorted her to the door, where they stepped out into the night.

"Oh, I was right," she exclaimed. "See the lightning? It is going to rain and spoil our party."

"That's nothing but heat lightning, ma'am," one of the soldiers said. "It's way across the prairie, and no threat to us. You just come on and enjoy yourself and don't worry about the weather." He tried to draw her into the hall, but she held back.

At the edge of the shadows she saw the outline of a familiar figure. Deftly dodging the young men, she was able to see Black Hawk disappear into the stables.

He had come to see her in her ball gown. She fluffed the creamy ruffles that covered the skirt from waist to floor. "You gentlemen will really have to excuse me," she said, smiling demurely. "I have to go and powder my nose."

Without giving them time to get over their shock at her blatant admission, she disappeared around the side of the building.

James Thomas and Beth Ann had danced almost every dance together. It wasn't until heat and exertion sent them to a bench outside the back of the building that they were able to talk.

"What's wrong, little one?" James Thomas asked when she looked over her shoulder for the tenth time in the same number of minutes.

"I'm expecting Rachael Bright to come and tell me it's time to go home," she admitted. "I've never been allowed to stay out so late."

"You look so lovely tonight."

"Do you really think so?" Delight shone in Beth Ann's eyes. "I wanted to look my age, so you wouldn't always think of me as a child when you have gone far away."

"I will remember you as everything bright and beautiful," he said. "I only wish it were somehow possible for you to share my life. Someday...somehow..."

Forgetting propriety, she clasped both her hands over his. "That is my wish, too. More than anything in this world, I want to be with you. I would wait for you to come for me forever."

He knew he could not take her with him. Not only did he doubt she could endure the rigors of the life he would be forced to live, alone in the wilderness, but he was aware that Beth Ann had become the bulwark of her family. Suzanna's health had forced her to depend on her younger daughter to the point of almost reversing their roles as mother and daughter. No matter how much he loved Beth Ann, no matter how empty his life would be without her, he could not ask her to leave her family and go with him.

"There is no need to wait forever," he said, raising her hand to his lips, "only until I can build a home and a life to share with the woman I love."

Was he saying she was that woman? Dared she believe that she, Beth Ann Cadwalder, was the woman he loved? "You will go away and forget all about me," she responded.

"Or you will forget me." He gestured toward a group of young men in military uniforms. "How can I expect you to wait for an old Indian scout when there are so many men closer to your age from which you can choose?"

"I would choose you above all of them," she told him. "I would choose you above all the men in the world."

"You say that now," he said with a smile, "but it will take months, maybe years, before I will be able to share my life with a woman. The country where I am going is wild and untamed. I could not, in good faith, ask any woman to share it with me until I knew she would be safe."

"I always feel safe with you." It was an honest answer, and she prayed he would know that the words came from her heart, as well as her lips.

"I would never want that feeling to change."

She could not find the words to answer, and she pressed her hand against his cheek, surprised at her effrontery but unable to stop herself.

He leaned forward and lightly touched her lips with his own, praying that God would forgive him for taking that first precious kiss from this child-woman on the night of her first ball. Praying that her words held true meaning and that she would wait for him, for he knew that he would come back for her.

She leaned toward him, her lips clinging to his as though she would never let him go. He placed his hands on her shoulders and gently set her away from him, aware that his heart hammered in his breast as wildly as hers must be hammering beneath the ruffles of her gown.

"I have something I want to give you. It belonged to my mother, and her mother before her, and now I want it to be yours. Something to remember me by."

She swallowed with difficulty, her lips tingling in the aftermath of his kiss. Not the kiss of a man and a child, but the kiss of a man and a woman. There was a difference, she knew—now.

"Wait here." He squeezed her hands and got to his feet. "I'll be right back. The ring is in my saddlebag in the stable. Wait here for me, Beth Ann."

"I'll wait," she managed. "No matter what happens, I'll wait. Forever."

As she watched him walk across the grounds toward the stables, a feeling of foreboding washed over her. Had she dared, she would have called him back, so great was her momentary panic. Then she chided herself for being childish. Here was a man who loved her. A man who had asked her to wait for him and had promised to return to fetch her once he had built a home for the two of them.

Her heart sang in harmony with the music, and her happiness drowned out her premonition. She hummed the tune struck up by the musicians and tapped her foot to its rhythm, waiting patiently for James Thomas to return.

James Thomas's eyes scanned the heavens. The distant lightning had come closer, and he could hear the sound of thunder announcing the coming storm. Heavy clouds swept across the night sky. His journey to join the wagon train would be a wet, and most likely, a cold one, but he didn't care, for he would be warmed by the memory of Beth Ann.

The door to the stable swung open silently. James Thomas paused before advancing into the building. He planned on sleeping in the stall beside his horse once his formal clothes had been carefully packed away. It was in the stall that he had stored the saddlebag, which held the little sapphire-and-gold ring he'd seen so many times on the hands of the women of his family.

Once again he paused. The feeling that something was out of place came to him again. But only the muffled snorts and grunts of the horses came to his ears. He spoke soothingly to his horse and took the saddlebag from the nail where it hung. He was bending over the bag looking for the pouch in which he had placed the little ring when a clump of hay fell against his back. He turned quickly and caught a glimpse of eyes watching from the loft above.

"Identify yourself," he called. "No one is to be in here during the ball." He knew that to be the absolute truth. Even the stable boy had been allowed to watch the festivities. There was no good reason for anyone to be in the stable at that hour of the night, and that left only circumstances that spelled trouble. Quickly he mounted the ladder and climbed to the loft.

"Don't come up here," a woman's voice pleaded as he neared the top.

It was too late. Realizing that he had stumbled upon a lovers' tryst, he was more than willing to ignore the whole situation and go back to Beth Ann, but the sound of the woman's voice struck a chord in his mind.

His eyes opened wide as he saw Melisue struggling with her gown, and to his abject horror he realized Black Hawk was trying to help her.

The consequences of their little romantic interlude would be quick, as well as devastating, should they be discovered. Indian braves didn't make love to white women, especially when the woman in question was the daughter of the most powerful man in the territory.

"What in the name of a merciful God do you think you're doing?" he burst out.

One look at James Thomas's face told Melisue it would be useless to lie. Even she couldn't think of a reason for being in the stable unless she wanted to be here.

She cleared her throat and brushed a piece of straw off the ruffle on her shoulder. "I wanted to show Black Hawk my dress," she said, with what dignity she could muster, while trying to tie the huge bow at the back.

"And what was he doing? Trying it on?" James Thomas could see the weeks he'd spent making the treaty going to waste. He turned in anger to his friend. "How could you allow this to happen?" he asked Black Hawk. "Don't you realize that if you're caught here with Melisue you'll be killed?''

Melisue gave a little gasp. She knew that her father had killed one man to defend her honor, and this was far more serious than the incident in New Orleans. She didn't want Black Hawk to die because of her—unless, of course, it was due to a broken heart when she told him she couldn't go with him.

''You mustn't let them hurt Black Hawk,'' she pleaded, real concern in her voice. ''He must get away.''

''If they even suspect that the two of you were here alone together, the treaty will be voided, whether Black Hawk is caught or not,'' James Thomas explained.

Melisue laid a soft hand on his arm. ''Oh, Mr. Montgomery, you simply must help us. I'd just do anything to keep from being the cause of a war with the Indians.''

Black Hawk grabbed her wrist and pulled her into his arms. ''You will come with me. We will go so far away they will never find us. You will be my woman. I will marry you in the white man's church if that is what you want. We will be very happy.'' He lifted her in his arms and carried her down the ladder, where he placed her gently on her feet.

''Think, man!'' James Thomas grabbed his friend's arm. ''They will come after you if you take the woman. They will say you stole her, and again the treaty will be worthless. Many people will die. Both white men and Indians.''

Melisue put her hands against him. ''Oh, Black Hawk, please go,'' she begged. ''I don't want anybody to die.'' She stopped short when she saw the determination in his eyes. He didn't care who died. He wanted her for his woman. He would kidnap her and make her live like a squaw. There would be no balls, no galas, no barbecues, no lovely dresses, and no chance of ever returning to civilization in Virginia or Boston. ''I don't want there to be a war with the Indians.'' She knew instinctively that, should such a war break out, their lovely new house would be abandoned and she would be forced to live inside the fort in a room with her mother and sister, and soon a squalling baby. The horror of the situation fairly took her breath away.

"Say your goodbyes," James Thomas ordered. "I'll take Melisue back to the dance."

"No! This is my woman!" Black Hawk crushed Melisue against him. "She comes with me. The treaty is your problem."

Before James Thomas could voice another protest, Black Hawk had scooped Melisue up in his arms and started toward the back of the stable. As he reached the door, they heard a man's voice.

"I tell you there was an Indian sneakin' around here earlier this evenin', and now Miss Melisue can't be found anywhere. He probably scalped her for that pretty hair of hers and she's lying in there stone-cold dead."

"They say that scout can't be found anywhere, either. She's probably off with him somewheres. He's in pretty thick with her daddy. Maybe he's out sparkin' her."

"Well, let's look in here first. If she hasn't showed up by the time we get back to the ball, we'll have to get a search party together."

Black Hawk slammed his shoulder against the doors, holding them shut.

"Damn things must be stuck. Let's go around and see if we can get through the doors on the other end."

Melisue allowed her breath to escape, but the man's next words brought her up short.

"There's Mr. Cadwalder. Have you seen any sign of your daughter, sir?"

"Let her go!" James Thomas told his friend. "If they catch you here like this they'll kill you. They'll probably kill us both."

Melisue's eyes narrowed as she felt Black Hawk's grip relax. She pushed away, leaving him standing in the shadows.

The door opened as she reached James Thomas's side. She could feel the tension in the man beside her, as well as that of Black Hawk. If the truth became known, both men might easily die right before her eyes.

Melisue looked up into James Thomas's face. She saw that he would not allow his friend to be killed and the treaty nullified by an all-out Indian war.

"Do you really believe there will be a war if my father learns the truth?" she asked.

"Yes, I do." James Thomas tried to read the frenzied excitement in her eyes but was unable to do so.

"If the war could be averted and the situation explained away to my father's satisfaction, what would you be willing to give?"

"I would give anything I have to stop this tragedy." The moment the words were out of his mouth, he wished he could take them back, for the look in Melisue's eyes was the same he had seen in the eyes of a rattlesnake poised to strike.

Without further indication of her intent, she turned to face the men.

"Papa, I have such wonderful news," she gushed, running to her father, a smile of happiness lighting her face. "Mr. Montgomery has asked me to marry him. We were just coming to ask your permission. Isn't that the most wonderful news you've ever heard?"

"So that's why you were away from the ball for such a long time, you sly kitten." He kissed his daughter and, with his arm around her, walked over to James Thomas and shook his hand. "We heard there was an Indian sneaking around here somewhere and thought you were about to be stolen away."

"Oh, Papa, how you do go on," Melisue laughed. "That wasn't just any Indian. It was Black Hawk, come to say goodbye to Mr. Montgomery.'' She turned and indicated the place where Black Hawk had been standing, only shadows now. ''I guess all the excitement was too much for him.'' She put one hand through James Thomas's arm and the other through her father's. ''Let's go back to the ball.''

''May I have a dance when we return?'' one of the young soldiers asked as she brushed past him.

''Oh, I'm afraid not. I'm an engaged woman now. I couldn't dance with anyone but my future husband.''

James Thomas felt as though the whole world were crushing down on him. He knew he must keep silent until Black Hawk was well away. If the young Indian was killed, there would indeed be war. He had told Melisue he wanted to avert that war at all cost, but he had not realized the price she would put on his words. With his free hand he fingered the little ring in his pocket. He looked for Beth Ann, but he could not find her in the crowd that blocked their path with questions and congratulations as the news spread.

Thunder shook the earth as the sky split with lightning. The storm let go its fury over the perfidious farce that was being played out. The heavens opened, and the guests scurried back into the hall as Brandt Cadwalder stepped onto the platform and held up his hands for silence.

''Ladies and gentlemen . . .'' he began, his words punctuated by the thunder. ''Ladies and gentlemen, it is my pleasure and my honor to announce the engagement of my daughter, Melissa Sue Cadwalder, to our good friend Mr. James Thomas Montgomery.''

Chapter Nine

The crowd of well-wishers surged forward to congratulate the newly engaged couple while the musicians struck up a lively tune.

James Thomas looked above the crowd to the open doorway, where Beth Ann stood waiting, her eyes filled with pain and disbelief. Before he could extricate himself from the throng the wind gusted through the hall, slamming shut the doors as the rain pelted down like tears from the heavens.

Beth Ann stared at the doors, unaware of the rain that soaked her gown, or the cold wind that buffeted against her. Her mind was numb, as was her body. The thing she wanted most in the world had been within her reach, and now it was suddenly snatched away by her sister. It was beyond her power of comprehension to understand how such a thing could have happened, and she stared at the closed doors as though they shut out all hope of happiness.

The plummeting rain took on the cadence of hoofbeats and she looked up in time to see a horse and rider gallop through the gates of the fort. Her mind must be playing tricks on her, for the man had looked like Black Hawk. But how could that be? What could the Indian be doing at a ball?

If she was indeed hallucinating, perhaps the announcement of Melisue's engagement to James Thomas was also a figment of her imagination. He had said he was going to get something from his saddlebag. He had told her he would return for her and take her to the home he would build for the two of them. He had asked her to wait. He had made her promise, and that promise she had given willingly and with all her heart.

Ignoring the wind and rain, heedless of the lightning and thunder, Beth Ann returned to the bench where she had been sitting when James Thomas had kissed her. If she stayed there, perfectly quiet, perhaps she would discover that this was all a bad dream, and he would return with his gift, and the night would again be clear and filled with stars with only a hint of disaster, far away, like heat lightning in the distance.

It was a distraught Rachael Bright who discovered the girl some time later. She wrapped a dry tablecloth around Beth Ann's shoulders and led her to the carriage, shivering and soaked to the skin.

By the time they reached the Cadwalder home it was evident that Beth Ann had a high fever. Rachael Bright put her to bed and stayed by her side, unaware of the drama unfolding in the parlor.

"I think a May wedding would be nice," Melisue purred as she entered the house, followed by her parents and a reticent James Thomas.

"May would give us the time to prepare a proper trousseau," Suzanna mused, her mind still numbed by the events of the evening. Everything had happened so quickly—and without a hint of warning. She felt so weak. How could she possibly assume the responsibility of planning Melisue's trousseau, much less the wedding?

For the past few months she had allowed Beth Ann to assume the responsibilities that should, by rights, have fallen to the lady of the house. Melisue's wedding was another matter, however, and Beth Ann could not be expected to rejoice at her sister's engagement, much less plan the nuptials.

During the commotion that had followed the announcement of her sister's engagement, Beth Ann had somehow been caught in the oncoming storm and had taken a chill. Suzanna looked at the door to her daughter's room, closed against Melisue's happiness.

It bothered her that she had been so wrong about the relationship between James Thomas and her daughters. She had been so certain that he cared deeply for Beth Ann, and yet it was Melisue to whom he had proposed marriage. Perhaps his interest in Beth Ann had only been that of a man for a younger sister. Yet she had been so sure. . . .

Exhausted both physically and emotionally, Suzanna excused herself and mounted the stairs, hoping that Beth Ann's illness was not the result of having been under the same misconception.

Brandt Cadwalder accompanied the couple into the parlor, noting the stiff reserve with which James Thomas held himself. There was none of the adulation he would have expected from a man caught up in a love that brought about such an abrupt engagement.

He offered his future son-in-law a chair and was about to seat himself when James Thomas made his request.

"I know it is unusual," he said, "but this engagement has come about rather abruptly. I would like to have a few words with Melisue, alone."

Sated with the congratulations of the guests at the ball, not to mention the personal pride she took from having pulled unlimited success from what might have been a disaster, Melisue lethargically nodded her agreement.

"We've had so little time to discuss anything," she said, smiling affectionately at James Thomas.

"I realize that," Brandt said officiously, "but I hardly think this is the time or the place. It's late, and we're all tired. I'm sure you can make your plans tomorrow."

"I'm afraid not," James Thomas returned. "I leave at first light. As I told you, I'm scouting for a wagon train and must join them as quickly as possible."

"But surely you don't intend to meet that commitment when you've just become engaged?" Brandt exclaimed before Melisue could speak.

"I see no reason to change my plans," James Thomas said.

"But what about the parties that will be given in our honor?" Melisue objected, suddenly alert now that her social life was being threatened. "I simply can't attend them alone. How would it look?"

Thinking they had been swept away by the heat of the moment, Brandt decided that the newly engaged couple did, indeed, need time to discuss their future. He beamed proudly at his daughter, certain that she would be able to convince James Thomas to stay.

"Very well. I can see you have things you must discuss. I'll go see how your sister is doing." He paused at the door. "Remember, James, that position I offered you is still available." He was halfway across the hall when James Thomas stopped him.

"What's wrong with Beth Ann?" The concern in the man's voice was obvious.

"She wasn't feeling well. Too much excitement, I suppose. Rachael Bright brought her home some time ago."

Without giving the younger man time to ask anything more, Brandt turned on his heel and went up the stairs.

The memory of Beth Ann's face haunted James Thomas as he returned to Melisue.

"I am leaving in the morning. I am going to settle near Montana. I have made no plans to come back here."

"Well, then, you'll just have to make some plans," Melisue challenged haughtily. "I want a May wedding, and there will be a million things to do before then. I need you here," she said as she ran her hand down the sleeve of his coat.

"I don't intend to change my plans," he said firmly. "And I don't intend to come back here in May."

"Well, when will you come back?" Melisue was taken aback by his failure to succumb to her overtures. A light touch on the arm usually made a man her humble slave.

"I'm not coming back," he repeated. "If you want to marry me and make this farcical engagement something more than a clever ploy to save yourself from a bad situation, you can be ready to leave in the morning."

"That's impossible!" she cried. "You said yourself that the place you intend to live in is no place for a lady. How would I survive?"

"I have no idea." He turned his back on her and looked again at the door, his mind shifting to Beth Ann, whom he had allowed to be hurt by this farce.

"Even if I were to go with you it would take several days before we could be married," Melisue said, stalling. Given time, she knew, she could prove to him that life in the wild was folly and returning to Virginia with a beautiful wife was the road to true happiness.

"There is a traveling preacher with the wagon train." His voice was hard, emotionless. "He can perform the ceremony for us. By the time we reach our destination, with any luck, you should be with child. The country needs to be populated."

Melisue's face turned red. "What a horrible thing to say! You can't really expect me to go off into the wilderness and have a baby every year like—like some Indian squaw!"

"I didn't expect to marry you. If you feel this contract is a mistake, perhaps we should break the engagement before it goes any further. You could wait a decent period of time and then tell the locals that you're tired of waiting for me and have found someone else."

Melisue's mind worked quickly. The men at the fort were, for the most part, Northerners of no social standing. It was highly unlikely that she would find anyone who could give her the home and servants she expected.

"I love you, James Thomas," she whispered, advancing on him again. "I've always loved you. You know that, don't you?"

"Somehow the factuality of your love evaded me when I found you in the stable with Black Hawk."

"I was just trying to make you jealous." She smiled tremulously, looking up through her lashes.

The thought of spending his life with a woman who twisted the truth into unrealistic lies almost gagged him. She spelled trouble wherever she went, and he knew it would be only a matter of time before she caused pandemonium should she be allowed to travel on the wagon train.

"You promised to do anything if I would avert an Indian war and keep Black Hawk from being killed. I did the only thing I could think of." Tears of self-pity welled up in her eyes. "Now you want to desert me and embarrass me before the whole community."

"Had you not been in the stable with Black Hawk, there would have been no need to fear an Indian war," he reminded her. "I will stand by my word. If you wish to be my wife, be ready at dawn."

Melisue flounced over to the settee and dropped onto it. "I would have been better off going with Black Hawk," she lamented.

"If I see him, I'll send him back for you," James Thomas said as he started toward the door, no longer able to contain his worry over Beth Ann. He had to know how she was faring. He needed to speak to her, to explain what had happened, and ask her forgiveness.

"Don't bother sending Black Hawk," Melisue returned. "I'll wait for you. Regardless of what you say now. Someday you'll come back, and I'll be waiting."

"Then you'll have a lifetime to wait, because once I leave here I won't return."

"You lie!" She threw the words at him. "You'll come back, if only to see Beth Ann."

Stung by her words, he bit back the angry retort and forced himself to control his voice. "That might have been true once, but no longer. There is nothing here for me."

"You can't desert me like this," she wailed. "I'll die of embarrassment. My mother is in a delicate condition. She might not be able to survive the trauma of having her daughter deserted at the altar."

He took a deep breath. "Then don't set a date to go to the altar." He should never have allowed Brandt Cadwalder to make the announcement, but he'd had no idea the man proposed to do so until he entered the hall and heard the words being spoken. Realizing that Black Hawk must have time to leave the fort, he'd kept silent, and now it was too late. "Once I have built a place to live I will send word to you. As to whether or not you come, the choice is yours."

Brandt Cadwalder was coming down the stairs when James Thomas opened the door.

"Have you settled your little differences?" he asked, aware of the angry flush on Melisue's face.

"We've come to an understanding," James Thomas assured him. "Is Beth Ann awake? I'd like to say goodbye before I leave."

Melisue gave a little gasp and stamped back into the sitting room.

"Rachael Bright is with her. Suzanna has gone to bed. I suppose it would be all right if you said your farewells. She's always been very fond of you." Without giving it another thought, Brandt went to see to the well-being of Melisue, wishing with all his heart that his wife were there to handle the situation.

James Thomas's light knock was answered by Rachael Bright. A frown creased her forehead when she recognized him. "What do you want here?" she demanded in a harsh whisper. "Haven't you done enough already? Leadin' Miss Beth Ann on and treating her like she was somebody special and then asking Miss Melisue to marry you. You should be ashamed of yourself."

"I'm more than ashamed," James Thomas said truthfully. "I'm leaving as I planned, and I'm not coming back. I had to see Beth Ann again. I have to tell her...to explain."

"She's sleeping, and what you might want to tell her couldn't do anything but hurt her more. You're going to marry her sister. There's no room in this child's life for you anymore."

Before she could continue her tirade, Suzanna called Rachael Bright's name. She glanced from the man to the sleeping girl. "Don't you wake her up with your false confessions. Leave her alone. If you marry Melisue, it's because you deserve her."

Rachael Bright brushed past him and hurried to answer Suzanna's call.

James Thomas paused only a moment before crossing the room to kneel beside Beth Ann's bed.

"This wasn't the way things were supposed to be," he whispered. "I went to get the ring for you and found Melisue and Black Hawk in the stable together. If your father had known Melisue was alone with an Indian, he would have killed Black Hawk. I want you to have the ring.'' His voice broke as he took his mother's ring from his pocket and slipped it onto Beth Ann's finger. It fit perfectly, as he had known it would.

When she awakened, she might throw it away in righteous anger, but that was her prerogative. He gave her the ring just as he had given her his heart—irrevocably, and forever.

It was wrong for a grown man to cry. He'd thought he had shed all the tears in his soul when his family had been torn apart by the war between the North and the South. Virginians all, they had possessed independent opinions on what was right, and brothers, cousins, uncles, as well as friends, had died for both sides before the fighting ended. It was a waste, such a waste.

For a brief moment he had thought to pull success from the tragedy by building a life with Beth Ann, far from men who gloated over their victory or were unwilling to admit defeat. Now, even that dream was lost, for he knew instinctively that Melisue would not let him go easily. But at that moment, with Beth Ann's sweet face before him, he could not accept the thought of spending the rest of his life with Melisue.

Pampered and petted, she would demand constant service in a territory where each person must carry his own share of the burden, or none would survive.

With tears in his eyes, he whispered his final goodbye to Beth Ann. He then left the room, the house and the whole Cadwalder family behind, without another word to any of them.

Ghost voices haunted Beth Ann's dreams. Again and again she heard James Thomas begging her to forgive him. Heard him explaining how he had gone to get the ring that had belonged to his mother and grandmother and... It was no use, she could not remember.

She struggled through the thick darkness until she awoke to find herself in bed, the anxious faces of Rachael Bright and her mother hovering over her.

Suzanna took Beth Ann's hand, pressing it against her cheek. "Oh, my precious child!" Suzanna cried. "You've been so ill. We feared for your life."

Rachael Bright's face acknowledged Suzanna's words, and Beth Ann allowed the dreams to swarm about her as she wondered which were real and which only nightmares. Then she saw the ring on her finger. She drew her hand away from her mother's face, desperately trying to focus her eyes. She did not remember having seen the ring before, yet she knew without doubt that this was the ring of which James Thomas had spoken. The ring he had promised her at...the ball? She remembered his words, the tender love that had shown in his eyes as he spoke of the future. It hadn't been a dream, for here, on her hand, was the ring he had offered as a token of his love.

She closed her eyes and pressed the ring to her lips, drifting gently in and out of consciousness as she relived the moments they had spent together. Yet, even through her happy memories, she felt a niggling of unrest. She turned to her mother to verify her recollections and wipe away the shadows.

"The ball! Did I really go to the ball?" Beth Ann asked.

"Of course you did, my darling," her mother told her. "And you were as lovely as anyone there."

"And James Thomas, where is he?"

"Why, Mr. Montgomery went out west somewhere," Suzanna said nervously, wondering if Beth Ann remembered her sister's engagement.

"Then he's already gone?" Beth Ann asked in a tiny voice.

"He left right after the ball," Rachael Bright said, plumping the pillows. "He stopped in to say goodbye, but you were already asleep. It wasn't until the next morning that we realized how sick you were. By that time he was gone."

"He stopped by to say goodbye to me?" Beth Ann felt like a fool, changing every answer into questions, but she couldn't seem to get the sequence of events clear in her mind. "How long has he been gone?"

"You've been sick well over a week," her mother said soothingly, "but you're better now, and the doctor says you're going to be all right."

"Yes, Beth Ann, you'd better hurry up and get well. I want you to help me plan my wedding," Melisue said once she had burst through the door. "It's to be in May, and that's not all that far away."

Beth Ann looked at her sister in confusion. Rachael Bright grabbed Melisue's arm and pushed her back toward the door. "Beth Ann isn't feelin' well enough to talk about weddings right now. You come back with your big plans some other time, when she's stronger."

"Oh, Rachael Bright, how you do fuss! There's few enough girls out here who are socially acceptable to be my bridesmaids. Beth Ann *must* be in my wedding. Now you hurry and get well," she called from the door. "James Montgomery and I would be devastated if you couldn't be there when we get married."

Beth Ann closed her eyes. Quietly her mother and Rachael Bright followed Melisue out of the room without noticing the tears that flowed silently down Beth Ann's cheeks and disappeared into her hair.

Spring came, and with it the birth of little Brandt Cadwalder III. Beth Ann devoted herself to her little brother while Suzanna took her time recovering from a difficult but highly gratifying birth. Her husband was euphoric over his son, showering his wife with gifts. Beth Ann remained in charge of the duties of the house. She even spent much of her spare time making the courtesy visits to the neighbors that her mother had instituted.

Oblivious of the fact that James Thomas had neither returned nor written, Melisue went on with her plans for a May wedding. But even her enthusiasm dwindled as no word came from her intended.

"I am going to have to change the date of my wedding," she announced one evening at dinner. "Mama isn't getting well as quickly as I had hoped, and goodness knows, a girl needs her mother to arrange a wedding."

She picked at her food and watched the faces of the others at the table. Her father was well aware that no word had come from James Thomas. Once the man had seen the members of the wagon train to their destination, he had apparently disappeared from the face of the earth. Therefore Brandt Cadwalder heard his daughter's decision to postpone the wedding with relief. It would be embarrassing to have a wedding without a bridegroom.

"Are you going to set another date for the wedding?" Beth Ann asked.

"Not at this time," Melisue said. She looked at her sister sharply, trying to find some hidden meaning in her words. "Why, for all I know, he might be lying out there dead. Killed by a beaver, or a fox, or one of those other animals he was telling me about before he left."

"Or he could be living with the Indians," Beth Ann said. "And speaking of Indians, they're back. I certainly hope they mean to honor the treaty."

"What do you mean, they're back?" Melisue demanded. "Who's back? How do you know?"

"Why, Mrs. Wexler saw Black Hawk down at the stream watering his horse the other day. She told me when she stopped here for tea this afternoon." Beth Ann frowned at her sister. "If you came in for tea occasionally you'd know all the gossip."

Melisue smoothed her napkin across her skirt. "Who wants to hear their old gossip? What's so interesting about a bunch of Indians, anyhow?"

"I have no idea," Beth Ann said noncommittally. "I just mentioned they were back. You were the one asking the questions."

Melisue jumped to her feet. "Well, I never! Here I am just trying to make dinner conversation and I get accused of being interested in the Indians. I've never been so hurt." She swooped out of the room, her skirts swishing with indignation.

Chapter Ten

By the time baby Brandt was eighteen months old, he thought of Beth Ann as a second mother. She spent every spare moment with him, unlike the other women in the house. The one called Mama had little energy left to play with him, and the one called Melisue screamed when he came near her, telling him he was not to touch her skirts. His happiness revolved around Beth Ann, who always found the time to play with him and tell him stories.

Melisue spent as little time as possible at the house. Although she had kept up the facade of an engaged woman, it finally became apparent, even to her, that James Thomas had disappeared into the wilderness and was either unable or unwilling to contact the woman he had agreed to marry.

Speculation abounded, for though every traveler was asked for news of the man who had forged the lasting treaty with the Indians, no one was able to give any news of him.

After months of silence, it was assumed James Thomas had been killed. While Melisue took on the status of a bereaved fiancée, it was Beth Ann who alternately grieved and hoped that the man might yet return.

Her shock had lessened, and although she didn't understand what motive might have made James Thomas propose marriage to Melisue, she accepted the fact that it had happened and that there was nothing she could do to change

the situation. Beth Ann was no longer a skinny little girl.
Her prayers had been answered, and she had blossomed into
lovely womanhood. The men at the fort swarmed around
the Cadwalder sisters, spoiling them with attention.

After the rumor of James Thomas's death spread through
the countryside, the men turned their attention to the viva-
cious Melisue, for Beth Ann kept them at a friendly distance and refused to consider their proposals. In her own
mind she still saw herself as a girl, a girl who, through lack
of physical attributes, had lost the man she loved.

"Your twin daughters are so lovely," one of the new settlers told Suzanna as they watched baby Brandt play in the
garden.

Suzanna stared at the woman in surprise before looking
at Melisue and Beth Ann. To her amazement, she found it
difficult to tell them apart from a distance. Had it not been
for the fact that baby Brandt ran unerringly to Beth Ann,
Suzanna would have had to move closer to tell the two girls
apart. It was amazing how Beth Ann had grown up in the
past months.

"The girls aren't twins," she told the woman. "In fact,
there is over a year between their ages. Beth Ann is like my
right hand. She oversees the making of the candles and soap
and sees that the mending and sewing is done. When Lucy
and Rachael Bright were busy harvesting the crop they
planted on their properties, she even cooked the meals."

"What a joy to have such a daughter," the woman exclaimed. "And the other girl? She seems so friendly and
popular. I see her at the fort almost every day."

"Oh, yes," Suzanna agreed, too quickly, "Melisue is very
popular."

"It's so sad about her young man. Dying out there in the
wilderness, I mean. She takes it so bravely. I do hope she
finds someone to take his place. They're both such lovely

girls.'' The woman twisted her hands nervously before continuing. ''I hope you won't think me forward, but my brother will be visiting here from Mississippi. I was hoping you would allow him to be presented to your daughters.''

''I'm sure they would be pleased to meet your brother.'' Suzanna smiled, unaware that Melisue had skirted the garden and come to a halt behind her.

''Honestly, that baby manages to smudge my clothes every time he comes near me,'' Melisue complained. She brushed at an imaginary spot.

Suzanna ignored her daughter's complaint. ''This is Miss Colfax,'' she said. ''She was just telling me that her brother is coming to visit from Mississippi. I told her we would do all we could to make him feel welcome.''

''Brother? From Mississippi?'' Melisue preened herself. ''How lovely. I shall be delighted to meet him. It's so seldom we meet a true Southerner out here.''

Miss Colfax squirmed uncomfortably. Her brother had seen Mississippi for the first time after the War between the States.

''Is your brother in business?'' Melisue asked, showing real interest.

Instinctively, the woman knew that if she gave the wrong answer neither she nor her brother would be welcomed by Melisue. How she wished she'd left well enough alone and quietly introduced her brother to Beth Ann, who would have paid him little notice and asked no questions.

''My brother is in the shipping business,'' she stumbled breathlessly.

''I hope he doesn't run one of those terrible little pig boats up and down the river,'' Melisue prodded.

''Oh, good heavens no,'' Miss Colfax responded. ''He is in steamboats. The big paddle wheelers.''

"How exciting," Melisue gushed. "I just can't wait to meet him. You must bring him around just as soon as he arrives."

Although the settlers found it more and more difficult to tell the Cadwalder girls apart, it took very little time for them to differentiate between Beth Ann's generous nature and Melisue's manipulative ways.

The girls did not acknowledge their pronounced resemblance, though Melisue gave several of her old gowns to Beth Ann, then teased her parents into buying her new ones. Although the styles had changed and hoops were much smaller, Melisue insisted on wearing her hoops as wide as possible, thus accentuating the smallness of her waist and the fullness of her bosom.

Beth Ann did not wear hoops except on special occasions, preferring to follow the example of the settlers. She was returning from a visit to the Wexler household when she stopped to water her horse at the stream. The air was hot and still, and she allowed the horse a much-needed rest.

Suddenly a hand closed around her wrist, almost toppling her from the saddle. She looked down to see the copper skin of an Indian and lashed out with the reins as she dug her heels into the sides of the horse.

The man grabbed the halter and brought the horse to a halt as he dragged her from the saddle.

"Why do you avoid me?" he asked, wrapping his arms around her. "Why do you refuse to meet me anymore? Always before when I came back to the plains you were happy to see me. You said you would never love anyone the way you love me, and now that snake from Mississippi takes all your time."

Beth Ann tried to push him away, but he held her tight, nuzzling her neck as he tried to invoke a response.

"I don't know you," she managed. "Let me go. I've never agreed to meet you."

"Don't tease me." He crushed her against his chest. "We know each other too well for that."

"We don't know each other at all!" Desperation gave her strength, and she shoved him away, stepping back far enough to get a look at her attacker.

A frown creased his brow. He walked around her warily. It had been almost a year since he had been near the white woman who fascinated him beyond understanding. And this looked like the woman—the same blue eyes, the same black hair—yet the skin was not the stark white color that intrigued him so. This woman had skin that carried a touch of the sun in its healthy glow.

"You are not Melisue," he said.

"I am Beth Ann," she returned. "And you must be Black Hawk. I remember the day we met you and Melisue told you not to water your horse at the stream."

"I remember that, too." He remembered something else. He remembered his friend James Thomas telling of his love for the younger Cadwalder girl. The one named Beth Ann. "My good friend Jim told me of you."

"What do you know of James Thomas? Have you seen him? Melisue believes he's dead."

Black Hawk watched the girl closely. She looked no older than Melisue had been when he met her, and she looked so much like her sister that he had been unable to tell them apart. Was she like Melisue in disposition, as well as appearance? Was her love as fickle as that of her sister?

"If Jim came back, he would be forced to marry your sister," the man said placidly. "Is that what you want?"

"I would be glad to see him married to Melisue if it meant he was alive." Beth Ann swallowed the lump in her throat. "He was my very dear friend. I cannot blame him for preferring Melisue to me. She is beautiful and charming."

"Did no one tell you what happened the night he became engaged to Melisue?" the Indian asked. He had promised James Thomas he'd watch out for this girl.

"I fell ill during the ball," she explained. "By the time I recovered, James Thomas was gone and Melisue was making plans for their wedding."

Beth Ann thought of the little ring she had discovered on her finger after her mind cleared and her illness was behind her. No one seemed to know where it had come from, and Beth Ann had slipped it into the little silver box lined with satin in which she had kept her treasures ever since she was a little girl.

"I am sorry that I thought you were Melisue. You look like her." He caught her horse and brought it back, patiently holding it while she mounted. He swung himself onto his pony, and he was about to leave when Beth Ann stopped him.

"Black Hawk, there has never been any proof that James Thomas is dead. If you were to learn that he is alive, would you tell me?"

"Why do you want to know?" the Indian demanded. "To tell your sister so she can again try to make him marry her?"

Beth Ann was taken aback by the vehemence of his words. "No, it's not that. It's just that, to me, the world would be a nicer place if I knew he still lived in it somewhere."

"You have my word that the world is indeed a very nice place. I have seen that this is so with my own eyes."

Reading the hidden meaning in his words, Beth Ann couldn't stop the tears of relief that flooded her eyes. "Thank you, Black Hawk," she whispered. "Oh, thank you so much."

He watched her ride away, so like her sister and yet so different. It would be many months before he again saw his friend Jim, and he wondered how he would tell him of Beth

Ann. These women were fragile. They could not take the hardships of the life lived by men like Jim and Black Hawk. Perhaps it would be wrong to tell him of the girl other than that she was well. Perhaps it would be better to forget that the conversation had ever taken place. Black Hawk had many months to think on the problem. When next he saw his friend Jim, he felt, he would have the answer. He had no way of knowing that James Thomas had already made a decision of his own.

The mountain man tied his horse to the hitching post in front of the Montgomery Trading Post. He waved to several townspeople as he secured his mules next to the horse before entering the building.

James Thomas's voice rang out. "Casey Stubbs! It's good to see you! How was the trapping?"

"Got some good skins," the man replied. "You can go over them and take your pick." He glanced out the window toward the street. "Town's growed some since I was here last."

James Thomas laughed. "Town's growed a lot," he agreed.

"Gettin' downright civilized." Casey Stubb's blue eyes twinkled above his russet beard. "Before long you'll be building a church and startin' up sewin' bees."

"The church may not be too far off," James Thomas admitted, "but it'll take a few more ladies to get the sewing bee going."

Both men laughed as James Thomas offered his friend a cup of rich, dark coffee from the pot on the stove in the middle of the store.

Casey took a sip and stared at the wall for a few minutes before he spoke again.

"You ever get lonely up here?" he asked finally.

James Thomas shot a quick look at the man. "Sometimes," he said. "What makes you ask?"

"I been gettin' lonely once in a while," the big man explained sheepishly. "That old horse of mine don't talk much, and the mules aren't big on conversation, either."

"I thought you were going to take up with one of the Indian gals," James Thomas observed.

"Thought on it, I did, but when it came down to makin' the offer, I knew it wasn't what I wanted. I don't want to live with the Indians any more than I want to live with the white men. When it came right down to it, I realized I want a woman I can bring into town with me. Somebody that can talk to me about how things used to be back before the war. Can't do that kinda talkin' with a squaw." He sighed and poured himself more coffee. "Guess I'm gettin' old. The winters seem longer and colder, and I keep thinkin' about how nice it would be to have me a woman to talk to of an evening."

"You mean you're actually thinking of settling down?"

"Been thinkin' about it for a long time now," the man replied. "More people settlin' around here all the time, and I kinda enjoy the company. Hasn't been any trouble with the Indians to speak of for quite a spell. Another couple of years and maybe I could persuade some lady to come up and spend the rest of her life with me. If I don't do it soon, I won't be able to remember how to carry on a conversation."

He drained the last dregs of coffee from his cup. "I'm goin' over to the boardinghouse and get cleaned up." He paused and looked at James Thomas. "Why don't you come back with me? You look like you might like to spend some time with a woman—in conversation, that is."

"If I need to talk to a woman I'll go over and see Ma Barker at the boardinghouse," James Thomas told him. "She likes to talk."

"She's eighty if she's a day," Casey grumbled. "Once I get me a cabin built, not in town, but out a ways, I'm gonna find me a woman to share it with. You're gonna wake up some morning and find yourself a lonely old man if you're not careful. You mark my words."

"I'll give it some thought," James Thomas called as the door closed.

After Casey left, James Thomas tried to laugh off the man's words, but there was too much truth in them for them to be funny.

At first it had been impossible for him to build his cabin without visualizing Beth Ann in it. Her ghost stood before the fireplace, sat in the wooden rocker, at the table—it even greeted him from the porch. It was only when he added the bedroom that he forced himself to cease his imaginings and face the reality that she would never share his life.

Black Hawk had told him that Melisue remained unmarried and held on to her claim of being an engaged woman like a dog with a bone. James Thomas had given up all hope that she would marry someone else.

He had never meant to live in this beautiful country alone. His whole purpose had been to see it settled by other people who would love the peace and beauty the way he did. His dream had been to share his life with the woman he loved. He had found that woman in Beth Ann, and he had lost her because of Melisue. And now Melisue refused to let him go. From halfway across the continent she clutched at him, choking the happiness from his accomplishment.

He slammed his fist against the wooden counter. Casey Stubbs was right. It was lonely without a woman. The little community was growing. In the past three years it had gone from a lonely trading post to a tiny, beautiful town with a boardinghouse and a nearby sawmill. Even a doctor had hung out his shingle, and although he doubled as a barber, the man had doctor's credentials displayed prominently on his wall. There were a blacksmith and a wheelwright who had come with their wives and families, lending the laughter of children to the song of the birds. Yes, it was time to bring in the women, while the town was still fresh and unspoiled, on the edge of being settled but not yet stodgy.

If he could not spend his life with Beth Ann, he must take the proper steps to secure his release from her sister. He had made himself a prisoner in his own world because of an ill-gotten promise. There was only one thing for him to do. He would beat Melisue at her own game. Either she could come to him and be his wife, or he would make it impossible for her to do anything other than break the engagement.

He smiled to himself. He had no doubt what her answer would be. No power on earth could drag her through miles of wilderness to live in a cabin. He thought of painting the bleakest picture possible of his living conditions, but then, remembering her reaction to Rachael Bright's little sod house, he discarded the thought. The unadulterated truth would seem like a nightmare to Melisue Cadwalder.

And on that premise he would stake the rest of his life.

Chapter Eleven

Melisue picked up the stack of mail on the hall table. She scanned through it until she found her daily letter from Reginald Colfax, and she was about to put the rest back on the table when she realized there was another letter addressed to her.

Curiosity overcame even her anxiousness to read Reginald's impassioned compliments, and she opened the letter with the unfamiliar handwriting and read:

Dear Melisue:

I hope this letter finds you in good health. I put pen to paper as the time has come for me to take a wife.

Everything I discussed with Beth Ann has come to pass. I have opened a trading post and have built a small log cabin. Men are settling nearby and bringing their wives and families. There has been no serious trouble with Indians or outlaws for some time and I feel you could come and live here in safety. Therefore, I will be sending a Mister Casey Stubbs, who will bring you back here if you still want to come.

I realize the trip is a rigorous one and that life here is lonely and hazardous, and I will abide by your decision to come, or stay where you are, but be assured I am satisfied with the life I have chosen and have no intention of returning to Fort Kearney.

My best regards to your parents and, of course, to your sister, Beth Ann.

Most sincerely,
James Thomas Montgomery

So, James Thomas was alive! If one could call existing in the situation he had described living.

Even so, had he written sooner, Melisue might have at least considered his request, but now that she had met Reginald Colfax, who offered her the life of luxury and ease she desired, following James Thomas to the ends of the earth was out of the question.

Besides, she thought, glancing at the letter a second time, the only person he'd mentioned by name was Beth Ann. But that was no surprise. He'd always been solicitous of the girl. It was no wonder Beth Ann was so smitten by him. Well, she could have him, for all Melisue cared. Life in a log cabin in the wilderness might be just Beth Ann's cup of tea, but it didn't suit her one bit. A woman would have to be crazy to give up a gentleman like Reginald Colfax and the life he offered in exchange for a cabin and a man who preferred to wear buckskins.

Melisue folded the letter and tapped it against her hand thoughtfully. If she wanted to live in the wilderness, it certainly wouldn't be with James Thomas. Not when Black Hawk walked the earth. She smiled to herself as memories swept through her mind like the prairie wind rippling across the fields. Then the smile faded, and she slapped the envelope against the table in frustration.

Why did Black Hawk have to be an Indian? There was no way she could spend the rest of her life with him, and there was no way she could forget him or the magical times they had spent together. No man had ever made her tingle all over the way Black Hawk did. Not even Reginald, with all his expensive clothes and elegant manners.

She wondered vaguely if Beth Ann felt about James Thomas as she did about Black Hawk. The girl had certainly shown no interest in any of the young men who had presented themselves as prospective beaux. If it was James Thomas Beth Ann was pining for, she was welcome to him.

Letter in hand, Melisue headed for the nursery, where Beth Ann would be minding baby Brandt. She stopped short before she reached the door. What if their parents insisted that Melisue honor her promise to marry James Thomas now that he had prepared a place for her? Suppose her father refused to let her marry Reginald and banished her to the wilderness under her prior commitment?

Heaven knew, Brandt Cadwalder had been less than enthusiastic when Reginald had asked for Melisue's hand in marriage. Had it not been for the fact that Melisue had acquired her wedding dress, as well as her trousseau, in anticipation of her marriage to James Thomas, there was no telling what sort of objections her father might have come up with. As it was, it took all of Reginald's considerable powers of persuasion, plus Melisue's own affirmation that her life would be ruined should she not be allowed to marry, to get her parents to agree to the wedding in the first place.

And Reginald was so anxious to make Melisue his wife as quickly as possible! He obviously realized that she could marry any man she wanted, and dared not wait to make her his own. He was so dear, and so impetuous.

It would be better for all concerned if she destroyed the letter. Chances were that the man James Thomas was sending wouldn't arrive until after she and Reginald were wed. Then it would be too late for her father to object. She slipped the letter into her glove box. After she left to get married, she would let Beth Ann know that her friend was still alive.

If Beth Ann wanted to write to James Thomas, she could give her letter to this Casey Stubbs and reestablish communication. It pleased her to think of herself as being instrumental in seeing that her little sister did not become an old maid—but Beth Ann's happiness would have to wait until after her big sister was safely wed.

"Just think of it, Beth Ann. I'm going to spend my honeymoon on a riverboat on the Mississippi. Have you ever heard of anything so romantic?" Melisue danced around the room in anticipation. "Isn't it just the most wonderful thing?"

"It sounds lovely," Beth Ann managed, "but where are you going to live after the honeymoon is over? You've never said a word about what's going to happen after the honeymoon."

"Oh, Beth Ann, don't be so dense. Reginald will take me to his palatial family home, where we'll live in style and elegance. Such things aren't ever discussed among people of our class."

"But what about James Thomas?" Beth Ann found it impossible to stifle the question.

"Mr. Montgomery's been gone for years, and Mr. Colfax wants to marry me right away. He can't stand to leave me even for a few days. Being away from me just breaks his heart. How could a girl ask for anything more?"

"But you hardly know the man," Beth Ann pointed out. "You only met him a few weeks ago. Papa hasn't been able to find out anything about his background. None of the people we know recognize the family name."

"Papa isn't acquainted with everyone," Melisue said. "Besides, I know all I need to know about Reginald. He dresses well. He lives well. He has expensive tastes. And I'd much rather spend the rest of my life with him than in some godforsaken cabin somewhere in the wilderness with Mr. James Thomas Montgomery.''

"I thought a cabin in the wilderness sounded wonderful," Beth Ann said quietly.

"Oh, you would. Well, you'd have been welcome to it. That is, if you really believe you could have made James Montgomery forget me, and that's impossible! Even if you could have talked him into taking you away with him, you could never have taken my place in his heart. He would have been comparing us forever. It's a moot point. You'd do better to do as I've done and find another man for yourself. Now that I've chosen Mr. Colfax, all the men at the fort are at your disposal, at least the ones who don't die of broken hearts when I tell them I'm lost to them forever."

"Your admirers have my deepest sympathy," Beth Ann said, trying to hide her smile.

"And think of it! A wedding right on the steamboat. There's not another girl in this territory who could even hope for such a thing," Melisue gloated.

"I thought riverboats made you ill," Beth Ann reminded her.

"That was years ago. I'm certain I'll be able to survive my wedding and my honeymoon with absolutely no trouble at all." She finished packing her trousseau and glanced around the room. "I'm sorry you can't come to the wedding with the rest of us," she said with a smile, "but, after all, someone has to stay here with baby Brandt. He doesn't like me anyway, and I'm sure he'd cry during the ceremony just to get back at me for slapping his hands when he got berry juice on my skirt."

"Babies aren't vindictive." Beth Ann told her, standing up for her little brother. "I don't know where you get these notions."

"Well, I know that's how I would have felt if I were him," Melisue said.

"You can't possibly remember what you would have thought when you were just a baby," Beth Ann exclaimed.

"I remember every thought I've ever had," Melisue assured her.

"And why not?" Rachael Bright observed from the other side of the room where she was making the beds. "Melisue's had so few thoughts that didn't involve men."

"What a nasty thing to say!" Melisue cried out angrily.

"It won't be the worst thing you ever hear if you go ahead and marry that Mr. Reginald Colfax," Rachael Bright told her. "That man spells more trouble than you do."

"He's a wonderful young man," Melisue said in defense of her intended. "He's handsome, ambitious, rich, and attentive. Everything I've ever wanted in a husband. How could I ask for anything more?"

"Truthful would be nice," Rachael Bright said.

"How dare you cast aspersions on Reginald's character! You should be ashamed of yourself, Rachael Bright. Telling tales out of school. You're just jealous, like the rest of the women around here. I'll be living in a beautiful whitewashed house overlooking the Mississippi and spending my holidays on the riverboat going from one gracious family residence to the other, while the rest of you are sitting out here in the middle of the parched prairie in your little sod houses." She tossed her head. "If you're not jealous, you should be!"

"I'm not jealous of you and the life you think you're going to live, nor am I the fool you think I am. In fact, it will be interesting to see just who turns out to be the fool in evaluating this situation," Rachel Bright replied.

"I'm not going to allow you to ruin this happy time for me. Mr. Colfax is coming to pick me up in a few minutes. If you're not careful, I'll tell him what you said, and you'll have to answer to him."

"That would be a pleasure. I can't help but wonder why your father hasn't investigated your Mr. Colfax's credentials more carefully."

"Because my father knows when he meets an honest man whose word he can trust."

"Either that or he's so all-fired anxious to get rid of you he's willing to do anything to keep from compromising the contract."

Melisue threw a silver powder box, but Rachael Bright dodged it easily.

"My, my..." She shook her head. "Look at that mess. And I have to go see to your mama. I guess you'll have to clean it up yourself, Miss Melisue. You'd better be careful. You must have the bridal nerves. You're gettin' clumsy." She opened the door. "Come along, Beth Ann. Master Brandt is waiting for you."

"Well, you could at least stay and help me clean up this powder. I'll get it all over my dress. Beth Ann doesn't have to go now. Brandt doesn't need her. I don't want to get powder on my dress. Reginald will be here in a minute, and..."

Her words faded into nothingness as Rachael Bright took Beth Ann's arm and they hurried down the hallway, doubled over with laughter.

Suzanna looked up from her needlework as her daughter and Rachael Bright entered the room.

"It's good to see you two laughing." She smiled. "I've been feeling so guilty because you're not going to the wedding, Beth Ann."

"There's nothing to feel guilty about," Beth Ann said. "I'd rather stay here and take care of baby Brandt than see Melisue marry Mr. Colfax. I don't like the man. He makes my skin crawl."

"Beth Ann," her mother said reprovingly, "what an ungracious thing to say."

"I'm sorry, but it's true." She kissed her mother's cheek and started toward the door. "Don't worry, I won't do or say anything to spoil Melisue's happiness. Now I must see to baby Brandt. I promised to take him for a walk this afternoon."

Suzanna's shoulders slumped and the needle fell idle in her hands as she watched the door close behind her daughter.

"He makes your skin crawl, too, doesn't he, Suzanna?" Rachael Bright let convention fall by the wayside and addressed her employer as she had when they were lonely girls growing up together.

"To tell the truth, he does. I have some serious misgivings about letting Melisue marry him."

"Then why did Mr. Cadwalder give his permission so readily?" Rachael Bright asked.

Suzanna hesitated, wondering just how much she should confide in Rachael Bright. Heaven knew, she needed someone to talk to, and Rachael Bright obviously already had her suspicions.

"It was that Indian, Black Hawk, that caused Mr. Cadwalder to allow Melisue to marry. She's been seen with him."

"Melisue has been seen with practically every male past the age of puberty," Rachael Bright pointed out.

So great was Suzanna's distress that she didn't even take exception to her companion's words. "The girl has been sneaking off to meet Black Hawk and spending hours with him, alone." She wrung her hands. "Mr. Cadwalder feared ... that is, he felt ..."

She was unable to go on. Rachael Bright finished for her. "He felt that any marriage was better than having a little papoose around the house."

Suzanna gasped. "Oh, Rachael Bright, Brandt never said *that.*"

"I'm sure he didn't," Rachael Bright observed. "But isn't there some way he could have arranged a marriage through his family back east?"

"We were trying to do just that, but then Melisue met Mr. Colfax and wouldn't consider anyone else. He is a nice-looking man, you must admit."

"That he is," the woman agreed, "but then, they say the devil was a beautiful angel."

"We don't know that he's anything other than what he presents himself to be," Suzanna replied, defending the choice she and her husband had made. Then she got to her feet, and her sewing tumbled to the floor unnoticed. "Regardless of what Reginald Colfax is or is not, I won't be driven from my home again by Melisue's escapades. We have worked hard to build a new life for ourselves, and I won't allow my daughter to ruin it again."

Rachael Bright's eyes widened in surprise, but she said nothing as she placed the material on the table. "Why don't we go join Beth Ann and baby Brandt on their walk? A little fresh air might do us good."

James Thomas glanced around the snug little cabin, took a deep breath and turned to the man sitting next to him before the hearth.

"I have a favor to ask of you," he said.

"After all the times you've had to stake me in my trapping, I owe you all the favors you can come up with," Casey Stubbs said.

"Something you said the other day got me to thinking."

"Something *I* said," Casey asked in disbelief. "What'd I say?"

"You were talking about a man needing a woman out here. About being lonely." James Thomas explained.

"Oh, that." The big man's laughter rumbled through the room. "I get that way sometimes after I've been out trapping for too long."

"What you said made sense," James Thomas told him. "I've never said anything much about this, but when I came out here I was engaged to a woman back in Fort Kearney. I was wondering if you'd stop by and see if she's changed her mind and wants to come up and join me here."

"A woman! You was engaged to a woman?"

James Thomas suppressed a smile. "What did you think I'd be engaged to? One of your mules?"

"You're about as stubborn," Casey grumbled. "I never heard nothin' about you leavin' a woman behind."

"I guarantee you, it's true. She's a pretty girl. Black hair and blue eyes. Quite the lady. That's why she didn't want to come up here with me. But now that I'm settled in, I thought maybe you could stop by and talk to her. If she's changed her mind, you could bring her back here with you."

"It's a long, hard trip for a lady," Casey observed.

"You don't have to try to talk her into anything. Just tell her about the cabin, and don't make it sound any better than it is. I don't want her coming up here expecting to live in Southern style. If she decides to come with you, I want her to have a clear picture of the life she will be leading." He got to his feet and poked at the fire. "Hell, for all I know she may already be married."

"What's this lady's name?" Casey asked.

"Her name is Melisue Cadwalder," James Thomas told him. "Her family lives in a big house outside the fort."

"Big as in the size of this cabin?"

"Big as in two stories, with five rooms on each floor."

"And you're just engaged to this gal? You ain't married or nothin'?"

"That's right." The memory of their brief engagement flashed through James Thomas's mind. "I left the morning after the engagement was announced."

"I'll bet she was real pleased about that," Casey observed, with more than his usual perception. "But if you're only engaged, how do you expect to marry her? There's no preacher up here, and not likely to be one real soon, either. If the girl's parents have a big house and a lot of money, they aren't gonna let their daughter come traipsing across the country to live with a man she's engaged to."

James Thomas took a deep breath. He was so certain that Melisue would turn down his offer that he hadn't thought about the fact that there could be no question of her coming unless they were married.

"I'll sign a paper and marry her by proxy. In other words, you'll stand in for me during the ceremony."

"You sure that's legal? I said I wanted a woman, but I want to pick her myself."

"I'm sure," James Thomas told him. "We'll write out an agreement the same way we do when you take my furs and sell them."

The big man nodded. "I guess that's all right, but how will I know this girl? You got a likeness of her or somethin'?"

James Thomas shook his head. "Just look for the biggest crowd of men you can find, and she'll be right in the center of them."

Casey wiped his brow. "You sure you really want me to bring her back here? She doesn't sound like the kind of woman who can pull her weight."

"There's a good chance she won't even come," James Thomas admitted. "But if she wants to be my wife, I want you to bring her back with you."

"If you're sure that's what you want, I'll do it," Casey promised.

"I'm sure." James Thomas took a deep breath. "And, Casey, don't go through with the proxy wedding while you're at the fort. Go to the nearest town where you can find a preacher and have the ceremony there. If you marry her at her home, she's likely to go through the ceremony and then decide not to come."

"Sure, Jim." Casey shook his head in confusion. "If that's the way you want it." He tried to put together all the things his friend had told him, but he just came up with more questions that he didn't want to ask. "She must be one beautiful woman for you to go to so much trouble to get her back here," he observed, hoping his words would cause James Thomas to tell him more. "Has she got a sister?"

"She's got a younger sister. The sweetest girl in the whole world. Way too good for you, Casey, you old horse thief." James Thomas slapped the man on the shoulder. "The little sister is way too good for either of us."

"If you're real sure this Melisue Cadwalder is what you want, I'll bring her back to you," Casey promised, "but the way you been talking about her, I almost wonder if you really wouldn't be happier alone. I seen men more excited when they was expectin' a plague of locusts."

James Thomas laughed aloud at his friend's analogy. A plague of locusts might be more welcome than a lifetime with Melisue—at least it wouldn't last as long. Once again he reminded himself that in all probability she wouldn't come.

"I've got to get out of here before first light," Casey said. "Better go get some sleep. It's gonna be a long trek goin' and a slow one comin' back. I just hope you know what you're doin'. Someday mebbe I'll learn to keep my opinions to myself and my mouth shut."

He was still mumbling when he stopped outside the door.

"You'll have those proxy letters ready for me in the morning?" he asked.

"They'll be here," James Thomas promised. "Along with the money for the woman's expenses, if it comes to that."

"Is there anything else I'm goin' to need?" Casey asked.

"There's one more thing you can do for me." James Thomas silently cursed himself, but could not stop the words. "Give a message to the younger sister, Beth Ann."

"What's that?"

James Thomas hesitated. What message could he give that wouldn't make the matter even more painful? "Tell her I wish her happiness."

"That's it?" Casey had expected something more, from the pained expression on his friend's face.

"That's it," James Thomas said quietly.

"Why don't you come with me? Then you can tell her yourself?"

"That's the one thing I couldn't do," he said, turning away quickly before the mountain man could see the tears forming in his eyes. As the door closed, James Thomas sank down beside the table, put his head on his arms and cried as he hadn't since he was a child, for, like that child, he had just seen all his dreams irrevocably destroyed.

Chapter Twelve

The road was dusty, the sun was hot, and Casey Stubbs was hungry when he arrived at Fort Kearney. He looked around for someplace where he might get some food. The thought of eating with the men at the fort didn't appeal to him.

Under any other circumstances he would have gone directly to the Cadwalder household, but the closer he had come to Fort Kearney, the more he found something unsettling in the situation involving Jim and his fiancée. He wondered if his friend was setting him up for some kind of practical joke, but then he dismissed the idea. Jim wasn't much for jokes, especially where women were concerned.

He noticed a group of men standing together just inside the gates of the fort. Jim had said to look for a crowd of men if he wanted to find Melisue Cadwalder. He started toward them just as a dark-haired woman burst from their midst.

"Next week I'll bring corn cakes," she smiled.

He couldn't believe his eyes, because here was by far the prettiest creature he'd ever set eyes on. If this was Jim's woman, he should have come after her himself, because if she so much as looked at him the right way he knew he'd never be able to give her up.

"Ma'am!" He started after her as she headed for a small buggy. "Ma'am!" He called louder. "Are you Miss Melisue Cadwalder?"

The woman stopped and looked at him with fathomless black eyes. "Why do you ask?"

He drew a sigh of relief. Jim had said the woman he was to fetch had blue eyes. Thank Providence, this wasn't Jim's woman. Now all he had to do was keep her talking until he could find out who she was. "I have a message for Miss Cadwalder from a friend of mine."

"And who might that be?" the woman asked.

"His name is Jim Montgomery."

The woman blinked but gave no other indication that the name meant anything to her. "There was a Mr. Montgomery here at the fort some years ago," she said. "He forged a treaty between the Indians and the settlers and then he left. Would that be the man you mean?"

"I don't know anything about him makin' an Indian treaty around here, but he sure did a good job of settlin' things down where we live."

"Well, I'm not Melisue Cadwalder, but I could show you where she lives. Would you like to follow me?"

Anywhere, Casey thought, but aloud he said, "That'd be right neighborly of you, ma'am." He was about to mount his horse when he found the courage to ask, "Could I drive your buggy for you? A lady like yourself shouldn't ruin her hands on the reins."

"I'm quite used to ruining my hands on the reins," she said, "but I would be happy to let you drive me to my home. From there I can give you directions to the Cadwalder house."

His heart lurching beneath his buckskin shirt, Casey climbed into the seat and clucked to the horses.

"My name is Casey Stubbs," he managed, hoping she would tell him her name in return.

Instead, she said, "I'm happy to meet you, Mr. Stubbs. How do you happen to be acquainted with Mr. Montgomery?"

"He runs a trading post up in the north country where I do my trappin'."

"You're a trapper?"

Now he'd done it. "I'm sorry, ma'am. I forgot how soft-hearted ladies are about little animals, but, yes, that's how I earn my living. I bring back all those furs they use to make coats and hats and collars and such." He ducked his head and wished he'd made up some other kind of occupation that wouldn't have set her against him.

"I'm sure you're very good at what you do, Mr. Stubbs, and there is a great demand for the goods you deal in."

The pleasant smile on her face led him to believe she wasn't horrified by his occupation. He breathed a sigh of relief.

"It's been so long since any of us have heard from Mr. Montgomery, we had begun to believe something might have happened to him." She watched the big man closely as she spoke.

"Only thing that's happened to Jim is that he's built himself a nice business. Runs the only trading post in the area. There's a whole town building up around it, and he got to thinkin' it's time to make a real home for himself. That's why he sent me down here for Miss Melisue Cadwalder. He said they was engaged, and if she still wanted to marry him, I was to bring her back with me."

"How lovely." She put her hand on his arm. "This is my house. Would you like to come in? I've been baking all morning and have dinner almost ready. It's lonesome eating alone. I'd like the company."

"I know how it feels to be lonely," he agreed readily. "I'd be real happy to join you." Then he amended his words. "It would be an honor, ma'am." he said, his blue eyes filled with admiration.

"Not 'ma'am,'" she said as he helped her from the little buggy. "My name is Rachael Bright, but please, call me Rachael."

She glanced around him as they started toward the house. In the distance the dust rose as a carriage started down the road at the end of the Cadwalders' drive.

"Could I ask a favor of you?" She gave him her loveliest smile.

"Anything," he answered. Even the furs he had kept back to give to Jim Montgomery's lady were hers for the asking.

"Would you mind taking the buggy to the shed at the end of the path there?" She gestured toward the well-defined pathway that disappeared around the side of the little sod house. "And please unhitch the horse. There's a fenced pasture a bit farther down. By the time you get back, I should have something ready for you to eat."

"Won't be no trouble," he told her. "No trouble at all." Without looking back, he led the horse down the side of the building. Just then, a carriage raced past carrying the Cadwalders off to Melisue's wedding.

Rachael Bright set the plates on the table and dished the food onto them. She doubted that this man had any idea of the trouble he could have caused by showing up and offering temptation to Melisue on the eve of her wedding. He seemed a nice man. Honest, and trying desperately to be a gentleman. His kindness made up for what manners he lacked. She would keep him with her until she was certain the Cadwalders were well away, and then tell him the girl was already married. Somehow she didn't think his friend Jim would be too heartbroken.

She felt no qualms about offering the hospitality of her home. For all that James Thomas Montgomery might have been misguided in allowing Melisue to railroad him into an unwanted engagement, Rachael Bright was certain he would never have sent a man to escort Melisue across the country if he was not completely trustworthy. She found herself looking forward to spending an evening in his company.

Casey took the halter off the horse before letting it loose in the pasture. He could see the gleam of water from a running stream. Remembering that there had been no time for him to clean up before he saw Rachael Bright, he went toward the water to get rid of the dust before going back to eat. He was wiping his face when he noticed the reflection of a figure in the water and looked up to see a woman so lovely she took his breath away. He wiped his eyes and got to his feet.

There, before him, stood the woman Jim Montgomery had described. The blue eyes, the shining black hair, the smooth white skin. No wonder Jim had sent him back for her.

"I know who you are," he said without introduction. "You're Miss Cadwalder. I came here with a message for you."

"You did?" the soft, well-modulated voice asked.

"Yes, it's from James Montgomery. He told me to tell you that he has a house and a nice trading post up in the north country. He said I was to bring you back with me, if you want to come, that is."

He felt more tongue-tied before this silent young woman than he had with Rachael Bright. Rachael had made him want to talk, while this cool young lady seemed shocked into silence at the mention of James Montgomery's name.

"I'm afraid you don't understand," she said tonelessly. "A young lady couldn't possibly travel alone across the country with a man she doesn't even know."

"Look, Miss Cadwalder, I shouldn't have put it to you like that, but I was surprised to find you here and didn't rightly have my thoughts together. Mr. Montgomery's taken all those things into account. He doesn't want to do anything that isn't right and proper. Could I come and talk to you a bit later?" I have an engagement right now, and I surely don't want to be late."

"Very well," she answered. "Was that all?"

"Wasn't that enough?" he asked, taken off guard in his hurry to get back to Rachael Bright.

"I mean, was that all the message?"

"Oh, well, that was all the message for you." He was backing slowly toward the sod house that held the best-smelling food and the best-looking woman he could ever have imagined. "The only other thing he said was that he wished Beth Ann happiness."

"Beth Ann? He sent a message to Beth Ann?"

"That's right," Casey said. "He said to bring Miss Melisue back if she wanted to come and leave the message for Miss Beth Ann."

"Thank you," the woman replied.

"You're welcome, ma'am, and I'll look forward to talking to you later."

She stood looking after him even after he'd disappeared into the soddy, but Casey Stubbs, his mind focused on Rachael Bright and the smell of food, didn't look back.

Beth Ann held the little ring in the palm of her hand, remembering the man who had given it to her. The hurt that had been inflicted during that dark time had dissipated. Melisue could talk the devil out of his pitchfork. What chance did a mere man have against her charms?

Over the years, Beth Ann had come to believe that she had misunderstood James Thomas's words and that the woman he had planned to take with him was Melisue. In her youthful wonderment, Beth Ann had heard only what she wanted to hear and had believed he meant the ring to be a token of his love for her rather than one of friendship. Her disillusionment had been intense, but she had learned to live with it, although she had never met a man who could take the place of James Thomas in her heart.

True to his word, he had sent for Melisue, and, with her parents gone, it would be up to her to tell Casey Stubbs that Melisue had grown tired of waiting and had married someone else. She pressed the little ring to her lips in a kiss of farewell. He would never return now, and she would never see him again.

Oh, why couldn't he have waited to make his commitment to her sister? Why couldn't he have come himself to fetch Melisue? Surely, if he could see how she had grown he would remember their friendship and sense the love she still bore him, and, perhaps, take her back with him. By sending a messenger, James Thomas had made it impossible for her to prove to him that she loved him as Melisue never could.

She put the ring back into its satin-lined box. Glancing up, she caught a reflection in the mirror. For a moment, her heart stopped. She moved closer through the shadow-shrouded room. For a moment she had thought Melisue had returned, but it was her own image she saw in the mirror.

"Oh, James Thomas, why must you want Melisue when I love you so much?" she said aloud as Caleb's footsteps echoed on the stairs.

"There's a gentlemen to see Miss Cadwalder," he intoned as she opened the door.

"I know." She slipped past him into the hall. "I've been expecting him."

Casey Stubbs was waiting in the sitting room when she entered. He got to his feet, obviously uncomfortable with all the finery of the Cadwalder home.

"It's nice to see you again, Mr. Stubbs." She held out her hand, over which he bowed, resurrecting long-forgotten manners.

"Miss Melisue, I understand your concerns about going all the way up to Montana, but I want you to know that Jim thought things out and has it all arranged." He held up his hand when she opened her mouth to speak. "Please let me finish before you say anything.

"Jim has a nice little house and a good business. The town is growing, and there are several families settled there already. It's beautiful country, and that's a fact.

"I know you were concerned about going up there without being married, but I have a paper here from Jim saying he wants to marry you by proxy, so you wouldn't have to worry about getting up there and having to wait until the circuit preacher comes along before you got married."

"You don't understand, I—"

Again he cut off her words. "There's a family that's going to be traveling along with us, so you wouldn't have to feel uncomfortable about no other woman being along, and of course, if you wanted to bring one of your servants, provided they was willing to come, that would be fine, too." A big grin split his face. "There's lots of room up there for everybody."

Beth Ann wrung her hands. Room for everybody, the man had said. Everybody except Beth Ann Cadwalder. She was doomed to stay here on the prairie, hundreds of miles from the man she loved.

"I don't know how to tell you this," she managed. "You see, my parents are away at my sister's wedding, and..."

"That must be Miss Beth Ann," Casey Stubbs said garrulously. "Then let me add my wish of happiness to Jim's. I hope she's just half as pretty as you. Why, from the description Jim gave me, I could have picked you out of a crowd."

"You could?"

"You'd better believe it," he assured her. "There couldn't be two women who answer the description Jim gave me so perfectly. And I'm sure Jim will be real glad to hear that your sister has found herself a husband. He spoke most kindly about the girl. I don't suppose it ever occurred to him she might be gettin' married."

"No, I don't suppose it did," Beth Ann agreed. "It's been such a long time since we've seen him."

Her mind was spinning. This man thought she was Melisue. More than that, he was sure she was Melisue. How many times had she heard people remark on their similarity?

It was only after James Thomas had gone away that she had grown to her present height and fullness of figure. The clothes Melisue had worn when he was with them had been handed down to her, and they fit her perfectly.

Once she was there, it would be difficult for James Thomas to send her back. It might be weeks, even months, before he realized he had the wrong sister. And she could make him love her, she knew she could. By the time he discovered her duplicity, he would be accustomed to having her around. He might even love her as more than just a friend. Besides, Melisue was marrying someone else. James Thomas couldn't marry her.

She batted her eyes flirtatiously, remembering all the times she had been reprimanded for mimicking her sister. "It will take me some time to pack my things. I simply couldn't travel without my belongings."

She held her breath, waiting to be struck dead for the lie she had just told. When nothing happened, she went on quickly. "When did you plan to leave?"

"I wanted to get out of here as soon as possible. Don't you have some servants that could help you pack?"

To get to James Thomas, Beth Ann would have traveled with nothing but the clothes on her back, but she must pretend to be Melisue from now on, and Melisue would have to take her wardrobe.

"It will take me several days to get my things together," she said haughtily. "Why don't you go and get a wagon and meet me here in two days?"

"Is there anything I can do to help?" he asked, slightly taken aback by her sudden change in manner. Once this little woman decided what she was going to do, she wasted no time getting started. He liked that in a woman, especially Jim's woman. For himself, he wanted something a bit less resolute.

"I wasn't plannin' on usin' a wagon just for the two of us. I usually do my packin' on a string of mules. If your bags aren't too large, we'll carry them that way."

"On mules?" she asked in surprise.

"Yes, ma'am," he nodded. "They're surefooted and don't break no wheels going over the roads we have to travel."

Beth Ann paused as though considering his proposal. "Very well, but I won't ride one," she told him.

Casey's laughter filled the room. "You don't have to do that, ma'am. Now, are you plannin' on takin' your maid with you? I need to know how many horses to get."

"You'll get two horses," Rachael Bright told the man before turning to Beth Ann. "You're not going anywhere without me."

Beth Ann blanched noticeably, certain Rachael Bright would give away her true identity at any moment. The only way to keep the woman from doing so was to get the man out of the house so that she could explain.

"Very well, Mr. Stubbs," Beth Ann said regally. "You may buy two horses, and what mules you need for my trousseau." She took his arm and maneuvered him out the front door. "I know you will excuse us. We have so many things to do before you return. This has been so unexpected. I'll see you day after tomorrow, and please don't be too early."

Casey Stubbs looked blankly at the closed door. When that little gal got the bit in her teeth, she was a real terror. Jim Montgomery was going to have his work cut out for him, and that was a fact. He ambled to the drive, where a boy held his horse, unaware that Beth Ann still stood on the other side of the door, her hand planted firmly over Rachael Bright's mouth.

"What do you mean, you're packing?" Rachael Bright demanded as she followed Beth Ann to her room. "It was bad enough when I walked in and thought you had accepted an invitation to go riding with Mr. Stubbs, but where are you going that you'd need to pack?" Warnings were sounding in Rachael Bright's mind. Casey Stubbs had said he'd come for Melisue, but Melisue was gone and Beth Ann was packing. She put a restraining hand on the girl's arm. "Honey, don't do this. Mr. Montgomery sent for Melisue. It isn't you he wants. It's your sister."

In reply, Beth Ann held up one of the hand-me-down dresses Melisue had worn when James Thomas was at the fort. Her eyes danced with excitement. "Do you really think that after all these years he'll be able to tell the difference?" she asked. "Why, you've remarked many times on how much we look alike."

"It's not just your looks. It's the way you act and think. He'll know who you are and send you back home." She shook her head despondently.

"He thinks of Beth Ann as a scrawny girl. If he sees any difference in personality, he'll think Melisue has matured."

"But you'll have to tell him sooner or later," Rachael Bright argued.

"I'll tell him when the time is right," Beth Ann promised. "Right now, I want to start packing." But instead of finishing she turned to Rachael Bright and took the woman's hands in her own. "I love James Thomas, Rachael Bright. I've always loved him. I'll never love anyone else. And I'm going with Casey Stubbs, no matter what happens."

"What about your parents?" Rachael Bright told her. "What about baby Brandt? You're supposed to be taking care of him."

"Mama and Papa will be back in a few days. You and Lucy can manage the baby until they return." Her heart ached at the thought of leaving her little brother, but the ache was less than the one she had carried with her over the years since James Thomas had gone away.

She looked out over the yard and saw little Brandt chasing a butterfly. How dear he was, and how she would miss him. But no matter how much Beth Ann loved her little brother, the fact remained that he was not her child. Brandt was the child of her mother and father, and sooner or later the time would come when Beth Ann would be forced to leave him and build a life of her own. She could not imagine building a life without James Thomas, and now that this God-given opportunity had been given her, she was not about to let it pass.

She longed for a family of her own. Her own little boy or girl. A baby with blond hair and dark eyes, the result of her love for James Thomas, and his for her. How wondrously happy they would be together! How beautiful their lives would be!

She knew she was right in her decision. She knew it in her heart, and she would not be swayed by Rachael Bright's predictions of doom.

"I will go, Rachael Bright. I must! If I don't take advantage of this opportunity, I know I will never see James Thomas again."

"Then Lucy will have to take care of the baby," Rachael Bright declared, "because I'm going with you. Your mama would die of shame if you went traipsing across the country with some stranger."

"Mr. Stubbs said there was another family going along," Beth Ann reminded her.

"Mr. Stubbs said a lot of things." Rachael Bright remembered their conversation over the meal they had shared. She liked the man. He seemed honest and solid, but she wasn't about to trust him with Beth Ann, especially a Beth Ann who was pretending to be Melisue.

Beth Ann realized there was no way she could stop Rachael Bright from accompanying her. "If you tell, I'll never forgive you."

"Don't worry about that. By the time we get to wherever it is Mr. James Thomas lives, I'll be calling you Melisue as though it was your name." She folded a petticoat and put it into one of the small trunks. "But I'm warning you. A life built on lies, even loving lies, is going to fall apart when the truth comes out. You better start thinking up some way to explain why you told Casey Stubbs you were Melisue."

"But I didn't tell him, Rachael Bright. When I said my sister had gone to get married, the man assumed I was referring to Beth Ann. He never doubted for a moment that I was Melisue."

"He never *saw* Melisue," Rachael Bright reminded her.

A troubled frown crossed Beth Ann's brow. "Do *you* think James Thomas will know that I'm not Melisue?" she asked.

"I think it'll be a lot less trouble if he does," Rachael Bright answered. She closed the little trunk and went to pack her own belongings, her mind already on the time she would spend with Casey Stubbs on the journey.

Chapter Thirteen

The flatlands of the prairie had developed into foothills, then mountain ranges, and now the little party were traveling along a path lined with trees that seemed to tower to the sky and march on forever. Beth Ann could hardly contain herself, for it was like having James Thomas's description of the land in which he had chosen to live become reality before her eyes.

Rachael Bright was beyond knowing, or caring. She saw nothing but the huge mountain man who rode beside her, expounding on the beauty of the country.

Had Beth Ann not been so nervous about meeting James Thomas and making him believe she was Melisue, she would have been amused at Rachael Bright's attraction to Casey Stubbs—an attraction that was returned in full measure by the mountain man.

Her unease was augmented by her guilt at leaving her baby brother and her other responsibilities with only a note to her parents explaining that she had gone to marry James Thomas and taken Rachael Bright with her. She justified the decision by assuring herself that her mother's health had improved greatly since baby Brandt's birth and there was no viable reason why Suzanna couldn't assume the duties of her household and child.

After all, Suzanna had found the strength to make the move from New Orleans to Fort Kearney despite her advancing pregnancy, enduring difficult travel conditions, even as the Borden family did now.

Beth Ann empathized with the family, remembering her own trip into unfamiliar surroundings to start a new life. The higher the mountains and the taller the trees, the more silent they became. It was as though they could not consume the sheer beauty of the place to which they had come. They had been little trouble, and about the same amount of support, as they followed along, almost unnoticed by Beth Ann and her companions.

Beth Ann had known a moment of panic when Casey Stubbs had spoken of the proxy wedding James Thomas had arranged. Although there had been little chance that anyone at the fort would have questioned her identity as Melisue, it had still been too close to home for her to feel comfortable about having the ceremony performed there. To her delight, Casey had said they would have the ceremony performed farther on in their journey, while they waited for the Borden family to join them.

Rachael Bright had agreed to watch for the Bordens' wagon while Casey Stubbs and Beth Ann went through with the proxy ceremony. After the ceremony, the minister had presented Beth Ann with a Bible.

"We don't have many weddings out here," he'd said sadly. "Mostly funerals, it seems. So my wife and I would like to give you and your new husband this fine Bible. Just something a little special so you can remember the day you were wed." He'd thumbed quickly through the pages. "Never know when you might feel like reading the word of the Lord. Even has a place to record births and such like when the time comes."

The Bible was wrapped in oilcloth and placed in her saddlebag. She reached back and touched it now, remembering all the stories of people within its pages who had gone forth into the unknown, trusting in the word of the Lord.

And Beth Ann was trusting in the Lord. She was also trusting in herself and her ability to make James Thomas believe she was Melisue until she could convince him to let her, Beth Ann, stay.

"That's the sawmill I was telling you about," Casey said, gesturing toward a building almost hidden except for the path leading through the trees. "The town—what there is of it—is around the next bend here."

Beth Ann's heart drowned out the clip-clop of the horses and the creaking of the wagon. She expected James Thomas to be waiting for them, and she searched the street as they rode along, but he was nowhere in sight.

"There's the trading post," Casey said, with an almost proprietary pride. "Looks to be closed." He squinted his eyes and stared at the building. "Guess Jim is waitin' to welcome you at the house."

They stopped in front of a cabin. There were flower boxes at the windows, and a low porch ran across the front. Wisps of smoke wafted from the chimney and climbed toward the clear blue sky. Beth Ann slid from her horse and found her legs almost unable to hold her. She had dreamed about how James Thomas would lift her from her horse, and how she would cling to him. Now she truly needed someone to hold on to. It wouldn't do at all to fall at his feet.

"Didn't you tell him we were coming?" Beth Ann asked.

"I sent him a message about a week ago," the mountain man replied. "Told him we should be in sometime today or tomorrow. Didn't rightly know when."

Casey lifted Rachael Bright from her horse and gave her hand a little squeeze before tying up the horses.

"Don't you go weak in the knees now," Rachael Bright warned. "This isn't the time to fall apart."

"I'm not falling apart," Beth Ann said. "I'm just rattling a little."

Casey held out his hand and led the ladies to the door. His brief knock was answered by the words, "Come in." The next moment, Beth Ann found herself in a big room that smelled of polished wood and good food. In front of the fireplace stood James Thomas with the same dark eyes and the same hair that seemed to capture the sun.

He looked no older than the day Beth Ann had first seen him. The only noticeable change was in the beard he now wore, as blond as the hair on his head. She remembered the days after he had been wounded, when he had gone unshaven, and how handsome she had thought him to be as his beard had grown. The memory of that time when they had established their friendship gave her back the courage she had lost. Surely it would be only a short time before she could tell him who she was and that she had come because she loved him. She longed to forget her hoax and tell him right away, to be done with this moment of deceit. But the presence of Casey Stubbs held her back. James Thomas had sent for Melisue, and if she divulged her secret before Casey went about his business, James Thomas might tell the man to take her back to Fort Kearney.

Somehow she must continue to pretend to be Melisue until Casey Stubbs was gone, or until she was secure in the knowledge that James Thomas loved the woman who had come to him, regardless of her identity.

She hesitated, waiting for him to welcome her. Hoping he would hold out his arms to her as he had when he returned to Fort Kearney before the ball.

He stared at her, unmoving. "I didn't believe you'd really come." He moved slowly through the shadowy room until he stood before her and took her hands in his. His eyes took in everything about her from her shining black hair to the little boots peering out beneath her riding dress. Her blue eyes seemed liquid with adoration, and, had he not known better, he would have sworn she loved him.

"A woman's place is with her husband," Beth Ann intoned, lifting her face for his kiss. It was a chaste kiss on the cheek, and once it had been bestowed he moved away. Unsure as to what was expected of her, Beth Ann looked around the room. "What a nice little house," she said, in her best Melisue imitation. "Did you build it yourself?"

"I had some help from Casey and some other friends," James Thomas said. Then he turned to Rachael Bright. "I'm even more surprised to see you, Rachael Bright," he told her, bowing over her hand.

"I couldn't let Miss Melisue come up here all alone." Her eyes met Beth Ann's, and she was rewarded with a smile. If the man had any doubts, he would forget them now. Surely, of all people, Rachael Bright would know which sister she was with.

James Thomas hung on to Rachael Bright's hand longer than necessary. It was obvious that he was not overcome with happiness at the arrival of his bride.

"I'm sorry, but our accommodations here are rather limited. There's a boardinghouse just down the road. I'm sure you'll be comfortable over there."

"There's no need for that," Beth Ann said. "Rachael Bright can sleep with me."

Casey dropped the ladle into the pot where he had been sneaking a taste of the steaming stew, and Rachael Bright covered her mouth with her handkerchief.

"Let me show you the rest of the house." James Thomas led her through the room. "Then perhaps you'll understand what we're dealing with."

The bedroom was by far the smaller room and held a bed and a chest of drawers, as well as an armoire. "As you can see, there's only one bed," he said, watching the color brighten and fade in his bride's cheeks.

"That will be quite adequate for Rachael Bright and my-self," Beth Ann said, with all the dignity she could muster. Of course, she knew that married people shared the same bed, but it had not entered her mind that this would be required of her. The wedding had been done by proxy and held none of the romance or excitement that must surely take place when the bride and groom were together. She had no idea what Melisue might have done in similar circumstances, but she knew what she must do. "Surely you can't think that I would jump into your bed after not having seen or heard from you in years? While I may be your wife, I understood that the ceremony took place because there is no preacher here. We need time to get reacquainted. I'm sure we've both changed a great deal in the time we've been apart. This is a time when we should get to know one another. So either I sleep in that bed with Rachael Bright, or I sleep at the boardinghouse."

Casey Stubbs gave a shout and clapped his hands. "I wrote you she was a spitfire," he laughed.

James Thomas did not push the point. "Very well," he agreed. "Until we become better acquainted, I will sleep in the loft." He gestured toward a little loft at the end of the room. "But be assured, Melisue Montgomery, this is only a temporary situation. I don't know why you decided to come, but I'll not be forced from my home, my bed, or my conjugal rights. You are my wife, and I expect you to behave as befits the position."

Beth Ann was taken aback. She had not expected the harsh tone of voice he used, any more than she had expected to go to bed with him. Her request seemed no more than normal considering the length of time they had been apart.

Seeing the brewing trouble between the newly married couple, Casey took Rachael Bright's arm. "You can show me which mules to unload first," he suggested as he maneuvered her out the door.

Once on the porch, the woman hesitated. "Do you think we should leave them alone just now?" Her worry for Beth Ann was obvious.

"I think that's exactly what we should do," he replied, helping her down the steps.

"I suppose you'll be leaving soon," Rachael Bright said as she pointed out the mules to be unloaded.

"Actually, I've about decided to stay around here awhile. Been thinkin' about building myself a cabin a short piece from here. Maybe after you settle in you might like to come with me and take a look at the place. It's only a couple hours' ride."

Rachael Bright squashed the hope that momentarily filled her heart. Casey Stubbs was a white man. No doubt he thought of her as no better than one of the Indian girls he could get to come and live with him. His attraction to her was probably no more than the fact that she could carry on a decent conversation, where perhaps the Indian girls couldn't. He knew of her background. She had made no secret of it as they had ridden together over the many miles they traveled. But she wanted to see where he would live, just as she wanted to cook for him, and take care of him, and talk to him, and sleep with him. She wanted him forever. She wanted to be his wife, and she knew she couldn't settle for less.

"I'd love to see the place where you plan to build the cabin you've been telling me about," she replied. "I'll have to see if Melisue can spare me for a few hours. I wouldn't want to be away too long. There's so much to do, with unpacking and everything."

He smiled at her obvious confusion. Rachael Bright usually had a good grip on any situation. It pleased him that she felt as flustered in accepting his invitation as he had felt in asking her.

"That's fine," he said. "We'll plan on going whenever you can get away."

Once the sleeping arrangements had been settled, Beth Ann wasted no time unpacking her belongings. Although she continued her ruse in letting James Thomas believe she was Melisue, she was able to send a letter to her parents telling them she had arrived safely and making certain, should her mother decide to write to her, that she would address the mail to Mrs. James Montgomery.

If James Thomas was surprised at his wife's domestic abilities, he kept his thoughts to himself.

Beth Ann was careful to address him as Mr. Montgomery, or sometimes, privately as James. She tried to remember all of Melisue's idiosyncrasies, but as the weeks went by she found herself modifying her behavior and allowing herself to be more the woman she herself had become rather than the lovestruck girl she had been when she had first met James Thomas, or the self-centered person Melisue had always been.

Though she said nothing, even to Rachael Bright, it troubled her that after the first suggestion that they share a bed, the subject had not been brought up again. James Thomas seemed quite content to sleep in the loft and did not suggest that the situation be changed.

Casey Stubbs spent as many evenings as possible in the Montgomery house. The mountain man gave periodic reports of the progress of the cabin he was building and often took Rachael Bright with him to see what he had done.

"I'm afraid you're going to lose your bunkmate," James Thomas told Beth Ann one morning as they watched their friends ride off toward the cabin.

"What do you mean?" Beth Ann was surprised at his choice of words, and she looked away quickly to hide her confusion.

"Casey wanted to build a cabin and find a woman to share it with. I think he's found the woman."

"You mean Rachael Bright?"

Although Beth Ann would have been the first to admit that Rachael Bright was attractive, the woman was the same age as her mother. It hadn't occurred to her that Rachael Bright and Casey Stubbs might actually be in love.

Her immediate concern was for her lifelong friend, and she was unable to hide it.

"He wouldn't ask her to go and . . . live with him, would he?" she asked in a small voice.

"I wouldn't doubt he's done that already," James Thomas said as he put on his buckskin jacket. "Hasn't she said anything to you?"

"No," Beth Ann admitted. "No, she hasn't." She twisted her fingers in the folds of her apron. "Do you think he wants to marry her?"

The troubled look in her eyes brought him to her side.

"Would there be a problem with that?" he asked quietly.

She took a deep breath, trying to form words that would not sound bigoted or overly righteous. "There's no preacher here," she reminded him. "And there are other problems."

"The circuit preacher should come through here anytime now. He shows up in the spring and fall. He'll be here before the snow flies."

"Do you think Casey Stubbs will ask her to marry him?"

"He loves her. Why shouldn't they marry?" James Thomas looked into her eyes, but she turned away.

"I wish I'd never allowed her to come with me. I should have insisted she stay at Fort Kearney." Tears of frustration slipped from her eyes and trailed down her cheeks.

"Once Rachael Bright makes up her mind, I'd say it would be almost impossible to stop her from doing what she believes is right." Seeing her concern for Rachael Bright, he didn't try to touch her.

"That's true," she nodded in agreement, "but I don't want her to be hurt."

"Neither does Casey," James Thomas said firmly. "Rachael Bright is a very special lady, and Casey knows it."

She turned and lifted her tear-filled eyes to meet his. "But will he marry her when he knows that her mother wasn't white?"

In the face of her obvious distress, James Thomas forgot his vow to keep his distance. He reached out and took her into his arms, resting his cheek against her hair.

"He already knows, little one. He knows, and it doesn't matter. He wants to share his life with Rachael Bright, just as I want to share my life with you. Up here there are no prejudices. What you were, or who you were, or who your parents were, doesn't make any difference. It's who you are now that counts, and Casey Stubbs wants Rachael Bright to be his wife."

Once in the secure haven of his arms, Beth Ann didn't want to move. His words erased her fears, just as his arms erased her inhibitions. She slipped her arms around him and nestled closer, listening to the steady beating of his heart and reveling in his warmth. She felt his lips against her hair and lifted her face to receive his kiss.

Perhaps it was because she had been crying that her lips parted beneath his, opening the floodgates for the searching, probing kiss that enjoined both passion and wonder as it deepened in its promise. This was not like the last kiss they had shared, when she had been a girl on the threshold of womanhood, but the full-blown kiss of a man for the woman he loved and wanted. The woman he had taken to be his wife. And, in that moment, Beth Ann knew that his wife was what she wanted to be. His wife, in every way.

Chapter Fourteen

As James Thomas had predicted, the preacher arrived before the winter storms. The day was warm, and filled with sunshine filtering through the towering trees.

"Wedding?" Preacher Fullbright said. "Wedding, you say? Well, that's exactly what I'm here for. Weddings and christenings. Anyone who wants to join the flock only has to come to me to be saved."

Beth Ann suppressed a giggle as the elderly, rotund man stood on the porch of the trading post, waving his arms, beckoning to the townsfolk to come forth.

The resonant tones of his voice made Casey Stubbs back away. He had quietly asked if the preacher would perform a wedding ceremony, and the man had echoed his words over the entire town.

"Now, who's the lucky lady?" the preacher expounded.

"Her name is Rachael," Casey said softly, wishing the man would keep his voice down, conveniently forgetting that his enthusiasm over Rachael Bright's acceptance of his proposal had made him rush up to the preacher before the man got off his horse.

"Rachael!" The little preacher glowed with approval. "A good name. Out of the Bible it is, you know."

"Yes," Casey agreed. "I know."

"When will you be wanting this marriage ceremony to take place?" he asked. "I'll only be here for a few days."

Casey was well aware of the miles the circuit preacher was required to cover on his semiannual rounds. "We'd like to be married as quickly as possible. We don't want to hold you up."

"Fine! Fine with me," the preacher said. "And now, when will I meet the bride?"

"She'll be at the ceremony," Casey assured him. "We want to have the wedding at our new house, with just a few of our friends present. Jim and his wife will stand up for us."

"Wonderful, wonderful." The preacher nodded. "Would tomorrow be too soon?"

"Tomorrow sounds fine," Casey said, breathing a sigh of relief. He wasn't sure of the laws of the area, and fear built up within him that someone would realize that Rachael Bright carried black blood in her veins and that the preacher would refuse to marry them. Once the deed was done, there was no way anyone would ever make him give her up, but making sure the marriage took place had him on tenterhooks.

"Tomorrow!" Casey clapped James Thomas on both shoulders. "Tomorrow! I can't wait to tell Rachael Bright. Is she still at the house?"

"As far as I know." James Thomas smiled at his friend's excitement.

The man was halfway across the street when he came to a sudden stop and ran back to the trading post. "A ring. I have to have a ring." He brushed past James Thomas and Beth Ann and went into the building. "You must have a ring around here someplace!" He checked out each counter and cranny before turning to the Montgomerys.

"I'll find something. I'll bring it with me tomorrow when we come out to your place," James Thomas assured him.

"You won't forget?" Casey wiped his forehead with his neckerchief. "I have to tell Rachael Bright. I have to tell her now."

He raced off down the street as though he were being pursued.

Beth Ann slipped her hand through her husband's arm and smiled up into his eyes.

"He certainly is excited, isn't he?"

"He certainly is." James Thomas agreed. "But right now I have to go try to find out what size ring will fit Rachael Bright's hand."

"And I have to go get something ready for supper. Not that Casey and Rachael Bright are going to be able to eat with all the excitement, but I feel we should offer it anyway." Beth Ann lifted her face for her husband's light kiss and hurried off down the street.

As Beth Ann finished putting the dishes in the cupboard, James Thomas took Rachael Bright aside. "I need to know what size ring you wear," he said. "Does my wife have a ring that fits your finger?"

Rachael Bright was somewhat taken aback. "Casey doesn't need to give me a ring to make me feel like his wife," she said.

"He wants you to have a ring. Now go see what you can find, and I'll look for one about the same size at the trading post."

Rachael Bright disappeared into the bedroom she shared with Beth Ann. A small smile played on her lips as she wondered what sleeping arrangements would be made once she moved into her own home tomorrow. Tomorrow! The happy thought filled her mind as she poked through the jewelry in Beth Ann's box.

To her disappointment, none of the rings were close to a good fit on the third finger of her left hand, the finger on which she would wear Casey Stubbs's wedding ring. The thought filled her eyes with tears of pure happiness. No, she didn't need a ring to be Casey's wife. As she closed the box, she noticed the chain Beth Ann usually wore about her neck. Without conscious thought, she picked it up to put it away. On the chain hung a ring. Rachael Bright slipped it from the chain and onto her finger. It fit perfectly.

She hurried into the other room and went directly to James Thomas. "This one fits," she told him.

She held her hand toward him. The smile of anticipation froze on his face.

"Where did you get the ring?" he managed.

"Why, it was in the jewelry box, but it was the only one that fit, and..."

She looked at the ring. At first it meant nothing to her. It wasn't one that she had seen on Beth Ann's hand, and it certainly wasn't one of the baubles that Melisue had left as being unworthy of her notice. Yet she was certain she had seen it before. Suddenly she remembered having seen the ring after James Thomas had left Fort Kearney. The ring that Beth Ann had hidden away and taken out only when she thought she was alone.

Taking a deep breath, Rachael Bright walked toward Beth Ann. "Isn't this the ring your sister, Beth Ann, gave you?" she asked meaningfully.

Beth Ann recovered enough to take the woman's hand in her own and look at the ring. "Why, yes, I believe it is. Beth Ann said it was for me, though I swear I don't know why. And it fits you perfectly. How lovely! Now you have the right size for Rachael Bright's wedding band. Once you're done with the ring, don't forget to put it back. I have little enough to remind me of my baby sister, and that ring seemed to have a very special meaning to her."

James Thomas looked from one woman to the other, took the ring from Rachael Bright's fingers and marched out into the night, while both women sank weakly into the chairs beside the table.

The light from the hurricane lamp danced across the shadows like flickering memories as James Thomas held the little ring in his fingers. How clearly he remembered slipping it onto Beth Ann's hand as she'd slept, leaving with it his love and his final farewell. Somehow he had believed she would feel his love and keep the ring, despite the unfortunate circumstances that had come with his forced engagement to Melisue.

It hurt to think that it had been a forgotten token given Melisue and tossed in a jewelry box over the past years. His grandmother had worn it throughout her lifetime, and he remembered it as part of the love and kindness that she had always shown him. It was because of that love that he had wanted Beth Ann to have it. He had found surcease from his misery in thinking of it on the hand of a woman who shared the same qualities as did its original owner.

With fumbling fingers, he searched through his supply of rings until he found one of the same size. He closed the case and turned out the light, but hesitated before returning to the house. Tomorrow Casey and Rachael Bright would marry, and again the life of James Thomas would change. Although he and Melisue had lived together for many months, they had not lived as husband and wife. Tomorrow the presence of Rachael Bright would not be there to deny him his bed.

He had never demanded his marital rights. Not that he had not thought about it as he'd lain up in the loft. Not that he had not chided himself for his lack of action. But the very fact that Melisue had come had stunned him. And the strangeness of her presence was augmented by the fact that she had mellowed over the years.

Her abilities in taking care of his home left him staring in surprise as she mended his shirts, cooked his dinner and talked quietly to him during the evenings. Many times he had found himself speaking of things he had mentioned to no one since he had confided in Beth Ann so long ago.

He wondered how Beth Ann was faring with her new husband. It seemed strange that she should be the one to go back to the South while Melisue came to the wilderness. But life itself was strange, and there was no way to explain its complexities or resolutions. He smiled to himself as he closed the door and started down the tree-lined road.

It was when they talked sometimes, or when he turned and caught a certain look on her face, that he could not help but be reminded of Beth Ann. But they were sisters. Beth Ann would probably never have the beauty of his wife. He stopped and looked up at the sky. No doubt Beth Ann had grown to womanhood, yet it was impossible for him to imagine her other than as a girl with that sweetness that still tore at his heart.

With resolve, he pushed the thoughts of Beth Ann out of his mind. Melisue was his wife. She had traveled the long, arduous miles to share his life, and he must shut his memories of Beth Ann away in his heart and learn to love and live with the woman he had married.

When he reached the house, he saw the two women, heads bent together in woman talk. He knew Melisue would miss Rachael Bright, and he silently vowed to be more of a companion to her over the days ahead.

"Try this on." He put the gold wedding band on the table before Rachael Bright, watching her delight as she put the ring on her finger.

"Where's my ring?" his wife asked.

He reached into his pocket, reluctantly returning it to her.

"Thank you," she said. "For a minute there I thought you had left it in the case to be sold with the others."

She slipped it on her finger, and once again he remembered it on Beth Ann's hand. He discounted the thought. At the time, Beth Ann's hands had been worn from working with the children of her neighbors, and now Melisue's hands were less than perfectly manicured through work in her own home. Still, he felt a certain disquiet at the longing that it might have been Beth Ann's hand that wore his grandmother's ring.

There was a certain amount of tension coupled with the light banter as the carriage brought them back through the twilight from the wedding. At Rachael Bright's urging, they had remained at the house after the others had gone and toasted the bride and groom once again.

Now as they approached their house, James Thomas realized that his wife was plagued by the same tension that affected him. This was to be their first night alone together.

As he lifted her from the buggy, he held her a moment longer than was necessary. Her body was tense and board-stiff at his touch. She started toward the house, and he took her arm, walking with her through the autumn night.

"Even though Rachael Bright was a beautiful bride today, there was no one there more beautiful than you," he said softly.

"Thank you." She swallowed. "This dress was always most becoming."

He waited, thinking she might complain because she had had no new clothes since marrying him, but she said nothing more.

"I have to go back and take care of the horse." The words sounded foolish even to him. Of course she was aware that the horse must be cared for. "The night air carries a chill. Do you want me to light a fire?"

She took the lighted candle he offered before walking toward the bedroom. "It doesn't seem cold to me," she said. "Besides, it's late. I'm so tired. All I want to do is go to bed."

Even the back of Beth Ann's neck flushed at the audacity of her words. She had thought of little or nothing else since Rachael Bright had said she was going to be married. Now she was alone with James Thomas. Tonight was to be not only Rachael Bright's wedding night, but the wedding night of James Thomas and Beth Ann, as well.

As she lit the painted hurricane lamp in the bedroom, she heard the door shut as he went out. With shaking fingers, she managed to remove her finery. Once again she realized how much help Rachael Bright had been and sent good wishes for her happiness across the miles.

She removed the pins from her hair, letting it fall loose about her shoulders. For a moment, she hesitated. She wanted to look like a bride in every way, and yet, deep in her heart, she wanted him to know her real identity. How she wished she dared tell him. But that would come later. That would come when she was certain he loved her unconditionally.

She adjusted the lamp until the tiny rim of fire barely showed above the wick, then climbed into the bed she had made early that morning, before they had left for the wedding. The scent of lavender pleased her, and she sank back into the feather bed.

She heard the door open and the bar swing across, locking out the night. The minutes ticked on, and her eyelids closed, heavy with weariness after the events of the day. It certainly wouldn't do to be asleep when he came in to her. For a moment she wished she had not closed the door, but it would have been indelicate to undress in full view of the living room, and she had not thought to reopen it.

Again her eyelids drifted shut, though her senses remained alert. She fought against the sleep that threatened to overtake her, but when she opened her eyes, James Thomas still had not come to join her in her bed. Wearily she got up and went to the door. Through the silence of the house she could hear the steady cadence of her husband's light snores coming from the loft.

The night she had thought would be so special had been nothing more than the end of an exhausting day for James Thomas. He had given no thought to changing their sleeping arrangements now that Rachael Bright had gone.

She wished she had not been so adamant about not sharing his bed when she had first arrived, but her fear had overcome her vow to emulate Melisue in every way. She did not know how long she could successfully continue to pretend she was something she was not, and she knew James Thomas often looked at her askance.

She sat down on the side of the bed and carefully parted her hair down the middle, dividing it into sections as she began the task of braiding it. There was no sense in leaving it down to become tangled during the night. She had wanted him to see her as a bride when he came to her, and he had not come.

She put out the little glimmer of light and lay tossing in the darkness. As she tossed, she relived the moments they had spent before she had come to her room. Her words came back to her, and she realized how poorly she had handled the situation. How easily he could have misconstrued what she had meant to be an invitation for him to come to her that night as a plea to be left alone.

Perhaps his offer to light a fire had been a suggestion that they spend some time together. Perhaps he was as disappointed as she that they were spending the night apart. But there was no reason for them to be apart. This misunderstanding must be rectified.

She slipped from her bed again and moved quietly across the floor. The moon threw a silvery shaft of light across the main room of the cabin, leading her easily to the ladder that led to the loft. His snores ceased when she reached the top of the ladder and stood before him, outlined by the moonlight.

Having lived in the wilderness for so many years, James Thomas was aware of the sounds around him. Even in his sleep he sensed movement in the cabin below. It wasn't until he heard the sounds of someone climbing the ladder to the loft that he pulled himself from the depths of sleep. His eyes opened to see an apparition in white at the foot of his bed. An apparition that floated ever closer.

The window at the end of the loft caught the glimmer of the moon, sending the shafts of light over the woman who now stood hesitantly beside his bed.

Fully expecting to see the determined and somewhat secretive features and flowing black hair of Melisue, James Thomas found it impossible to believe his eyes when the quavering light revealed the soft, girlish face of Beth Ann. The love he remembered so clearly shone in her eyes. The tenderness of her lips, the sweetness of the sound when she whispered his name. Even the long dark braids against the white of her gown were as he remembered.

If this was a dream, he prayed that he not waken until he had held her in his arms—until he had touched the beauty and known the love that had been denied him.

And it was to Beth Ann that he held out his arms. It was to Beth Ann that he made his full and final commitment of love as he drew her down beside him. And because it was Beth Ann, he was gentle. His lovemaking was tender and painstakingly slow, for this dream, this miracle dream, might never come again, and he must live every moment to the utmost.

He made love to her as he had never dared imagine he could. Guiding and discovering at the same time. Learning each wondrous secret as his quest for fulfillment intensified. As he explored the lush curves of the beautiful body that shared his bed and his passion, his mind told him this could not be Beth Ann, but he thrust the thought aside.

He knew that Melisue was experienced in making love, that she had given her favors to Black Hawk. Had he gone to her room earlier that night, he would have taken her quickly, but here, lost in the shadows of illusion, he could believe he gave his love to the blessed innocence of Beth Ann, and, to become one with her, he must first earn her trust and her willingness to share in his passion.

So it was Beth Ann that he kissed, and Beth Ann's body that he worshiped with his hands and his lips, and Beth Ann's love that joined with his.

And it was Beth Ann's name he cried out as he felt himself hurled into a void beyond passion.

His wife's body stiffened, but it was too late. He could only hope she had not understood his words. He forced himself back to reality, reluctantly abandoning the dream that had inspired his lovemaking, and lay back, holding her in his arms. He was aware that he had made a major mistake, but the warm, soft body curled gently against his, and after a few moments he knew she was asleep. He lay listening to her steady breathing while thoughts as quick and irritating as flies buzzed through his brain, giving him no rest. He realized that Melisue, for all her beauty and fire, could never take Beth Ann's place deep in his heart.

Chapter Fifteen

At first Beth Ann didn't know where she was. Startled and disoriented, she found herself in the loft. James Thomas had gone. The sun was high in the sky.

She scrambled into her nightgown and hurried down the ladder. Only when she had closed the door to her bedroom was she able to sit down and try to still her racing pulse. Her mind went back to the previous night. A night such as she had never dared imagine. She held each moment within her heart, savoring them one by one.

His breath, warm against her skin as he whispered words of love. His hands, gentle and loving as he awakened her to the wonders of love. His lips, dropping kisses over her body until he could stand no more, devouring her. His body, hard and strong, yet so very sensitive to her every reaction, burning against her skin as he soothed away her fears and carried her with him on waves of delight.

Where she had expected pain, he had given her joy. Where she had hesitated, he had carefully guided her along the path of pleasure. And where she had steeled herself against hearing him make love to her in her sister's name, their crescendo of happiness had been so great that even his cry of release had sounded, to her ears, like an echo of her own name, Beth Ann. And though she knew she had heard only what she wanted to hear, she gratefully accepted, without question, this last miracle that had blessed their night of love.

From now on it would be different, she assured herself. Soon there would be no need for subterfuge. Soon she would reveal her identity and he would realize it was Beth Ann he loved, not her sister. And how he had loved her. Their love had been all that she could have hoped for.

Quickly she readied herself for the day—this glorious day in which her troubles would dissolve as the night had dissolved into sunshine.

She longed to run over to the trading post to talk to him, but she held back, contenting herself with a quick glimpse of her husband as he moved around the store.

His dinner was ready and waiting when he came in.

After the love they had shared the night before, Beth Ann had expected something more than the courtesy kiss he always gave her in greeting.

He sat down at the table and commented on the meal. Beth Ann sat opposite him, unable to hide the disappointment on her face. It was obvious that James Thomas felt ill at ease. He could not meet her eyes, and he centered his attention on the food before him.

Her questions regarding the customers that had come to the trading post were met with short answers, and she finally gave up all hope of conversation.

Her heart sank. She had been so certain that everything would be all right once they had made love. She had been so sure that he would know that she loved him above all else in the world. She had been so positive he would return her love, and she had been so wrong. If anything, he was even more silent, and impossible to reach.

As she was clearing off the table, she turned and found him watching her with an expression of infinite sadness. She wanted to run to him, to explain why she had come in Melisue's place, but before she could move, the expression changed to a dark scowl and she found herself shut out again.

Tears ran down her cheeks and dropped into the water as she began washing the dishes. James Thomas knew she was crying. He didn't know what to say. His mind was spinning with the happenings of the past night. None of it made sense. His head ached from trying to sort it all out.

He had waited, ready to apologize for calling out another woman's name as he made love to his wife, but she had not spoken of the matter.

Surely she didn't expect *him* to bring the subject to light. Still, she had watched him closely, expectantly, throughout the meal, even as she made her inept attempts at small talk. He couldn't understand her attitude. It wasn't like Melisue not to vent her wrath over so obvious a blunder.

Perhaps she had not understood his words. Yet there was no doubt in his mind that she had stiffened when he had spoken them. Just as there was no doubt in his mind that his wife had been a virgin.

That fact he could not fathom. He knew Melisue had been seeing Black Hawk, and though the Indian had never bragged about having a white woman, James Thomas knew his friend well enough to know the man would not turn down what was freely offered.

He closed his eyes and sat back in his chair, remembering the lovely apparition that had come to him in the night. Perhaps it had all been a dream. Perhaps she had not come to him at all.

"I brought your things down to the bedroom."

Her voice brought him back from his musings. He went to her and lifted her face with his hand.

"Thank you." He searched her face as he spoke. There was no accusation there, only tenderness and traces of tears. He softened his words with a light kiss on her upturned lips and returned to his chair to recount the problems of the day.

The tension had been broken, but the problem remained unresolved.

If there was one lesson James Thomas had learned from life, it was acceptance. When his wife did not berate him for his mistake during their lovemaking, he willingly endeavored to ignore the lapse and made certain it didn't happen again.

As the weeks passed, they became closer, sharing one another's thoughts through the long evenings. When the weather permitted or when necessity prevailed, Rachael Bright came into town to pick up supplies at the trading post and talk to Beth Ann.

"You mean you haven't told him?" the woman demanded. "But why not? Surely you know he loves you."

"He loves Melisue. If I told him now that I'm Beth Ann, he might not even believe me." Beth Ann twisted her fingers in the folds of her apron. "Every time I try to tell him, I see the frown on his face and I know it is the wrong moment."

"I know that you love him. But you can't build your marriage on lies," Rachael Bright said sagely. "Until you tell him who you are, you can never really be his wife."

"But I *am* his wife," Beth Ann protested, "and it's because I want to remain his wife that I dare not speak the truth."

Rachael Bright shook her head. "You're beginning to *think* like Melisue. I don't like it. I don't like it a bit."

"I'm not like Melisue." Beth Ann protested. "I've carried this pretense so far I'm ashamed to admit I've deceived him, but I promise to tell him the truth at the first opportunity."

Rachael Bright finished her tea and picked up her parcels. "Very well, Beth Ann. But remember, if James

Thomas ever asks me straight out about your true identity—I'll tell him.''

The last snow had fallen and melted with the warm winds of spring, leaving the ground uneven from the hooves of the horses and the wheels of the wagons.

James Thomas watched as his wife picked her way across the frozen mud that served as a road in front of the trading post.

"Come in here, little one," he said as he took her hand and helped her up the steps to the entrance of the store. "You're out early," he remarked.

"I brought you some hot rolls." She set the basket she carried on the counter, and the scent of hot bread and cinnamon filled the room.

"You'll have every man in town in here begging to buy some," James Thomas told her, proud of his wife's baking abilities. It seemed as though she had surprised him in some way almost every day since Rachael Bright had moved to her own home. He was pleased with her accomplishments, and he'd told her so. Still, he did not feel she was completely at ease with him, and he'd redoubled his efforts to make up for his mistake during their initial lovemaking. She watched him when she did not think he would notice and turned away when he did.

Often he asked, "What did you say?" knowing she had said nothing aloud, but feeling strongly that there was something she wanted to say to him. Her answer was always a quick shake of the head as she went about her business, leaving him to wonder once again what was bothering her.

He poured her a cup of coffee from the pot on the stove that heated the store. After taking a bite of one of the steaming rolls, he broke off a little piece and popped it into her mouth.

"If you don't quit hand-stuffing me, I'll be as fat as one of Ma Barker's prize geese," she protested, licking her lips.

James Thomas didn't take time to think. He bent down and kissed the sugar from her mouth. She did not push him away, despite the fact that they were in a public place, but remained in the curve of his arm as he finished the roll.

It was James Thomas who pulled away at last.

"Customers coming," he said as he walked toward the door. "You'd better get back to the house. It looks like a band of Indians. They'd probably rather trade their furs for you than anything I have in the store." He kissed her again as he helped her down to the road. She scurried along, her now-empty basket waving precariously as she fought to keep her balance. When she reached the path to their house, she paused, laughing back at him. He waved and turned his attention to the newcomers who stopped in front of the trading post.

The Indians did not go inside. Instead, they waited for James Thomas to come and inspect their wares. Jim Montgomery was known as a fair man, and they knew he would give them the worth of their labors.

"Jim, my friend, I need to speak to you."

James Thomas stopped short at the sound of the voice. "Black Hawk!" He clasped the man's arm. "It's been so long since you came this way. I thought never to see you again." For a moment the joy of seeing his old friend overpowered his concern over Melisue's reaction when she realized the handsome young Indian was in the vicinity.

"We did some hunting along the way. We camp far up in the mountains. The white man has taken everything below." He shook his head sadly. "That is one reason I came to speak to you," Black Hawk told him. "There is no trading post within many miles of where we go. I think it would be wise to build one."

James Thomas rubbed his forehead thoughtfully. "Even after you put up the building, it would take money to stock a trading post."

"I have worked as Indian guide. I have money." Black Hawk said bluntly.

"There is another obstacle." James Thomas wondered how he could phrase the problem to keep from hurting Black Hawk's pride. "It is very possible the U.S. government wouldn't let you own a trading post, even in a remote place, because you are an Indian."

Black Hawk put his hand on his friend's shoulder. "I am aware of that possibility, but if you were my partner they would say nothing."

When James Thomas did not speak, Black Hawk asked, "Would you become my partner, Jim Montgomery?"

"I can send for the supplies you will need," James Thomas said, calculating quickly, "and perhaps even give you enough from my own surplus to get you started, but I would not be able to go with you and help set up the place. I have a wife now and cannot leave her for any great length of time."

"I heard you had married. Does life treat you well?"

"The trading post is busy, my wife is beautiful, and, though she has said nothing as yet, I believe there will be a child sometime this summer."

"You must be a proud man," Black Hawk said.

"Melisue manages quite well."

"Melisue is here?" Black Hawk's usually stoic expression changed to one of surprise.

"Black Hawk," he explained patiently, "Melisue is my wife."

The Indian shook his head. "Jim, my friend, I cannot guess what game you play, but the woman I saw is not Melisue. I made the mistake one time, and will not do so again. Your woman is Beth Ann."

"That's ridiculous. She even brought Rachael Bright with her. There has never been any question of her identity. I sent for Melisue, and she came. Why would she lie to me?"

The Indian laughed. "Why indeed! Beth Ann has always loved you. Melisue went off to get married, and Beth Ann was left at home to care for her little brother. When her parents returned, they were told she had gone away with a mountain man."

James Thomas stood silently, mulling over the many inconsistencies he had noted and ignored over the past months. He could not deny the possibility that Black Hawk's words might be true, yet he could not believe Beth Ann would have lied to him and been able to carry off the lie to the point where he believed it. One of the things he had loved most about Beth Ann was her inherent honesty.

He voiced his doubts aloud. "But why would Beth Ann lie to me?"

"She would lie because she loved you and believed you had willingly chosen her sister to be your wife," Black Hawk explained. "How could she know that it was not Melisue you loved, when it was Melisue you were to marry?"

"I had not seen either of the sisters since I left Fort Kearney," James Thomas said. "The last time I saw Beth Ann, she was hardly more than a child. It is impossible to imagine she could have grown to look so much like Melisue that I could not tell them apart."

Black Hawk's laughter filled the air. "I knew Melisue far better than you, my friend, and when I came upon Beth Ann, grown to the beauty of womanhood, I thought she was her sister." He placed his hand on the white man's shoulder. "If you saw them together, there would be no doubt in your mind as to which woman shares your life."

Before he could say more, the voices of the other Indians called out for attention. James Thomas forced his mind back to the business at hand.

"We will draw up an agreement, but our partnership will be on paper only. The trading post you build will belong to you." He held out his hand.

Black Hawk shook hands gravely. "It is good," he said. "And deal gently with the girl. Her lies are loving ones."

Had it not been for the Indians, James Thomas might have confronted her then and there, but the trading took several hours, and it was late in the day before he was able to go to his home and his wife—whoever she might be.

Beth Ann looked up from her cooking as he entered the house. "You were gone so long I was afraid you had indeed traded me for a bundle of furs." She laughed, lifting her face to receive his kiss.

"I declined their offers," he assured her, "but the trading took longer than usual, because my friend Black Hawk was among them."

The spoon clattered against the kettle, and Beth Ann grabbed at it, holding it steady with both her hands.

"Black Hawk? Whatever is he doing here?" Perspiration formed on her face, and her hands turned cold. Had Black Hawk seen through her subterfuge when he'd passed her on the road? Had he exposed her to James Thomas?

"He came with the others. They are going far into the wilderness, away from the white man. They will be able to live as they always have, at least for a while longer." James Thomas noted his wife's trembling hands. Why didn't she admit she had seen Black Hawk? If she was indeed Beth Ann, she had nothing to hide. But Melisue's attraction to the Indian would seal her lips with guilt.

"Did he...has he seen my parents? My little brother? Did he say if they were well? Did he say anything about my sister?"

"Only that she is happily married and hasn't returned to Fort Kearney. I was surprised. I thought Beth Ann was close to her family and would visit them often."

"Perhaps it is impossible," she said quietly. "Doesn't the Bible say a woman should cleave only to her husband?"

James Thomas sat down at the table. "I hope it's nothing more than that. It would be too bad if Beth Ann's life hadn't worked out as she had hoped and she didn't want her family to know of the circumstances."

With great effort, Beth Ann began eating her meal, willing her hands not to shake, and hoping the pallor of her face would go unnoticed in the dim evening light.

James Thomas had never loved Beth Ann except as a little sister. She was sure that once he discovered her secret he would send her away. She was not the wife he wanted, and she had come to him under false pretenses. And, although she had tried to make him happy, she was acutely aware that he often looked at her askance.

She dared not confess her subterfuge to him. Dared not tell him that it was love that had brought her across the endless miles. She would wait until he had finished eating, and then she would talk to him. Perhaps the child she carried would make the difference. Surely then he would love her just as he would love their baby.

When she had finished her evening chores, Beth Ann pulled over a low stool and sat down beside her husband's chair.

"What are you up to now?" he asked gently, touching one of the dark curls that had escaped around her face.

"There's something I must tell you," she began.

"Is it a secret?"

"It has been until now." She watched his face, but was unable to make out anything other than mild interest. "You see, well, I'm ... that is, we're going to have a baby."

A smile lit his face, and he bent down and kissed her tenderly. "That's the most wonderful secret I've ever heard."

He took her hand and held it in both of his. "Was there something else?" he asked.

Beth Ann closed her eyes. What would he do if he learned it was not the child of the woman he loved?

"When will the baby be born?"

"Sometime this summer." She began twisting her apron. "Or at least that's what Rachael Bright says."

It hurt to know that Rachael Bright had been informed before he had. He got to his feet and walked around the room. His eyes lit on a beaded band tucked away on the sideboard.

"Where did you get this?" he asked, recognizing it as the same pattern Black Hawk wore.

"I found it," she mumbled.

"Found it where—on Black Hawk's buckskins?"

"I found it after I passed him on the road." She clapped her hand over her mouth, but it was too late.

Her husband's face clouded with doubt. "You didn't tell me about the child, you didn't tell me you'd seen Black Hawk. What else are you not telling me?" James Thomas demanded.

"You never give me a chance," Beth Ann objected.

"I've given you every chance. You'd rather live a life filled with lies than come to me with the truth."

"That's not so. I've tried to tell you the truth, but each time I start, you stare at me as though you are accusing me of..."

"Of lying?" he finished for her.

"Not lying." Tears filled her eyes. "I've never meant to lie to you."

He turned from her, pacing the floor. "Very well, not lying, then, but certainly not telling the truth. If it's truth I want, I can see I'll have to go elsewhere."

"No, James Thomas. I'll tell you. I'll tell you anything you want to hear."

"That's just what I'm afraid of," he said as he took his coat and gun from the pegs by the front door. He paused and looked back at her. He ached to hold her and kiss away her tears, but there were too many lies between them. Too many lies that had to be cleared up, and quickly, because if this woman was not Melisue, their marriage was illegal and their child would be born a bastard.

"James Thomas, James Thomas!" she called. "Where are you going?"

"I'm going to see Casey Stubbs."

Without looking back, he rounded the corner of the house and disappeared from sight.

Beth Ann buried her face in her hands. She should run after him and tell him everything. Surely the baby would make the difference. He wouldn't send his own child away, regardless of his disappointment at the identity of the mother. Before she could open the door, the sound of hooves faded into the distance and she knew he was gone. She had lost the chance to tell him the truth. The chance to tell him how she loved him—how she had always loved him.

She leaned weakly against the door. He had said he was going to Casey Stubbs. Casey had brought her here. Was James Thomas going to ask him to take her back to Fort Kearney and bring Melisue back?

Her heart stopped. Bring Melisue back! But James Thomas didn't know Melisue was at Fort Kearney. She hadn't told him of the letter she had received from her mother saying that Melisue's husband was dead.

Beth Ann dug into her sewing basket. The letter was still at the bottom, beneath her handiwork. Her husband couldn't know that Melisue was available to share his heart and his home. But Beth Ann knew, and the ache in her heart was as great as her fear that her deception had caused her to lose the man she loved.

Chapter Sixteen

"I knew it would come to no good. You told him, and he left me. He went back to search for Melisue. It's Melisue he wants. He didn't even say goodbye." Tears streamed down Beth Ann's face as she spoke.

"He sent us to take care of you while he's gone," Rachael Bright said soothingly. "It was imperative that he leave as quickly as possible." The agony she had seen on the man's face was burned into Rachael Bright's soul. How she wished she had never been party to this deception.

"Then where is he?" Beth Ann asked, as she did a hundred times a day. "Why hasn't he come back?"

"He went to get supplies for Black Hawk's trading post." Rachael Bright hugged the girl tightly. "He loves you. He's never loved anyone else. Believe me. The only reason he left so suddenly was because he was hurt and angry that he had to hear the truth from me."

"I wanted to tell him the truth!" Beth Ann cried. "I was so afraid he would tell me he really loved Melisue and I was a poor substitute. Baby or no baby, I thought he'd send me back to Fort Kearney."

"No need to worry about that," Rachael Bright assured her. "Now let's see that pretty smile. That's better," she said when Beth Ann managed a watery smile. "I have to go back home tomorrow and take of things there, but Casey will be staying at the trading post and handling the business. Don't you worry about James Thomas. He'll be coming back as quick as he can. And don't worry about Casey, either. He'll sleep in the store, but if you could manage to see to it that he eats regularly I'd appreciate it.''

"I'll be glad to fix Casey's meals,'' Beth Ann told her. "It's the least I can do when he's taking the time to run the trading post for us.''

"That's my good girl.'' Rachael Bright gave her another little hug and went off in search of her husband.

The doubt that Rachael Bright spoke the truth sent Beth Ann into a shell of silence. In Beth Ann's heart she was certain that James Thomas would not accept her as his wife when Melisue was available.

There was no denying the fact that she had married James Thomas under her sister's name. According to the laws regarding proxy marriages, it was Melisue who was married to James Thomas. What would he do when he was faced with the living proof that Beth Ann had lied to him? Would he cast her out and open his arms and his heart to the woman he had thought he had married?

Night and day she agonized over the web in which her lies had trapped her.

"I dare not stay,'' Beth Ann said aloud as she emptied the dresser drawers. "I'd better leave while I have the chance. James Thomas might decide he wants to keep my baby. I couldn't bear to have my child call some other woman mother, even if that person was Melisue.'' She slammed a drawer shut to emphasize her words. "I couldn't stand it if he sent me away and kept my baby. I couldn't stand it.'' As an unmarried woman, her only chance of keeping James Thomas's baby was to get away now, before the child was born. Before anyone could stop her.

If she could get back to her parents, perhaps they would protect her, regardless of the shame. There was no other way. She must leave as quickly as possible. Beth Ann felt she had no right to the home she had tended and loved, the man she adored, or the child she carried.

Panic seized her. When James Thomas found Melisue, he would soon forget that Beth Ann had ever existed—despite the hollow promises Rachael Bright had made concerning his love.

She hurried toward the stagecoach and called out to the driver. "I must get back to Fort Kearney. You have room, don't you?"

The stagecoach driver swallowed hard. The last thing he needed was a pregnant woman jolting over the horse trails he was forced to follow. There hadn't been once that he hadn't lost at least one wheel on this trip. He dreaded every minute of the trail down to the flatlands, and he dreaded doubly making the trip with this delicate-looking girl as a passenger.

"We don't take pregnant women," he said gruffly. "You'd be better off to stay here. Anything's better than havin' a baby out in the middle of nowhere."

The young man riding shotgun hesitated as he was about to put Beth Ann's bags on the coach.

"I'm not that near my time," Beth Ann assured them. "Just get me out of here and everything will be fine."

Fear, brought about by the driver's words, as well as desperation at the thought of leaving the home she had thought of as her own and never seeing James Thomas again, drained Beth Ann of the last remnant of pride. Tears of determination streamed down her cheeks and her hands shook as she reached out toward the coach.

"You sure you want to do this, ma'am?"

Beth Ann nodded numbly.

"I thought you said we didn't carry pregnant women," the young man reminded the driver.

"We don't, but from the look on that woman's face I think she'd walk to get where she wants to go." He turned to Beth Ann. "I'll need the money now," he said.

"Very well. I'll be right back."

She went into the trading post. Casey Stubbs was busy talking to a customer and paid little mind to what she was doing until he saw her hurry out of the building with a handful of cash. He glanced at the money box and realized it was open.

"Hey, Mrs. Montgomery! What are you doin'?" He raced to the door in time to see her hand the money to the driver as the stagecoach started down the street.

"Wait! Come back! Don't take Miz Montgomery! Come back!" He chased the coach until it disappeared out of sight in a thick stand of trees.

"What was all that about?" he asked aloud as he limped back into town. "Where's Miz Montgomery going?"

The blank looks on the faces of the townsfolk told him they knew no more than he did. "I'd better go tell Rachael Bright," he said to no one in particular.

James Thomas breathed a sigh of relief when the final papers were signed. His proxy marriage to Melisue Cadwalder was annulled. It was declared void by a judge on the grounds that the woman had been married to someone else at the time.

It had taken him much longer than he had anticipated to find the record of Melisue's marriage to Reginald Colfax. He looked ahead to the weary miles between himself and Beth Ann. He had written to her, but he doubted the letter would arrive much before he did.

How he longed to hold Beth Ann in his arms. How he longed to tell her of his love for her, and only her. Even in his anger at her deceit he loved her and wanted only her happiness. He was forced to move slowly because of the string of mules that carried supplies not only for his trading post, but for Black Hawk's, as well.

He had found no sign of Beth Ann's sister. It seemed the woman had taken her servant and disappeared into thin air. And good riddance he told himself as he urged his horse to a brisker pace, dragging the reluctant mules along behind him.

Perhaps if she had believed in James Thomas more, or believed in herself more, she would not have found herself in this position. Beth Ann silently berated herself as the stagecoach jolted along the rutted trail. Regardless of Rachael Bright's assurances, Beth Ann had never been able to believe that James Thomas really loved her and not Melisue.

How she longed for the constant bumping to stop. How she wished she could lie down on her own soft bed, and how she wanted to feel the safe assurance of James Thomas's arms around her again. She closed her eyes to keep the tears from running down her hot, dusty cheeks.

"Why don't you trade places with me?" a man offered from the other side of the coach. "Sittin' over here will get you out of the sun. You look as though you have a headache. My wife had headaches something awful when she was in the family way." He scratched his head thoughtfully regarding his own words. "'Course, she had headaches pretty regular when she wasn't in the family way, too, now that I think on it."

"Leave the little lady alone," a second passenger roused himself enough to say. "We'll be changing direction soon, and you'll have to move back. Better off staying where you are."

"Thank you," Beth Ann said to them both. "I appreciate your kindness, but I'll be all right."

The words held more assurance than did her heart. She ached in every muscle and bone in her body. She knew she must be black-and-blue. Even her poor baby must be black-and-blue. She wondered where James Thomas was at that moment. How wonderful it would be if she could see him once more, if only from a distance. It was that thought alone that sustained her. Her eyes scanned the landscape.

There were very few travelers on the road. She saw a wagon train. James Thomas was not with them. On the afternoon of the third day, Beth Ann had just about given up even that last hope of ever seeing James Thomas again, when she saw movement in the distance. She watched as the dots became larger. Horses—or perhaps mules; although they seemed to be moving too quickly for mules—were coming single file, the way James Thomas led his mules. Her heart lurched.

"You enjoying the scenery, ma'am?" one of the men asked, noticing how she stared out the window.

"There's someone coming along the ridge there." She pointed. "It looks like it might be a trader with a string of mules."

The man shot across the seat and nearly landed in the lap of the other passenger. He looked out the window and rubbed his eyes. "Mules, hell! Them's Indians." He reached up and banged on the front of the stagecoach. "There's Indians out there. You'd better git them horses movin'."

The stagecoach lurched forward, almost knocking Beth Ann from the seat.

"Are you sure they aren't friendly?" she asked as she tried to right herself.

"I'm sure I don't want to stick around to find out," the man said as he checked the bullets in his gun.

"You know how to use one of these?" the second man asked, shoving his pistol under Beth Ann's nose.

"Yes...no...that is, I've fired one before, but I'm not a good shot."

"As long as you don't shoot one of us, you don't have to be good," he said. "If worse comes to worst and we have to fight, you can use this. I'll use my rifle." He fished around on the floor until he came up with the weapon.

"You don't really think we're going to have to fight them, do you?" Beth Ann gasped. "I thought there were treaties with all the Indians."

"There's always renegade bands that break the treaties—if the white men don't do it first. You're never safe out here. If the Indians decide they don't want you traveling through their country, they come after you. And that's about the size of it."

Beth Ann shrank back into the seat. There was a little puff of dust as a bullet hit the ground near the coach.

"Get on the floor," one of the men shoved her down. "You'll be safer there." He glanced at her as he climbed into the seat she evacuated. "Damn fool women have to go visit Mama when they should be home taking care of their husbands. And keep your head down, unless you want a hole in it."

But it was the man who ended up with a bullet in his shoulder. The other passenger thrust a gun into Beth Ann's hand and shoved the wounded man to the far side of the seat.

"Get up here and shoot the best you can. You might as well get your licks in, too. Way things look, we're all dead anyways."

Before Beth Ann could move, the coach swayed, tilted and pitched over onto its side. She fell, facedown, striking her head and struggling for breath, the wounded man on top of her. She could still hear gunfire, and it seemed to be coming from all sides now.

"There's more of them comin'," the driver yelled as the passengers tried to scramble out the door. His heel caught Beth Ann in the head as he vaulted out of the overturned stage. Someone called to her to follow, but her head was spinning, and she found it impossible to grasp the hand that reached down to her.

The sound of galloping horses became louder, and everything around her faded into darkness as she gratefully allowed herself to drop into the void of oblivion.

Suddenly, rough hands jerked her back to consciousness.

Still dizzy, she looked around as she was lifted from the coach and placed on the ground. The men who had been with the stagecoach were nowhere to be seen.

"Where is the driver?" she asked aloud.

One of the Indians turned to her. "Take horses and go." He pointed to a cloud of dust far in the distance.

"Oh" was all the answer Beth Ann could manage as the seriousness of her situation struck her.

She watched as the Indians opened her baggage and began digging through the items. She wanted to cry out in protest that she had been hurt enough and couldn't stand to have the last reminders of her life with James Thomas defiled, but she bit her lip to hold her silence. Then an Indian held up the bead band Black Hawk had dropped on her porch. She had stuffed it into her apron pocket when James Thomas began badgering her. The men examined it closely before one left the group and started toward her.

The Indian came nearer and lifted her chin, looking into her face. "I see you," he said. "At Fort Kearney."

Beth Ann's mouth was dry. Her throat closed. She didn't recognize him. But then, the only Indian she remembered from Fort Kearney was Black Hawk. She tried to smile. "Fort Kearney. I'm going there now to visit my mother."

He pulled her to her feet and stared openly at the bulge beneath her skirt. Then his eyes returned to her face. "Me-li-sue..." He pronounced the name carefully, watching for her reaction.

"Yes!" She nodded. "Melisue is my—"

She was about to say "sister" when the man held up the band of Indian beads and intoned, "Black Hawk."

Again she nodded, putting her hands over her baby to shield it from his eyes. "I know Black Hawk," she said, hoping this man was one of Black Hawk's friends.

"Sit!" He eased her to the ground and went back to the others, who were sifting through the rest of the baggage on the coach.

A few minutes later her bags were repacked and set apart from the rest. "Yours?" the Indian asked, pointing.

"Yes," Beth Ann said. Surely he wasn't going to take her back to his village and expect her to live like a squaw. Of course, it was preferable to being killed, but not much.

"Come!" He helped her to her feet and escorted her toward the horses. Several of the others followed, carrying her bags.

Before she could protest, he had lifted her onto one of the ponies and jumped on behind her. "You feel good!"

She could not tell whether he was asking her or telling her, and before she could clarify the matter he put his heels to the horse and they thundered off across the prairie.

It was dark when they came to a town and stopped before an impressive structure that might have served as either the town hall, a church, or both.

Beth Ann was relieved when she realized it was a white man's settlement with small houses, neat gardens and green grass.

The Indian lifted her from the horse and led her to a house next to the structure. The door was opened by a tall man with graying hair.

The Indian nudged her forward. "Black Hawk's woman," he said, as though no more explanation were necessary. Then, sensing Beth Ann's confusion he added, "Bishop Henry."

The man opened the door wide, and Beth Ann could see a dark-eyed woman with a puzzled expression in her compassionate eyes.

"Please come in," Bishop Henry said in a richly modulated voice. Then he turned to the woman. "Caroline, we have a guest. Will you see to her needs?"

The woman hurried forward and ushered Beth Ann to a chair, making little clucking sounds of sympathy. Beth Ann's attention remained on the two men.

"Where did you find her?" Bishop Henry asked.

The Indian began speaking in his own language, and Beth Ann was unable to follow the conversation. She looked at the woman, who seemed to understand. "What did he say?" Beth Ann asked.

Caroline answered without taking her eyes from the Indian. "He says the stagecoach overturned and the men left you for dead." She spoke in a low monotone. "He says he brought you here because you are the woman of his friend Black Hawk and you carry his child."

"But that's not true!"

Beth Ann would have gotten to her feet, but the woman's hand held her firmly in her chair.

"Be still. Your life and the life of your child depend on your silence."

The Indian glanced their way, and the woman patted Beth Ann's shoulder solicitously while her eyes sought those of the bishop.

"We will see that Black Hawk's woman is cared for until he can come for her. She will be my honored guest," the man said with warm assurance.

"It is good." The Indian gave Beth Ann a nod in parting and followed the white man out the door. "Stay well, Black Hawk's woman," he said as the door closed between them.

Beth Ann opened her mouth to protest, but the woman put her finger to her lips. Moments later, the Indians dropped Beth Ann's bags outside the door. When the sound of horses faded into the distance, Bishop Henry came back into the house. He pulled a chair from beside the table and sat down in front of Beth Ann, taking her hands in his.

"How long has it been since you've eaten?"

Beth Ann shook her head. "I don't know. I don't remember. But you don't understand. He wasn't telling the truth. The Indians attacked us. They chased us until the stagecoach turned over. The men rode off on the horses, but I had hit my head and must have been unconscious for a while. When I woke up, the Indians were going through the luggage. They found a bead band that had belonged to one of my—" she stopped herself before calling James Thomas her husband, and she choked back a sob before continuing "—the customers at the trading post."

The sob came, unbidden, and the bishop put his arm around Beth Ann's shoulder. "There's no need to speak of it now. You've been through a lot. Here comes my sister, Caroline, with some food. I'm sure you'll feel better once you've eaten, Mrs.—?"

"My name is Beth Ann," she said as the woman placed a steaming bowl of stew on the table. "Beth Ann Cadwalder."

"Don't you worry about a thing, Beth Ann." Caroline fussed around the table, watching every bite Beth Ann took. "We'll see that you're taken care of until you're able to continue your journey." She hesitated, then said, "How far are you going?"

"I'm on my way to Fort Kearney, in Nebraska, to visit my mother." Tears started down her cheeks.

"You'll see your mother in good time," the bishop assured her. "Right now you need all your strength for yourself and for the child you carry."

"It's not Black Hawk's baby," Beth Ann tried to explain. Realizing any further explanation would only make these good people think less of her, she forced herself to be silent and resume eating. How could she explain the web of lies she'd spun in her desperation to find happiness, and to give happiness to the man she loved? She covered her face with her hands, only vaguely aware of the sympathetic voices discussing her plight.

When she could eat no more, Caroline bundled her off to bed. The room was cheerful, even in the gloom of night. The white walls were set off by yellow curtains that matched the flowers on the washbasin and pitcher.

"I'll stop back when you're ready for bed and make sure you have everything you need," Caroline said as she turned back the covers.

"Thank you. You've been very kind," Beth Ann managed to reply.

The woman stopped by the door. "When you feel ready to discuss your problems, please feel free to come to me, or to my brother. I don't know if we can help, but we're more than willing to try. Meanwhile, put your faith in the Lord." With that, she slipped out into the hall, closing the door behind her.

Beth Ann wished she could confide in someone. Despite her good intentions, nothing she had done had turned out right. Rather than bother these people with her problems, she would get on the next stage and continue her journey.

She wouldn't impose on their generous hospitality any longer than was necessary.

Having made the decision, Beth Ann felt better. Regardless of the rigors of the journey, and the possibility of more Indian attacks, she would go on.

"Please let me be doing the right thing," she prayed aloud. "Please show me the way."

She pushed down the doubt in her heart as she made herself ready for bed. It was only when she removed her petticoats and saw the ominous bloodstain that she knew she must impose on the hospitality of the bishop and his sister for a while longer.

Chapter Seventeen

The circuit preacher rode into Montgomery, stopped at the trading post and climbed out of his buggy.

The townsfolk followed like a flock of sheep.

With a sweep of his hand he gestured toward the woman on the seat he had vacated. Her traveling dress was burgundy velvet. A little hat sat atop her neatly coiffed hair. She looked entirely out of place, as did the black woman riding astride a mule behind her.

She held out her gloved hands, wiggling her fingers impatiently at the preacher. "Help me down, Preacher Fullbright. I declare, I cannot abide another moment in this buggy."

Obediently the preacher hurried back to her side and lifted her to the ground.

Melisue brushed off her skirts. "I swear, I cannot travel another mile." Her eyes centered on a big, bearded man in the door of the trading post. That ruffian certainly couldn't be James Thomas!

"I've come to see Mrs. Montgomery," she announced. "Where does she live?"

Casey stared in disbelief at the woman, who looked so like his friend's wife. He looked her up and down. "You must be the sister I heard about."

"I've come to straighten things out between my Beth Ann and her husband." She sighed, as though it were a burden only she could bear.

"Jim ain't goin' to like that," Casey muttered.

Melisue continued undaunted, "I'm Melisue Colfax, Beth Ann's sister."

He glanced up and down the street. "Where's Mister Colfax?"

"My husband is dead," she said, dabbing her eyes and relishing the sympathetic groans from the crowd.

Casey Stubbs shook his head. "Jim ain't goin' to like that, neither." He started back toward the trading post, but her voice stopped him.

"Now show me where my sister lives and go on back to work. I don't want James Thomas blaming me for your dawdling, any more than I intend to blame him for your lack of manners."

Casey Stubbs wasn't sure what this woman meant. Short of dropping to his knees and kissing the hem of her skirt, he had shown her the same courtesy he showed any woman. He wasn't about to do any more. But her supposition about his being hired help riled him.

It didn't take Melisue long to march over to the cabin.

As she reached the porch, the door opened. For a moment she couldn't believe her eyes.

"Rachael Bright, as I live and breathe! Whatever are you doing here? Aren't you glad to see me?"

"Of course I'm glad to see you. I'm just surprised. I had no idea you were coming."

"We'll talk about it inside," Melisue said as she gave Rachael Bright a perfunctory embrace and swept past her into the house. Her skirts swirled as she examined the main room.

"Is this all there is?" she asked. "Just one room?"

"There's a loft, too." Rachael Bright gestured toward the back of the house. Melisue meant trouble, and Beth Ann didn't need any more trouble than she already had.

"A loft?" Melisue gave the bright little alcove a critical look. "It certainly isn't what I'm used to, but I'll have to make do." She spied the door at the side of the room. "Where does that lead?"

"To the bedroom," Rachael Bright said flatly.

"Beth Ann's bedroom?" Melisue asked.

"Beth Ann has gone back to Fort Kearney."

"But that's impossible. She wrote that she and James Thomas were having trouble, but she also wrote Mama that she was pregnant. She shouldn't be traveling all over the countryside at a time like this!" Melisue dabbed at her eyes. "How could she just up and walk out on James Thomas? And after all I've done to make sure they found each other!"

"All you did?" Rachael Bright's jaw dropped in surprise.

"Well, of course." Melisue tucked an arrant curl beneath her bonnet. "James Thomas sent me a letter saying he was coming back for me, and I knew Beth Ann was pining for him, so I went off and married Reginald Colfax. I couldn't stand in the way of Beth Ann marrying the man she loved." She hesitated, then lifted her head and met Rachael Bright's eyes. "He did marry her, didn't he?"

"Well, yes... I mean, actually, no... You see, we came out here with Casey Stubbs."

"Casey Stubbs?"

"Casey Stubbs is my husband," Rachael Bright said proudly.

"Your husband?" It had never occurred to Melisue that Rachael Bright might marry.

Rachael Bright nodded. "He's taking care of the trading post while James Thomas is away."

"That great big man with the beard?" Melisue gasped. "But he isn't black!"

"Neither am I." Rachael Bright placed her hand on Melisue's arm. Long hours of being in the sun had darkened the cherished whiteness of Melisue's skin, and both arms were the same color.

"My husband knows all about me," Rachael Bright said. "And, speaking of husbands, where is yours? The last I heard, you were off to marry into wealth and luxury."

"That's exactly what I did." She took a deep breath, then sighed. "We spent most of our time on the Mississippi. It was so beautiful watching the scenery float past. So relaxing. Reginald was always so entertaining and interesting. He knew about so many different things."

"I thought you were looking forward to having a home of your own," Rachael Bright observed.

"We weren't ready to settle down in one place. We wanted to be free to move around and go where we pleased."

"Will he be joining you here?"

Melisue buried her face in her handkerchief. "My poor, dear husband was killed in a duel. I am overcome with grief at losing the poor, brave man. A handsomer, kinder, more honorable human being never breathed the air, but when Yankee carpetbaggers cheated his family out of all their possessions, it was too much for him. He challenged one of them to a duel, but Yankees know no honor. My poor Reginald was shot before the count was reached."

Rachael Bright's eyes met those of Melisue's maid, who fought to keep a smirk from her face. "Please accept my sympathy," Rachael Bright said. "Is there anything I can do to help you?"

"Well—" Melisue sniffed "—actually, there is. I can never get LuAnn to fix my hair correctly. Not the way you used to do it, Rachael Bright. Could you take the time to teach her?"

Rachael Bright looked from LuAnn to Melisue. There was no sign of tears on Melisue's face, although she had sobbed meaningfully into her handkerchief. "I'd be glad to spend some time with LuAnn," she said.

"Oh, Rachael Bright, you always were a darling," Melisue said beaming. "Now I'll just go along and freshen up after that dreadful journey."

"Miss Melisue traveled on the riverboats, all right," LuAnn said as she manipulated another curl on Rachael Bright's head. "That Mister Reginald was a gambler, and a poor one at that. His family was from Ohio, not Mississippi, and I doubt they ever owned anything—including the roof they lived under. Sometimes, when he was on a winning streak, they'd ride the boat in high style, but that didn't last very long."

"But what of the houses Melisue was talking about?" Rachael Bright asked as she watched the girl arrange the hair into Melisue's style.

"Sometimes one of the wealthy men on the riverboat would ask Miss Melisue and Mister Reginald to visit their homes, but mostly we lived on the boats. It wasn't so bad when he was winning, but when he had a losing streak we got packed into a tiny cabin so tight we couldn't all stand up at the same time."

"Then Reginald Colfax wasn't a rich man."

"Mister Reginald Colfax was a riverboat gambler, and a cheatin' one at that!" LuAnn emphasized the words with a shake of the brush.

Rachel Bright pushed on. "And he didn't die to avenge his family's demise at the hand of a scoundrel?"

"Oh, he was shot, all right, but it surely wasn't a duel," LuAnn said in a whisper. "He got caught cheatin' at cards, and one of the men shot him dead right at the table. Miss Melisue took on something terrible. The men went running every which way to try to get help for her. When they got back, there was nary a cent left on the table, but no one was going to suggest they search the grieving widow. I got to hand it to her. She took enough money to get us out here, and now she expects to live off her sister.''

"Why didn't she go back to her parents?" Rachael Bright thought she knew the answer, but she wanted to hear the girl's opinion.

"I don't think she was happy with her mama. They closed the fort down and sold the government the land around it. Miss Melisue says she'll never go back there. Says it's worse being a widow than it is to be dead.''

Rachael Bright covered her mouth to stifle her laughter. "With all those men around, I doubt Melisue would have any trouble finding another husband.''

"Most all the soldiers are gone, Miz Stubbs,'' LuAnn explained. "They didn't stick around long after the government closed Fort Kearney. Besides, Miss Melisue don't want another husband.'' The authority in LuAnn's voice left no room for speculation. "She didn't much like the one she had, but she liked the pretty gowns and the parties every night when her husband was winnin' on the riverboats.''

"I can't imagine why Melisue would want to come out here, of all places,'' Rachael Bright said again. "Surely she would have been happier living with her mother's people in Virginia, or even her father's family in Boston.''

The girl shook her head. "The family in Virginia are as poor as church mice. She couldn't wait to get away from there. It was all she could do to spend the night. And the Cadwalders in Boston wouldn't have her after they heard the truth about Mr. Reginald's death.''

"I don't rightly think she made up her mind to come out here until the preacher delivered Miz Beth Ann's letter and offered to bring Melisue to her sister. He told her how Mr. Montgomery was all successful with his trading post and the town, named after him, was growing. But I think she saw it grown a bit more than it is.''

Rachael Bright glanced down the one and only street, with deep wagon ruts and little billows of dust spiraling upward. "I wouldn't doubt but what you're absolutely right," Rachael Bright said as the girl bent over her head again.

It didn't take Melisue long to see that the men in the town were either married or busy. The trappers had no time for social graces. They came to town, sold their goods, bought supplies and rode out. Civilization didn't appeal to them, nor did the pretty little woman who flirted and flicked her fan and wore hoops that sent clouds of dust up around her. They were fascinated by her, but they knew instinctively that she would be more of a hindrance than an asset to their way of life.

"I swear, I'm guarded just like a prisoner," Melisue complained. "I can't even go for a ride without that old Casey Stubbs following me."

"All the trees look alike," Rachael Bright told her. "If you got lost out there, we'd never find you."

"Where are all those wonderful Indian trackers your husband was always bragging about?"

"I've never heard him bragging about anything like that." Rachael Bright was somewhat taken aback. Casey wasn't a bragging man.

"Of course, when I think of Indians, I always think of Black Hawk." Melisue fluttered her fan and dabbed her face with a handkerchief soaked in rose water to cool herself. She took a sip of water and put the glass on the table beside her. "You remember Black Hawk, don't you?"

"Yes," Rachael Bright said. "He was the man you used to meet down by the stream at Fort Kearney."

Melisue smiled. "That's the one. There was a man! It would have grieved me immensely if I had gotten him killed."

"There's no law against talking to someone while you're watering your horses," Rachael Bright pointed out.

"Oh, Rachael Bright, you're such an innocent. I can tell you, Black Hawk and I did more than talk." She leaned back, a dreamy glaze in her eyes. "A lot more."

Rachael Bright had suspected as much, but she feigned surprise, allowing Melisue to go on with her story. "How lucky you were not to have been seen!"

"Seen? Seen? Why, we were caught! And it was James Thomas who did it. It was the night of the ball at the fort. I looked so lovely. You remember, don't you?"

Rachael Bright nodded and sank down at the table opposite Melisue. She remembered the night of the ball, all right. "Well," Melisue continued, "I wanted Black Hawk to see me in my ball gown, so I told him to meet me in the stables. We had this little signal that sounded like an owl hooting, and when I heard it, I went out there and, sure enough, he was waiting. He vowed he'd never seen anything so absolutely beautiful. But, well, you know how men are. Before I knew it, he was kissing me and telling me how lovely I was and how he wanted to make love to me—right there in the stable, with the dancing going on across the way. I was just getting all mussed up, and it took me longer than I would have imagined to pull myself back together, since Black Hawk wasn't any help at all. And then who showed up but James Montgomery?"

"Go on."

"Well, James Thomas scolded us something awful. He accused Black Hawk of trying to ruin the treaty by getting himself killed, but he never said a thing about Black Hawk ruining *me*." Again the fan fluttered. "I thought they were going to fight right there, but before anything happened we heard voices outside the stable and realized that some of the men had joined Papa to come looking for me." She took a sip of water and fanned herself again. "I can tell you, I've never been so scared in my life. I just knew they were going to come in and make me marry that Indian. But when I told James Thomas how I felt, he said Papa would probably kill Black Hawk and nullify the treaty. I could tell that James Thomas was just jealous of Black Hawk. I'd known all along that he wanted me to be Mrs. Montgomery, so Papa wasn't a bit surprised when I told him that James Montgomery had asked me to marry him, and it wasn't any time at all before Papa announced our engagement at the ball." She ignored the look on Rachael Bright's face. "Now isn't that just the most romantic thing you've ever heard?"

"Actually, I don't see anything romantic about it at all. You endangered all our lives. If you and Black Hawk had been caught, it could have started a full-scale Indian war."

"Oh, that's just not true!" Melisue protested. "James Thomas would never have let anything happen to me. He loves me. The only reason he married Beth Ann was that I wasn't available. And I can tell you, I never dreamed I'd end up out here in this godforsaken place at the end of the earth to try to keep them together. I can only hope that my efforts will be rewarded and I'll find a man who enjoys comfort and beauty."

"If that's the kind of man you're looking for, you've come to the wrong place," Rachael Bright said bluntly.

Much to Melisue's disgust, there were no eligible men in the area. The only single man who could carry on a conversation was the circuit preacher. The trappers answered in monosyllables, yes or no, and looked highly uncomfortable if she so much as smiled at them.

Melisue was tired of the dust and being cooped up in the little house Beth Ann so proudly called home. Above all,

Melisue was bored. She was so bored she had taken to reading Beth Ann's Bible.

It was a relief when Preacher Fullbright drove his buggy up before the house.

The preacher beamed with approval as he knocked on the door. "What a delightful angel you are, setting there with the good book in your hands."

She didn't tell him that even a Bible story was more interesting than wondering where the next bug was going to light.

The preacher bent over her solicitously. "Why, look here." He pointed to the center section of the book. "The family record. From what I hear, it won't be long before there's an entry under Births. Didn't you say your sister's baby would be born toward the end of the summer?"

"In August," Melisue said, feeling somewhat uncomfortable talking with a man about her sister's delicate condition.

He reached over her shoulder and thumbed through the pages, pausing on the one marked Marriages.

"I thought you said your sister's name was Elizabeth Ann," he mused.

Preachers—especially Preacher Fullbright—shouldn't be allowed to think, Melisue decided as she snatched the Bible from the man's hands. What would he do if he realized Melisue's very own sister might be living in sin? Would the pious preacher help or hinder her? Why, if the words in the Bible were correct, Beth Ann might be disgraced, and Melisue would be disgraced right along with her.

"Why don't you tell me where you've been since I saw you last? I can read this old Bible anytime."

Melisue put the Bible aside, silently chiding herself for having let the preacher see the entry. But until he'd pointed it out, Melisue hadn't realized the Bible listed Melissa Suzanne Cadwalder as wife of James Thomas Montgomery. She batted her eyes and smiled in her most flirtatious manner, silently praying that the preacher would make his visit a short one, because she had to find out the truth about the situation between her sister and James Thomas, and the sooner the better.

Casey Stubbs looked up in surprise as Melisue came through the door of the trading post.

"Hello, Mister Stubbs," she said with a smile. "Do you have any of that good coffee left? I could surely use a cup."

"Could be," he grunted as he poured a cup of coffee, watching the woman speculatively. Mrs. Colfax looked like Beth Ann, but had none of the younger woman's sweetness. He was glad he hadn't had to travel the many miles from Fort Kearney with her. "Was there something I could do for you?"

Melisue looked innocently over the rim of her cup. "Well, I don't want to buy anything. But there are a few questions you could answer, if you would be so kind. I'm only concerned about my little sister."

He flicked some imaginary dust off one of the saddles that sat along the far wall. "She was fine the last time I saw her. 'Course, that was better than a month ago, now."

"Oh, I don't mean her health." Melisue blinked her eyes prettily. "I understood you brought her back with you from Fort Kearney, and I was thinking how it is outside the realm of decency for a single woman to travel that distance alone with a man."

"In the first place, Mrs. Montgomery wasn't alone. Rachael Bright was with her, and later, we picked up a family by the name of Borden. In the second place, we was married at the first town outside Fort Kearney."

"Married? You married my sister?"

"Married her in Jim Montgomery's name. Proxy wedding, they called it."

"Then you weren't married to her at all?" Melisue tried to understand what the man was saying.

"I wasn't married to her, and she wasn't married to me. I just stood in for Jim at the wedding."

Melisue put her coffee on the stovetop and walked slowly across the floor. "Let me get this straight. You said the words, but you didn't get married. And James Thomas wasn't even present, but he did get married."

"That's right. All nice and legal. Even recorded in that nice Bible the preacher's wife gave Miz Montgomery as a remembrance." He nodded his head and began straightening the blankets on a shelf.

"What if my sister couldn't have been there? What if the rigors of the trip had incapacitated her but she wanted to get married before going on? What would you have done then?"

"Well, I guess Rachael Bright would have taken her place. It was a proxy marriage, after all. As long as the right names got on the marriage certificate, that's all that matters." Why was this woman asking so many questions? It was none of her business how Jim and her sister became husband and wife. "I've got to get back to work."

Melisue narrowed her eyes thoughtfully. Somehow she had to find James Thomas and make him understand that he had to marry Beth Ann again, nice and proper—and preferably before the baby was born.

"O what a web we weave," she said softly.

"What did you say?" Casey asked from across the room.

"I just don't understand things sometimes," she improvised. "It's so nice to have a man to rely on to set things straight." She stood on tiptoe and kissed him on the cheek.

He watched as she hurried out the door, rubbing at his cheek as though it had been burned by a hot iron and wondering what he'd done to earn such gratitude.

* * *

James Thomas knew he should take his load of supplies on up to Black Hawk's trading post without delay, but he was within a day's ride of his home, and he longed to see Beth Ann again and tell her the news. He wanted to take her in his arms and explain that he understood why she had come, and why she had masqueraded as her sister. He wanted to beg her forgiveness, not only for having allowed Melisue to rope him into an unwanted engagement, but also for not having realized that his wife was his own Beth Ann. As soon as the circuit preacher made his rounds again, they would be married, as they should have been from the beginning.

He stopped the mules in front of the trading post as the townspeople peered from doors and windows. It seemed strange that they didn't come out to greet him, but his mind was on his meeting with Beth Ann, and he paid the townsfolk little mind.

Leaving the mules, James Thomas hurried to his house. The moment he opened the door he sensed that something was amiss. The room was dusty, the floor was unswept, and the furniture lacked the careful polishing that had been Beth Ann's pride.

He glanced into the bedroom. The furniture was the same, yet he sensed a difference. Casting one last glance at the kitchen, he hurried out the door.

At first glance, the trading post seemed deserted. But then he saw a dark head of curls at the far end of the store.

Where was Casey Stubbs? Why was Beth Ann minding the store, he wondered as he moved silently across the floor? At the moment, it didn't matter. Nothing mattered but the fact that they would be together again.

A creaking floorboard gave him away, but the woman didn't turn.

"What do you want?" she demanded. "Can't you see I'm busy?"

Stunned by the shrill edge to her voice, James Thomas laid a hand on her shoulder. She turned quickly, striking out at him as she did.

"Don't you dare touch me!" she exploded, her eyes blazing. "You dirty, filthy mountain men think you can come in here and paw me. Well, you're wrong! If you come near me or this store again, I'll take my gun to you. Now get out of here. Get out, I say, or you'll wish you had."

James Thomas stared in disbelief. This was not his beloved Beth Ann, although the coloring and the features were much the same. It was as though some evil spirit had taken possession of the beautiful woman he loved so much.

She had aged and hardened. Her voice was bitter with anger, and her mouth was set in a thin, hard line. Unable to move or even speak, James Thomas stood frozen in disbelief as she raised a derringer and pointed it at his chest.

Chapter Eighteen

"Melisue! What are you doing here?"

Melisue did not remember the man before her. She did not remember his voice, and she did not recognize his features under the thick growth of beard he wore as a result of his weeks of hard travel. She had never cared enough about James Montgomery to remember his voice, regardless of his unkempt appearance, as Beth Ann would have done. "How dare you address me by my given name!" she continued with hardly a breath. "Now get out of here, or you'll answer to Mr. Montgomery."

"I am Mr. Montgomery," he said as he deftly twisted the little gun from her hand.

"James..." she managed as realization hit her. Before he could move, she threw her arms around his neck. "Oh, James, I'm so glad to see you. I didn't recognize you with your beard. I've been so frightened here, trying to cope with everything all by myself. Thank God you've come back."

James Thomas removed her arms from his neck and stepped away as his eyes took in the disarray in the usually neat store. "Where is Casey Stubbs?"

"That smelly old mountain man?" Melisue sniffed. "He got a message and went running home to Rachael Bright. He isn't a gentlemen. I don't know how you could have hired someone like that to look after your interests while you were gone." She drew herself up in righteous indignation.

"Did Beth Ann go with him?"

The conversation wasn't going at all the way Melisue had planned. James was angry, and not the least bit happy to see her. She had to make him understand that what she had done was all for his benefit.

"I don't know where Beth Ann went," Melisue dabbed her eyes with her handkerchief. "She wrote that you didn't love her. That you had always loved me. I came to help you straighten out your lives, but by the time I arrived she was gone." She placed her hand on his arm. "I know how disappointed you must have been when Beth Ann came to you instead of me, but she always thought so highly of you, and you must realize that I couldn't commit myself to spending my life up here, away from all the things I love."

He stepped away. The last thing in the world he needed was Melisue's "help." "You don't understand, Melisue. I don't love you. It's Beth Ann I love. It's always been Beth Ann."

Melisue smiled uncertainly. "You don't mean that, James. After all, you asked me to be your wife."

"No, Melisue, you told your father we were engaged to save yourself from disgrace and Black Hawk from certain death. There was never any mention of your love for me, or mine for you. If there was any love included in that situation, it was between yourself and Black Hawk."

Melisue placed the back of her hand against her forehead. "Oh, the sacrifices I've made to save those I love," she said with a sigh. "First Black Hawk, and now you and Beth Ann." She caught a glimpse of his face through half-closed eyes and knew things were not going as she wanted. "I'm sure Black Hawk would do anything in this world to help me, after all I did for him."

"You'll have to talk to him about that," James Thomas told her.

"How can I?" She dabbed her eyes with her handkerchief. "I have no idea where he is."

"He lives about a five-day ride from here," James Thomas told her. Then, unable to tolerate any more of Melisue's dramatics, he turned on his heel and strode out of the store.

"Where are you going?" Melisue called after him, ignoring the startled looks on the faces of the people on the street.

"To find my wife."

He mounted his horse and rode away, stopping only to ask the boy at the livery stable to take care of the mules and store the supplies in an empty stall until he returned.

It was nearly dark when he arrived at Casey Stubbs's house. The lights in the window beckoned, and James Thomas felt a pang of sorrow when he remembered how he had thought he would return to such a welcome in Beth Ann's arms.

Casey opened the door. "Have you been to the trading post?" he asked, without preamble.

"And found Melisue," James Thomas replied. "She said Beth Ann had gone away. Is she here?"

Casey hung his head. "Last I saw of her, she was on the stagecoach, headed out of town. Musta been about six, maybe eight, weeks ago. Come into the house." He took in his friend's condition. "You look like you been rode hard and put up wet."

Rachael Bright cut into the conversation, her frustration over her husband's lack of action obvious in her manner. "I told him he should have ridden after her. By the time he got out here and told me, the stage was too far ahead to go after it."

James Thomas shook his head. He'd been in the saddle for the most part of the past month. A bone-aching weariness settled over him. "Maybe she felt the baby would have a better life elsewhere."

Rachael Bright put her hand on his shoulder. "That's just not true." She looked into his tired eyes. "Believe me, Beth Ann didn't want to leave. She would never have risked the baby's life by making a trip over roads like that if she hadn't believed you loved Melisue and had gone back to find her. She feared everything, from public exposure to having her baby taken away from her, because she was a fallen woman having a child out of wedlock."

James Thomas slumped into a chair and buried his face in his hands. "How could she think that of me?"

"You left her without so much as a by-your-leave and went off to find her sister," Casey reminded him.

"I went to get the proxy marriage to Melisue annulled so Beth Ann and I could be married. Everything took longer than I'd planned." Frustration and weariness overcame James Thomas, but there would be no rest for him. "Where did she go?"

"Apparently she was thinkin' of going back to her parents in Fort Kearney, but I don't guess things worked out that way." Casey pulled a crumpled letter from his pocket. "One of the traders brought this. He went to the trading post, but you weren't there, so he gave it to me." He fished into his pocket again. "This money was with it."

James Thomas scanned the note. "This is from the stage driver. He says he's returning part of the money because the woman didn't reach her destination."

He got to his feet. "Do you know the name of the man who brought the note?"

"Name's William, that's all I know. He's long gone into the wilderness by now," Casey said morosely.

"Will you take the supplies up to Black Hawk for me?" James Thomas asked.

"Don't need to. Black Hawk should be here in a few hours. I sent for him to help me find Mrs. Montgomery."

Rachael Bright began setting some food on the table. "There's nothing you can do tonight that won't be done better in the morning. Why don't you eat and then get a good night's rest? As soon as Black Hawk gets here, you can decide what you're going to do."

James Thomas hesitated. He wanted to go after Beth Ann. He wanted to go now, without wasting another moment, but he saw the sense in Rachael Bright's words. He smiled for the first time.

"Very well," he agreed. "I'll wait for Black Hawk. At least he'll be able to take charge of his supplies. That'll leave me free to go and look for my wife."

Rachael Bright's eyes met those of her husband in a shared silent prayer that he wouldn't be too late.

Rachael Bright had just finished clearing the table of the breakfast dishes when Black Hawk rode up to the house.

"I'm glad to see you here, Jim Montgomery," he said when the men came out to greet him. "It will save us both much travel."

"I thought you were going with us to find Beth Ann," Casey reminded him.

"My plans have changed." Black Hawk's expression remained the same, but there was a spark of amusement in his eyes. "You will go find Beth Ann. I will take my supplies to my trading post."

"Danged Indians," Casey grumbled, "always changin' their minds."

"You do not need me to find the girl," Black Hawk contended.

"That may be so," Casey agreed grudgingly, "but you'd probably save us a heap of time."

"I can save you the time without going with you." Black Hawk nodded his head stoically while the men looked at each other in disbelief.

"How is that?" James Thomas asked.

"An Indian came to me as I made ready to leave. He looked at the building we have made for the trading post and asked to see where I would live. My hogan is large and will house many squaws and papooses, I said, but the man shook his head. 'Your woman will not want to share her dwelling,' he said. 'White women never want to share!'

"I told him I had no white woman, and he laughed. 'I have seen this woman, and she is big with your child. I do not think the white people will welcome her when they learn she is carrying a papoose,' the man argued. 'You must go after her as quickly as possible. I told her you would come.'

"Again I told him I had no white woman, and no papoose. Then he described the woman. He said she was young, with eyes the color of the sky and hair as black as night. He had found her in an overturned stagecoach. This man knew me at Fort Kearney and had seen the woman there. Although she did not speak his language, she recognized the name Melisue."

"It's Beth Ann." Rachael Bright dropped the plate she was washing and clasped her hands against her breast. "Oh, thank the Lord. It's Beth Ann."

"You said he found her in an overturned stage?" James Thomas could not control the anguish in his voice. "Is she all right? Where is she now?"

"He did not think she was harmed, and she still carried the child," Black Hawk told them.

"Did he take her to his village?"

"He took her to the house of a man of God. He is called Bishop Henry. The woman was left in his care in a town near

Fort Laramie." Black Hawk watched James Thomas closely. He did not understand why Beth Ann would have left the man she loved, a man who also obviously loved her. He had never seen his friend so shaken.

"We will go at once." James Thomas began collecting his things, but Black Hawk stopped him. "If this woman is Beth Ann, why did she go from your house, Jim?" His eyes searched his friend's face as he tried to see into his heart.

"She went because she thought I loved Melisue."

"That is foolish," Black Hawk said. "Why would you carry love in your heart for her?"

"There is no love in my heart for Melisue." James Thomas could not hide his bitterness. "You were right, my friend. When I saw Melisue, I recognized her immediately and knew it was Beth Ann I had lived with and loved these past months."

Black Hawk could not hide his excitement. "Melisue is here?" He looked around as though expecting to see her appear in the cabin.

"Melisue was at my trading post when I left. She said she came to straighten things out between Beth Ann and me."

Black Hawk laughed. "Melisue has always enjoyed ruling the roost." The men chuckled at Black Hawk's assessment of the situation. They leaned over the kitchen table when Black Hawk said, "I will show you where you can find Beth Ann. Then I will go pick up my supplies."

His need to be gone was so obvious that Casey commented, "I wouldn't be that all-fired anxious to see that Melisue if I were you."

Black Hawk tried to feign surprise, with little success. Realizing his friends had seen through his ruse, he shrugged his shoulders. "I have never forgotten Melisue," he admitted.

"Neither have I," James Thomas agreed, "but for different reasons."

Not to be left out, Casey added, "I've been trying to forget I ever laid eyes on her. I can't see why you should be so stuck on a woman who always thinks of herself first."

Black Hawk was undaunted. "My people believe that no man can love another person more than he loves himself. If this is also true of women, then Melisue has a great deal of love to give, and I intend to be the man to receive it." Before either man could speak, he looked at James Thomas. "Who's going to take care of the trading post while you're gone?"

"Since I know where Beth Ann was taken, I can go after her alone." James Thomas looked at Casey, hoping the man would offer to resume his duties.

"All right," Casey said, after meeting Rachael Bright's eyes. "I'll go back, but I'm not lookin' forward to it."

"I understand," James Thomas assured him. "Right now, the only thing on my mind is finding Beth Ann and bringing her back before the baby arrives."

"If it's not already here," Rachael Bright added, shaking her head.

"The child's not due for another month," the prospective father reminded her.

"When a woman has had half the trials Beth Ann has experienced over the past weeks, a baby sometimes comes early." Rachael Bright didn't want to think of Beth Ann being with strangers when her baby came into the world. "Let me go with you," she said, taking them all off guard.

"If there's any chance of the child coming early, I want to be with Beth Ann when it happens," James Thomas told her, "and I can ride faster if I ride alone. I appreciate your offer, but I'm going by myself, and I'm leaving now."

Black Hawk nodded. "That is good. Rachael Bright will make things ready for when you return with your wife. Casey Stubbs will watch the trading post, and I will see Melisue."

Casey remembered Melisue's outspoken opinions of mountain men and Indians. She had no use for either. "You better hope you see her before she sets her eyes on you," Casey mumbled, "because I got a feelin' she's not going to be real happy when she finds out you're lookin' for her."

"You worry about running Jim Montgomery's trading post, friend Casey," Black Hawk said. "I will worry about making Melisue happy."

Casey shrugged as he went to help James Thomas saddle his horse. "If you're goin' to try to make that woman happy, you've got your work cut out for you."

Melisue wandered aimlessly around the living room of her sister's house. "I'm going to have to leave," she said to LuAnne. "I've done all I can to make James Thomas realize that he's better off with Beth Ann than with me. After seeing how she's forced to live, I'm sure she's more than welcome to this kind of life, although I can't see how she can enjoy it. I'm sure James Thomas realized I was not meant to live up here in the wilderness. He was so brave and self-sacrificing, saying he loved Beth Ann and would take her back even after she'd lied and said she was me. But I must leave as soon as possible. I don't want to be here when he brings Beth Ann home. There's no sense in breaking his heart." It was beyond Melisue to imagine that any man would prefer her little sister to her. "I don't know how we'll manage. I spent nearly everything I had to come out here and help my sister. You might be able to take in some laundry or sewing to make ends meet." She looked meaningfully at LuAnn. "The only man here that could even be considered eligible is Preacher Fullbright, and heaven knows he's nothing special. Still, there's a certain distinction in being the preacher's lady."

Of course, James Thomas had mentioned that Black Hawk was out here somewhere, and while he might not be suitable for marriage, he was certainly qualified in all other respects, Melisue thought. If the area weren't so uncivilized, she would be free to go looking for him. As it was, it was virtually impossible for a woman to travel alone.

"I didn't think the preacher was the marryin' sort," LuAnn grumbled as she sorted through Melisue's clothing. The idea of taking in laundry did not set well with her.

"Any man is the marrying kind if he finds the right woman," Melisue said, with an assurance she didn't feel. "Besides, we traveled all the way out here together and no one gave it a second thought. Preachers are above the sins of the flesh, according to Preacher Fullbright."

"I wouldn't be too sure about that," LuAnn said sagely, but Melisue paid her no mind.

She was too busy with her immediate problems to heed the girl's veiled warning. There was no way she could support herself in this backwoods wilderness without a man, and she refused to consider leaving the territory until she saw Black Hawk again. The very thought of him made her blood quicken and her heart pound. And since he didn't know where to find her, she would go to him. And the preacher would take her.

LuAnn looked at Melisue over the bag she was packing. She didn't understand the expression on the woman's face, but she recognized the determination in the set of the jaw. She hoped they wouldn't have to move to the boarding-house. LuAnn was tired of moving around and wished her mistress would settle down.

Melisue was closing the last bag when there was a knock on the door.

"Why, hello, Mrs. Colfax!"

The sound of a masculine voice caught Melisue's attention, and the sight of the circuit preacher was a welcome one. "Why, Preacher Fullbright..." Melisue went toward him, holding out both hands. "I can't tell you how happy I am to see you."

The portly preacher reddened satisfactorily. "And I am happy to see you. Has your visit to your sister been enjoyable?"

Melisue caught her breath. What was she to tell this man about Beth Ann? Certainly not the truth. However, she might be able to tell him part of the truth and enlist his help and his patronage.

She looked up at him through her lashes. "You are the answer to my prayers."

He squeezed her hands, thinking how small and helpless she seemed, and made a silent prayer that God would give him the wisdom to give succor to this beautiful angel. "I'm sure it can't be as bad as all that. Jim Montgomery has a reputation for being a good, fair man, and your sister is well liked hereabouts."

"She's no longer here. And I must leave. I don't know where I'll go." She buried her face in her hands and began to sob. Her shoulders shook so pitifully that without a moment's hesitation the preacher put his arms around her and patted her in his most comforting manner.

"There, there, now," he said, thinking that her hair smelled of rose petals. "Tell me about it, and I'll do everything in my power to make things right for you."

"Oh, you are such a good man." Melisue leaned against his shoulder pathetically. "I can't tell you what a relief it is for me that you're here. You see, the wedding ceremony between Mr. Montgomery and my sister may not have been legal. When my sister found out, she ran away. And now James Thomas has gone to fetch her, leaving me to try to deal with running the trading post and keeping the house and—" She buried her face in her handkerchief, seemingly unable to go on. "I must find another place to stay until my sister returns."

"Oh, certainly, certainly," the preacher said, barely able to concentrate on Melisue's words, so overcome was he from holding her in his arms.

Again Melisue gave the man her most pathetic look. His expression was one of absolute adoration. "You will help me, won't you?" she asked.

"With all my heart," he said, patting her shoulder awkwardly. "I'll protect you with my life. Now let's hurry along. You can travel with me until we can decide the best way to proceed."

Melisue smiled through her tears, congratulating herself on having found the solution to her dilemma. Surely the preacher's travels would eventually lead her to Black Hawk. Once again she had snatched victory from the jaws of defeat. "Oh, you're so kind to me," she said, wondering how she would get rid of this old tub of lard when he was of no more use to her.

The day after James Thomas rode out in search of Beth Ann, Casey rode into town and opened the store, while Black Hawk went to the house, hoping Melisue would still be there. To his disappointment she was gone. He returned to the trading post, a dour expression on his handsome face.

"Melisue is not there," he told Casey.

"If I were you, I'd quit while I was ahead, but since you're all-fired determined to find her, you might ask at the boardinghouse," Casey suggested as he straightened the merchandise.

"You lookin' for that woman that used to work here?" one of the customers asked.

"That's right," Casey answered, before Black Hawk could open his mouth. "You know where she went?"

"Sure do," the man said obligingly. "She took off with that preacher fellow. According to the preacher, her only desire is to dedicate her life to saving the souls of all the sinners west of the Mississippi. From the look on his face, I'd say that wasn't what he desired, but bein' a confirmed sinner who does most of my prayin' just before I throw the first punch, what would I know about some preacher's thoughts?''

"Probably just as much as the preacher does, my friend." Casey clapped the man on the back. "I doubt his desires are all that different from any other man's—at least where Mrs. Colfax is concerned."

Black Hawk cut the conversation short. "You know where they went?"

"They didn't say, and I didn't ask," the man replied. "As long as they weren't tryin' to save my soul, I didn't care."

Black Hawk gave a contemptuous snort. "I will pack up my supplies and go back to my trading post," he told Casey. "I have work there."

"You opening a trading post?" the customer inquired.

"With Jim Montgomery," Black Hawk told him. "Near the mouth of the Yellow River."

"Having a trading post up there sounds like a fine idea to me," the man told him. "And, who knows, maybe someday that circuit preacher and his fancy lady will pay you a visit."

Everyone laughed as they wished Black Hawk well and bade him goodbye, but there was no laughter in his eyes as he packed up his string of mules and rode away. He had never been able to forget Melisue. The whiteness of her skin, the shimmer of her hair against his chest, and the soft touch of her hands, so unlike the callused palms of the Indian girls. She was like a flower, with her hoops and petticoats, her ruffles and lace; when the petals were plucked there remained a body as soft and pliable as the skin of a deer, and as wildly fulfilling as the Indian dances that sent him into an ecstasy of exhaustion. No, there would never be anyone who could take the place of Melisue. He loved her and cursed her in the same breath, for he knew her well enough to understand that, given the aura of respectability she had found with the preacher, she would never willingly come to him again.

Beth Ann stayed in bed most of the time during the weeks after her arrival in the Henry household. Caroline cared for her with all the dedication of a mother hen, while the bishop divided his time between his flock and his houseguest.

"But surely there must be someone we could notify that you're here. Your family will be worried," Caroline argued as she fluffed the pillows on the bed. "Your mother will be beside herself, I'm sure."

"My mother had no idea I was coming to visit," Beth Ann hedged. "It was to have been a surprise."

Remembering the Indian's allegations regarding the child Beth Ann carried, Caroline murmured, "It will be a surprise, and that's the truth." But she did not push for the particulars of the situation, and for that Beth Ann was grateful.

The arrival of summer brought long, hot days. The night breeze cooled the air only a little, and sleep came sporadically. Caroline went to the porch to try to catch the breeze that sometimes crept through the shadows.

Seeing a sliver of light beneath Beth Ann's door, she paused and asked her guest to join her. It was there on the porch, during the summer night, that Beth Ann told Caroline of her plight, her heartache and undying love for James Thomas, and her guilt for not staying and fighting for the life they had built together. As the dawn was breaking, the women returned to their rooms.

"I have a favor to ask of you," Caroline said as she paused outside Beth Ann's door. "I want to tell my brother. Perhaps he can help."

Beth Ann hesitated. She hadn't really intended to tell Caroline, but the conversation had come about so naturally that she had found herself doing so without inhibition. The weeks they had spent together had bonded their friendship. "Very well," she finally agreed. "I owe you both so much, the least I can do is present my situation without excuses."

"Friends don't need to make excuses to one another for situations that are out of their control," Caroline assured her, "and I hope you consider us your friends."

Beth Ann gave the woman a warm hug. "I am honored to be your friend," she said, blinking back the tears that came so easily and often.

"Now get some sleep," Caroline urged. "This next week will be a busy one. My brother is dedicating the new bell at the church a week from Sunday, and there will be quite a celebration."

But Beth Ann was not destined to join the festivities, for when she awakened a few days later, she found the sun high in the sky and her baby fighting to be born. Days and nights of pain passed before James Thomas's son was brought into the world.

Chapter Nineteen

An agonized scream filled the air, followed by deathly silence, as James Thomas dismounted in front of the Henry's house. Sweat beaded on his forehead as he raced up the stairs and across the porch to pound on the door. His insistent knocking was answered by the cry of a newborn baby; angry, loud and strong. His legs began to shake, and he leaned weakly against the door, aware that it was his child who had come into the world and now protested his illtreatment.

Though early by Rachael Bright's calculations, the baby sounded healthy, but the scream he had heard as he rode up still sent chills through his body. If the child that cried so lustily inside was indeed his, then the scream had come from Beth Ann, his Beth Ann, and he hadn't been there for her. He had been too late. Could anyone scream like that and live? he wondered as once again he began to pound on the door.

A tall man with graying hair answered. "I'm sorry to have taken so long in answering your knock. I was witnessing a miracle."

James Thomas swallowed hard. "I'm James Montgomery," he managed. "I'm looking for my wife, Beth Ann."

The man's expression changed imperceptibly. His eyes scanned the yard in front of his house, noting the single horse, obviously ridden hard.

"Come in, Mr. Montgomery." He stepped back to allow James Thomas to enter. "I believe you're the father of our miracle."

"Is Beth Ann all right?" James Thomas ignored the smile on the bishop's face, which included both satisfaction at the man's concern and relief that he had asked about his wife even before learning the sex of the child.

"Beth Ann has had a very difficult time. The child is early, but strong. My sister is the best midwife in the area. That's why the Indians brought Beth Ann here."

James Thomas nodded. "Until now, I couldn't understand why they would bring her to you rather than take her with them."

"The brave who brought her here believed she was carrying the son of an Indian named Black Hawk. He knew the woman was near her time and didn't want to take the risk of his friend's child being born somewhere along the trail. Had the child died, he would have answered to Black Hawk. He indicated that he would apprise his friend of the matter."

"He did so," James Thomas assured him. "Black Hawk is my friend, also, but I assure you, neither the woman nor the child is his."

Bishop Henry put his hand on James Thomas's shoulder and guided him into the study. "I'm well aware of that, and even had I not been informed of the situation, I would have known the moment I saw the child. Your son looks very much like you, Mr. Montgomery. Now, would you like to toast your new son with a glass of port?"

James Thomas would have preferred something stronger. A double shot of whiskey sounded more to his liking, but in deference to his host's religious calling, he accepted the offer gratefully.

"When may I see my wife?" he asked as he downed the drink.

"I'm afraid you'll have to wait until my sister has tidied up a bit. Beth Ann was—" he paused, choosing his words carefully "—sleeping when I left."

No need to tell the man she had passed out from the pain, the bishop thought. James Montgomery looked to be at the end of his endurance. The child was alive and healthy, and only time would allow Beth Ann to regain her strength.

"While we're waiting, there is something I would like to ask," the bishop pushed on boldly. "Beth Ann confided in my sister, so I am aware that she is not legally your wife, but that is not my question. I'm puzzled that you could live with a woman and not realize who she was. Did you not know it was Beth Ann rather than Melisue who had come to be your wife?"

Realizing that without the aid and succor of this man and his sister both Beth Ann and the baby would have died, James Thomas agreed to answer. "I never bothered to question the identity of the woman who came to my home. I hadn't seen either of the Cadwalder sisters for almost three years. The one who came to me as my wife looked like the Melisue I remembered. Beth Ann was hardly larger than a child in pigtails when I saw her last. Any changes in the woman I married in a proxy ceremony were attributed to the length of time during which we had made no contact. Any doubts I might have had at our initial meeting were erased when she was accompanied by Rachael Bright, who had been her mother's maid and confidante for many years.

"It was Rachael Bright who explained to me that Beth Ann had often imitated her sister." He bowed his head. "I'm not trying to make excuses, but it wasn't until a few months ago that I became certain the woman I had been living with was the woman I had loved since she was a child, my Beth Ann."

"Beth Ann indicated that you left her with hard feelings between you."

"She refused to admit that she was not Melisue. I had to go to Rachael Bright to learn the truth. I have loved Beth Ann for so long. I couldn't understand why she needed to continue to lie to me about her identity."

"Did it never occur to you that she had no way of knowing you loved her?" the bishop asked.

James Thomas jumped to his feet. "That's not true. I told her I loved her many times."

The bishop's smile irritated James Thomas as much as his next question.

"Did you simply say, 'I love you,' or did you say 'I love you, Beth Ann'?"

"How could I say 'I love you, Beth Ann,' when I thought she was Melisue?" James Thomas shouted in growing frustration.

"So you said, 'I love you, Melisue,'" the bishop concluded.

"I didn't use a given name. I just told her I loved her."

"But, since she was pretending to be Melisue, it was Melisue she believed you loved."

James Thomas wiped his face with his hands. "I never loved Melisue. You must believe me. Beth Ann must believe me, because although I didn't get here in time to make Beth Ann my wife before our child was born, I want to marry her before returning home. The proxy marriage to Melisue has been annulled. I have the documents to prove it. There's no reason why we should wait. Could a wedding be arranged?"

The bishop gave a sigh of relief. He had wondered if this man would be anxious to wed Beth Ann after she had deceived him. Aloud he said, "I'm sure that if the lady is willing, a ceremony can be arranged. Now, I see my sister gesturing to me from the stairs. Perhaps you'd like to meet your son.'' The bishop had to hide his laughter beneath a cough, for James Thomas paled visibly at the suggestion.

Beth Ann slept fitfully. Her dreams were real and fraught with problems. Over and over, she dreamt about losing her child and leaving everything she loved behind. And what if James Thomas found her now? What if James Thomas came after her and discovered the child had been born? Would he take the baby from her? No, he could never be that cruel. James Thomas would never deliberately hurt another person. That was one of the things she so loved about him.

She drifted on the edge of consciousness, sometimes believing she heard his voice telling her he loved her. ''I love you, Beth Ann, my little one,'' he would say again and again, and she would feel the warmth of his hands holding hers as his strength and love flowed through her. But when she tried to open her eyes, it was Caroline or the bishop who sat beside her bed, never the man she loved so desperately.

Her fevered brain told her he wouldn't come, and if he did, more likely it would be to take their child home with him and leave her behind. She must get better and quickly. She must get back to Fort Kearney. Back to the haven of her parents' home, where she could raise her baby in safety.

Mustering the last remnants of her strength, she managed to open her eyes. A man's figure was outlined against the window. Her heart jumped when she recognized James Thomas, his blond hair catching the morning sun. His back was to her, and she watched him greedily and at great length without his knowing. He bent his head toward the bundle cradled in his arms. It was several seconds before Beth Ann was able to focus her eyes so that she could make out the tiny head of a baby. Her baby! Their baby! The child made a tiny mewling noise, and the man turned toward the door.

He was leaving. He was taking her baby with him. Her worst fears were realized. She struggled to a sitting position as he stepped into the hall, calling out to someone in the house. With the strength of desperation, Beth Ann staggered from the bed and into the hall. She collapsed at James Thomas's feet just as Caroline reached the top of the stairs in answer to his plea for her to come and take the fussing infant.

Frantically shoving the baby into the woman's hands, James Thomas lifted Beth Ann in his arms.

"Don't take my baby away from me," she whispered as he carried her back to the bedroom.

"No one will take your baby from you," he promised. "Nor will they take you away from me."

The church bell rang gaily in celebration of the wedding of James Thomas and Beth Ann, but the people of the town gave their congratulations to the happy couple on the christening of their child. Bishop Henry arranged to have the wedding ceremony take place in privacy, before the church service, but the baptism was witnessed by the whole congregation.

The next morning, amid tears and promises that Caroline and her brother would come to visit, the Montgomery family began their trip to their home in the mountains. James Thomas sent a message to let Casey Stubbs know they would be returning and to set Rachael Bright's mind at ease regarding the birth of the baby and the welfare of Beth Ann.

Casey wasted no time in announcing the child's arrival to the customers, and word spread throughout the territory that the Montgomerys had a son. Melisue heard of it while she was taking tea with some ladies in a small community Preacher Fullbright visited on his rounds.

"This part of the country is certainly growing," one of the women said. "It's reassuring to know that families are settling instead of savages and mountain men."

The other women nodded in agreement, but Melisue remained silent, lost in her own thoughts.

So James Montgomery had found Beth Ann and was bringing her back with him. No doubt he intended to continue his life of sin with her sister, living without the benefit of a legal marriage. But Melisue intended to see them married, right and proper. Of course, to accomplish that she would need the services of the preacher. It was up to her to see that those services were made available without delay. But Melisue had not realized the depth of the preacher's determination to make her his own.

"But, Melisue, my dear, if what you've told me is true, I cannot perform the ceremony between your sister and Mr. Montgomery. My job is to save souls and show people that they must live a good, God-fearing life. That is what I was sent here to do." Preacher Fullbright had tried to explain his vocation to the irate woman for the better part of an hour and was no closer to gaining her understanding than he had been when she first broached the subject. "Your sister and Mr. Montgomery have been living in sin for years. They have committed adultery, in the worst sense of the word. I couldn't call myself a man of God and look the other way when people blatantly break His laws."

Melisue tried again. "If they want forgiveness, it's your job to see that they get it. Why are you being so mean and stubborn?"

"They don't want forgiveness. They want social acceptance," he declared. "Think of my reputation when the people learn that I am condoning the fact that they have been living in sin. The decent people will protest to my superiors, and I'll be forced to take a menial position in some

little church out on the prairie.'' Melisue wouldn't like that
at all, he thought manipulatively. She probably wouldn't
stay with him. And it was mandatory that she stay. He
couldn't let her go. He had to do something that would bind
her to him, if not in gratitude and love, then through intim-
idation.

He lived in constant fear that Melisue would leave him.
She was so beautiful, and she carried with her an aura of
aristocracy. His reception in the villages he visited had become warm, and together they were welcomed into the most
comfortable homes.

From the day he had taken her from the Montgomery
house, she had been an asset to his ministry. The townspeople willingly overlooked the fact that her voice was sharp
and reedy and that she stumbled over the words of the sim-
plest hymns, as well as the fact that she invariably sang off-
key. Her beauty alone caused men and women alike to stare
in awe as she took her place at the front of the church, the
hymnal in her hands, to lead them in musical worship.

He was also very grateful that she shared his life, for his
flock generously moved out of their own rooms to make a
place for the preacher and his lady.

He knew there would be the devil to pay if his ruse was
discovered, but not even the threat of exposure, or the
knowledge that, should their liaison be discovered, his life's
work would be destroyed, could make him give her up.

As far as Melisue was concerned, the respectability that
surrounded traveling with the circuit preacher was enough
to sustain her. She was pleased to be honored and feted in
the homes they visited. She enjoyed the admiring looks of
the men and the envious stares of the women. Her clothes,
with their wide hoops and flounces, were not of the latest
fashion, she knew, but they were becoming and feminine
and far more elaborate than anything the work-worn wives
had in their possession. But her longing for happiness was

not fulfilled. She continually watched for a man who would take her away from the preacher and offer her the life she felt she deserved.

Beth Ann was greeted by the scent of fall flowers and fresh air when she entered her home. Even James Thomas could not hide his surprise at the gleaming wood and shining windows.

"Rachael Bright must have been here," he said, "because the house didn't look this good when I left."

Beth Ann sank into the little armless rocker before the hearth, and her husband placed their baby in her arms.

"We're home, Jason," she told the child, "and I can't wait to show you off to Rachael Bright. Where do you suppose she could be?" she asked James Thomas.

"Probably at the trading post," he replied, his eyes already straying toward the building.

"Why don't you go over there now?" Beth Ann suggested. "I'll feed the baby, and you can send Rachael Bright back to me."

But Rachael Bright did not come until late in the afternoon, when Beth Ann was looking through the spotless kitchen for something to cook for supper. After tearful greetings and much enthusiastic admiration of little Jason, Beth Ann offered her thanks to Rachael Bright.

"I can't tell you how much I appreciate the way you cleaned up the house. I expected to find weeks of dust waiting for me."

"I'm afraid I can't accept your thanks for that," Rachael Bright said honestly.

"But if you didn't do this—" she gestured toward the room "—who did?"

"I believe I have the answer to that question." Rachael Bright walked to the center of the room and looked up at the loft. "LuAnn, are you up there?"

An anxious face appeared from the shadows.

"Yes'm."

"This is Melisue's maid," Rachael Bright announced.

"Not anymore," the girl said as she came to the front of the loft and began climbing down the ladder. "When Miz Melisue went off with that preacher man, I stayed behind. Mr. Casey, he knew I was here and that I didn't have anyplace else to go. I promised that if he'd let me stay in the loft until you folks got home I would take care of the house."

The thought of Melisue traveling with a preacher was almost more than Beth Ann could comprehend. She had the wild urge to laugh, but she recovered her composure and told the girl, "You've done a good job. What do you intend to do now that we've returned?"

LuAnn shifted nervously from one leg to the other. "I was hoping you'd need some help, with the new baby and all. I like babies, and I can take care of them."

"If you could put up with Melisue, a baby should be no problem at all," Rachael Bright observed. "We already know LuAnn's a good lady's maid and a spotless housekeeper," she added. "If you don't need her, maybe I'll take her home with me."

"But I do want her," Beth Ann insisted. "I can't think of anyone I'd rather have help me with little Jason."

LuAnn was beside herself with happiness when Beth Ann nodded her approval.

"James Thomas was going to try to find one of the girls in the area to come in and help me," she confided to Rachael Bright, "but this is so much better."

"I'm glad you feel that way," Rachael Bright said. "From the look on your face when you first saw the girl, I thought you were going to send her away."

Beth Ann looked at her wedding ring. "I didn't want to face Melisue just now."

Rachael Bright laughed. "You probably won't have to face her for a long time. As LuAnn said, she took off with the circuit preacher and is traveling around the country passing herself off as his wife."

Beth Ann was aghast. "You mean she's living in sin with a minister of the gospel?"

The men overheard her words as they entered the room.

"With Reginald Colfax dead and the proxy marriage null and void, Melisue is a free woman," James Thomas observed. "Maybe she married him."

"Oh, I hope she did," Beth Ann exclaimed. "I do so want Melisue to find happiness."

"I doubt if old Fullbright has it in him to make any woman happy," Casey observed caustically, "much less Melisue."

Melisue was holding court with the ladies of a relatively large settlement when a man rode into town looking for the preacher.

"There's been an explosion at the mill up near Round Ridge," he told the assembled townspeople. "A couple of men are dead. One of the widows wants the preacher to say a few words over her husband."

Melisue wasn't interested in going any farther into the wilderness, but Preacher Fullbright began packing up immediately, and there was nothing for her to do but follow. The ride was rough and difficult, and Melisue complained all the way. She found it gratifying to be met by a crowd of people who had clearly been watching the road anxiously.

"I must say it was nice of you folks to watch for us so diligently," the preacher expounded. "Now, which of you is the bereaved widow?"

"The widow is waitin' inside the cabin just out of town," a man said, pointing down the road. "And while we're right glad you've come, the truth of the matter is that we're waitin' for supplies from the tradin' post. We got to try to repair the damage before winter sets in.''

Melisue caught the man's words and was about to give him a piece of her mind for finding supplies more important than the visit of a man of God when she realized that the trading post belonged to James Thomas and he would most likely bring the supplies himself.

The possibility of seeing James Montgomery was much more important than listening to the sobs of the bereaved family, and Melisue wasted no time letting Fullbright know she preferred to wait while he went in for his initial visit. But by the end of an hour Melisue had reached the limit of her patience. Excusing herself, she skirted the crowd and started toward the house. The sound of wagon wheels brought her to a halt. Unable to see over the heads of the men gathered around the wagon, she burrowed her way through the crowd. She had almost reached her objective when the driver jumped from the wagon. Just then, a man stepped back on her foot. She gave a scream of outrage, and would have lost her balance had not a pair of strong arms caught her, holding her tightly. As the initial pain subsided, she struggled to free herself.

"Thank you for saving me from falling," she said breathlessly, "but I'm quite all right now. You can let me go."

The man did not loosen his grip. Instead, she felt herself being lifted in his arms.

"No, Melisue, I can never let you go," a deep voice whispered in her ear, and she found herself looking into Black Hawk's dark eyes.

Chapter Twenty

It took Melisue less than five minutes to realize that she wanted Black Hawk to make love to her. It took two days, however, before the opportunity arose.

Preacher Fullbright and the rest of the settlers were busy trying to repair the damage done by the explosion. The women had prepared food and had taken it to where the men were working and Melisue was left alone when Black Hawk drove up on his buckboard. She knew that he, too, had been waiting for the opportunity to be alone with her. The naked desire in his eyes was so intense it melted her bones. She stepped from the house, praying her legs would hold her, and started toward the wagon.

"I thought you might like to go for a ride with me," he said, his eyes centered on her mouth.

"That would be delightful," she managed, wondering how long it would take to get out of sight of the town so that she could experience the promise she saw in his hot gaze. "Let me get a wrap." She started toward the house, but he grabbed her arm.

"You will be warm with me," he said, drawing her toward the wagon.

Melisue giggled nervously. Her heart pounded hard and fast. She hadn't felt like this since she was a girl, long before she had met and married the disappointing Reginald

Colfax. "You shouldn't talk that way, Black Hawk," she teased. "After all, I'm a respectable woman. What would Preacher Fullbright think if he heard you?"

Black Hawk lifted her to the seat, his hands resting far longer than necessary on her slim waist.

"Respectable you will never be, Melisue, but woman you are, in all the ways that matter to me."

"Oh, Black Hawk, what a thing to say! If I thought you really knew what you were talking about I'd have to slap your face." She smiled, looking up at him through her lashes, and was pleased to see that the old ploy still entranced him.

"You will be surprised at what I know," Black Hawk told her as he sat down beside her.

"I simply can't wait to find out," Melisue simpered.

Black Hawk wiped the sweat from his brow. "If you keep talking like that, you'll find out right here."

Melisue pushed herself from the seat, only to fall back against him as the horses started to move.

"If you're going to talk to me like that, you can let me off this old wagon right now," she said sulkily. "Every time I speak, you try to make something nasty out of it."

"There's nothing nasty about wanting to make love to you," he assured her. "And there's nothing wrong with your wanting to make love to me. That's what we're talking about, because that's what we both want, and no matter what we try to say, that thought is always the most important in our minds."

"Speak for your own mind," Melisue reprimanded. "The last thing I'd ever think about is making love to you."

But Black Hawk only smiled, for they both knew she lied.

"I was certainly surprised to see you drive up on the wagon when the people said they were expecting supplies from the trading post. I thought James Thomas would bring the goods," Melisue said, changing the subject.

"Jim Montgomery's trading post is many miles from here," Black Hawk told her. "My trading post is closer, so the people come to me."

"You have a trading post, Black Hawk?" Melisue was sick of trading posts and hoped she never had to see another one, but if it took Black Hawk's mind off sexual innuendos until they were well out of the town, she'd encourage him to talk. "Is it like the one James runs?"

"There is very little difference," Black Hawk told her.

"Do you have a little house like his, too?"

"My house is large. There is a main room, and then there are the places to sleep."

"You mean bedrooms," Melisue corrected. "How many of those do you have?"

"Five, maybe six." He clucked to the horses.

"That must make your squaw very happy." Melisue tried to squelch the bitterness that rose within her at the thought of Black Hawk's squaw.

"I have no woman. The squaw in my lodge is the wife of a dead warrior. She cooks for me. Her daughters help clean."

"How nice for you." Melisue's mind was not on his words. She couldn't concentrate, with him so close. She could feel the heat of his thigh through the material of her dress. It seemed to burn right through her hoops and petticoats. "Are there many white women up where you live?"

"Not many," he said, flicking the horses again. "None like you." His eyes roamed the length of her body. "You should come and see it."

"Well, I should think not," Melisue protested with a smile. "Even with your servants and large house there's no place for a lady like me out in the middle of nowhere. What would I do with my time?"

He pulled the horses into a thick grove of trees overlooking a running stream. "Same as you will do now." Smiling, he lifted her from the wagon and carried her to the thick grass at the edge of the water.

She opened her eyes wide in feigned innocence. "Ride out in the country and go on picnics?"

"Make love to me." His lips closed over hers, and he drew her breath into himself as he pressed her down against the grass.

With Black Hawk there was no reason to be coy and reserved. As when she had been a girl, Melisue could let her sexuality take over, giving and taking with complete abandon. With him there was no question of being reprimanded for her uninhibited appetite. Black Hawk responded with the greatest appreciation to any innuendo. Even the skirts, petticoats and hoops were a hindrance that he patiently removed, one by one, before laying them aside.

His careful slowness began to irritate Melisue. "Had I known you would insist on such neatness, I would never have worn such an intricate dress," she told him impatiently.

Then his hands were on her, tantalizing, teasing and worshiping, before returning to remove another article of clothing with slow deliberation.

"When you pick a flower, you must first enjoy the beauty of the petals before taking in its sweetness," he told her as he placed the last article of clothing with the others and bent down to taste the sweetness of which he had spoken. But she held him back.

"You're not being fair," she protested, running her hands beneath his buckskins. "When you're hungry for an ear of corn, you must first strip away the husk before satisfying your appetite."

"Then strip the husk away," he managed as he felt the afternoon sunlight touch his skin.

* * *

The room was comfortable and well furnished, much of the furniture obviously store-bought and shipped across the country. The food was good, and her host and hostess were solicitous of their guests. Melisue felt quite at home as the center of attention in the parlor.

At any other time she would have been in the height of her glory, but today her mind continually wandered back to the hours she had spent with Black Hawk.

How sad it was that he was an Indian and unable to give her the life she deserved. She patted her flawless hair and smiled at one of the gentlemen. Why, of all the men on earth, did Black Hawk have to be the only one who could fulfill her needs? The only one who understood her? It was so unfair!

And there was no way Black Hawk could pass for a white, as did Rachael Bright. He was an Indian. The rich color of his skin, the dark, intense eyes, the straight hair that hung to his shoulders, all cried out his origin. The thought of his strong, handsome face sent shivers through her, and she was vaguely aware that one of the men placed a light shawl across her shoulders. She willed herself to stop thinking of Black Hawk before her thoughts wandered to their recent lovemaking. Heaven forbid she should do anything as uncouth as perspiring in someone's parlor.

Yes, it was too bad that Black Hawk couldn't have had a religious calling like Preacher Fullbright. She would have to be out of her mind to give up the toil-free life she led as the preacher's lady. She was petted and pampered in every town, village and home they visited. She definitely had found her place in life, and even Black Hawk's passionate lovemaking couldn't sway her. And it wasn't as though she would never see Black Hawk again. Part of the ministry, Preacher Fullbright had told her, was to spread the word and give succor to the savages. It was just that Melisue intended to spread a different word from the preacher's, and give succor on an individual basis.

She was troubled by only one thing. She had been with the preacher for the better part of a year, and he had yet to find another man of God who could marry them. Of course, it was only a matter of time. Heaven knew the preacher's intentions could be nothing less than honorable. After all, he was a preacher.

"I'll be more than happy to take your letters to the Montgomery Trading Post." The preacher's words caught her attention. "I'm sure they'll send them on for you."

"I didn't know we were going back to Montgomery." Melisue's sugary voice belied the anxiety in her eyes.

"It's part of my circuit," the preacher expounded garrulously. "Part of my little flock. I couldn't possibly omit them from my rounds." He shifted in his chair, uncomfortable under her accusing stare. "Besides, word has it they have built a church. I must be there to see that it is dedicated with a proper sermon."

"How wonderful." Melisue rose to the challenge. "And have you chosen your theme?"

"Why, not as yet," he blustered, "but you can be certain it will be for the greatest benefit of my flock. I know exactly what that town needs to hear."

When Melisue saw the power he had over the churchgoers, she would be forced to stop thinking she could get support from her sister and would depend completely on him. Of course, it was sad that he had to expose a man like James Thomas, whom he had always admired, but the man was living in sin, and it was his duty as a man of God to expose that sin and purge it from his fold.

Montgomery was all taken to overflowing when Melisue and Preacher Fullbright arrived. The rooms at the boardinghouse were filled, and every spare bed in the private homes for miles around was filled.

"I do believe we can find you a place, if you don't mind traveling a short distance," Ma Barker told them when they stopped for accommodations. "I'll send one of the men to show you the way. The house is out a piece, but I'm sure they'll be able to put you up for the night."

The preacher took in the expression on Melisue's face and asked, "Isn't there any way you could convince one of your clients to let us have their room? After all, I must be here early to dedicate the new church. If this place is any great distance, it would mean getting up in the middle of the night to be here in time for the service."

"I'm sorry," Ma Barker said, shaking her head, "but I'm afraid it's all I have to offer. The people in my boarding-house are settled and paid. I couldn't ask them to leave."

The preacher sighed and climbed up beside Melisue, who sat primly on the seat of the buggy, her parasol held stiffly above her head.

"They have no room. But we've been promised accommodations a short ride out of town. I'm sure we'll be most comfortable there."

"Let's stop my sister's house and see if they could take us in," Melisue suggested.

"I refuse to be party to their sinful situation," the preacher declared. "We'll do very nicely without having to stay in this Sodom and Gomorrah."

The short ride turned into hours on bumpy trails, and Melisue spent her time alternately whimpering and com-plaining. It seemed like days before they turned into a well-leveled drive and stopped before a cabin.

"I certainly hope the lady of the house has a hot cup of tea and something for us to eat," Melisue said as she al-lowed the preacher to help her from the seat. "I declare, I couldn't travel another inch."

As she spoke, the door opened. "I hear we have guests," Rachael Bright said as she stepped onto the porch. "How nice of you to come, Preacher Fullbright, and Mrs. Colfax. Please come inside. Your beds are ready.''

"Why, Rachael Bright!" Melisue couldn't hide her shocked dismay. "Whatever are you doing here?''

"I live here, Melisue. This is my home. Now, would you care to come in, or would you rather sleep outside tonight?''

"We'll come in, to be sure," the preacher said ingratiatingly. "I can't tell you how much your hospitality is appreciated." He ushered a reluctant Melisue into the house.

"There's food on the table," Rachael Bright told them. "You must be hungry after that long ride.''

The preacher ate with gusto, but Melisue picked at her food.

"I'm sorry the chicken and dumplings don't suit you," Rachael Bright said to Melisue, but it was the preacher who answered.

"Everything is just delicious," he expounded. "These dumplings are light as a feather, aren't they, my dear?" He turned to Melisue.

"I'm afraid I'm just too tired to eat much," Melisue said yawning.

"Fine, fine." The preacher wiped his chin and pushed his chair away from the table. "We will have to be up bright and early in the morning if we're to make it to the dedication of the church." He beamed at Rachael Bright. "Would you mind showing us to our room?''

"Not at all," Rachael Bright beamed back. "You can sleep on the bunk in the corner near the stove. Mrs. Colfax can share my room, since my husband is staying in town to help put the finishing touches on the church for the dedication tomorrow." She pointed to a door opposite the preacher's designated sleeping area. "You just go right ahead and settle in," she said graciously. "I'll take care of Mrs. Colfax.''

The preacher's face was a livid puce as he waddled over to the bunk in the corner and adjusted the blanket that separated it from the rest of the room.

"What do you think you're doing," Rachael Bright said the moment the bedroom door was closed, "running around the countryside with that man? You're living like a loose woman. Your mama would be ashamed of you."

"That man is going to marry me as soon as we can find another preacher to officiate at the ceremony. You know about the scarcity of preachers out here."

"Has the preacher told you that?" Rachael Bright asked.

"Well, he doesn't have to," Melisue replied defensively. "After all, he is a respectable man of God. What other reason could he possibly have for not marrying me?"

Rachael Bright narrowed her eyes. "Why don't you ask him?"

Melisue tossed her outer garments on the bed and stepped out of her hoops. "That's exactly what I intend to do," she replied, her hand on the door latch. Then, realizing her state of undress, she asked, "Do you have a wrapper I could slip on?"

Rachael Bright handed her a wrapper. "I'm going to sleep," she said. "Tomorrow will be a busy day."

"It surely will," Melisue agreed as she bolted out the door, to be met by the snores of the preacher.

Angry and frustrated, Melisue stepped out the door into the star-studded night. She walked to the edge of the porch and leaned against the post, taking in the silence.

"She's right, you know," a deep voice said as strong hands gathered her into his arms. "The preacher will not marry you. But I will."

Melisue gave a little yelp before Black Hawk's lips smothered the sound. Then, after returning his kiss, she pulled away with all the indignation she could manage.

"You were eavesdropping," she accused. "Besides, I couldn't possibly marry you. I can't imagine myself living in a tepee."

"I don't live in a tepee," he reminded her.

"I want a house like the one my father built at Fort Kearney for my mother."

"And do you really believe your preacher will give you that?"

"He'll give me anything I want," Melisue declared, with more confidence than she felt. "I simply haven't asked him yet."

Black Hawk's eyes pierced the darkness. "Come away with me and be my wife."

She had seldom seen him so intense. The thought filled her with excitement—and fear. He had always been so gentle with her, but now his hands were rough as they moved across her shoulders. What would it be like to wake the savage in him? To be made love to without the facade of propriety? Uninhibited by the bonds of civilization, lost in uncontrolled passion?

She put her hands against his chest, letting Rachael Bright's wrapper fall open.

"It isn't that I don't care for you, Black Hawk, it's just that I would never be happy as your wife. You know that as well as I."

"You're happy when I make love to you." His voice was soft and rough with desire.

"But we can't do that all the time." The words flew out of her mouth, and she heard his low laugh at her admission. "Besides, I'm quite content with the life I lead as the preacher's lady. I'm going to marry the Preacher Fullbright, and there's nothing you can do about it."

"I could carry you off with me." He held her close, his lips caressing her hair. "Your preacher would never find you, even if he bothered to look."

She pushed him away. The threat of being physically taken into the wilderness was too great a threat to be tolerated.

"You can take your hands off me. I don't want to marry you. I don't want to be your squaw and raise a bunch of little half-breeds. You can't give me what I want, so let me go." She spun from his grasp and started for the door.

Without a sound, he scooped her into his arms and started across the yard, his jaw set in angry determination.

"I can give you what you want, Melisue," he said as they reached the trees where his horse was tethered. "I may not be able to give you the kind of life you think you want to live, but I will give you a night you'll never forget."

He tossed her on his horse, then jumped up behind her. The animal shot forward through the shadows.

She pounded on his chest. "Take me back! They'll hang you. There are laws against Indians abducting white women."

"Tonight there are no laws but the ones we make."

The timbre of his voice sent a chill through her. She was at his mercy and she knew instinctively that all the flirting in the world wouldn't sway his intent. How she wished she'd never challenged him with her talk of marrying the preacher. Black Hawk had always been gentle and sensuous in his lovemaking. But the rough way he handled her let her know it would not be so now. The embers of a fire glowed like cat's-eyes in the darkness as he brought the horse to a halt and dismounted, pulling her with him.

Jerking away, she made a run for the horse. Her wrapper came away in his hands. He threw it aside as he grabbed her and carried her to the ground.

He spoke no loving, poetic words now as he tore away her chemise, exposing her cool white breasts to the moonlight. Then his lips touched her, working the magic that was his alone. And with the touch of his lips, the anger evaporated, but the wildness remained, surging from his body into Melisue's entire being until there was nothing that mattered more than becoming one with him.

Untamed and uninhibited they came together, fighting the need that could not be denied and the love that she would not acknowledge.

She grasped his hair and pulled his face above hers, savoring the passion in his eyes before grinding her lips against his. His hands knew her secrets, and his lips made silent promises as they explored her loveliness. Madness filled the night as unquenchable desire sent them tumbling through the thick grass, each desperate in the desire to feel, to know, to be absorbed by the other. "Love me, Melisue," he whispered against the cushioned softness of her breasts. "Love me as I love you."

Her fingers clawed his back. Her body arched and merged and became one with his, and the shadows of the night stood still as the earth trembled with the power of their passion.

And, had he asked, in that moment, she would have agreed to marry him, for he had become her whole world.

The night became a blur of lovemaking, each time more devastating than the last, before the embers burned to ashes with the coming of dawn.

"I'll take you back," he said, drawing her to her feet. "I'll take you back, if you still want to go."

To save herself, Melisue could not speak the words that would separate them forever. She knew he would never come to her again. She knew that this night would, indeed, live only in her memory.

She nodded her head. Outside the haven of his arms the world was cold, but his arms could not hold her always, and life in his world was impossible for her. She dressed and pulled the wrapper around her still-throbbing body without speaking, for to speak would be to betray herself. Long ago she had set a goal, and Black Hawk was not part of it.

They rode before the dawn until they were in sight of the cabin. He did not dismount, but let her body slide the length of his until her feet touched the ground. She looked up at him, willing him to kiss her once more. He touched her lips gently, without passion, for the passion between them was spent.

"Goodbye, Black Hawk." Her voice broke, but it didn't matter anymore. His kiss told her it was over.

He watched her for endless moments, his hand against her cheek, his fingers in her hair, wishing he could fathom her willful, selfish mind.

"Goodbye, Melisue. I will always remember this night." His hand slowly fell away and, putting his heels to his horse, he disappeared into the mist of morning.

The house was quiet except for Preacher Fullbright's snores. Melisue slipped inside and curled up in a rocker near the fireplace. When Rachael Bright came out of the bedroom, she found Melisue asleep.

"If you folks are going to the dedication ceremony at the new church, you'd better wake up," Rachael Bright said, loudly enough to stop the preacher in the middle of a snore.

"We're coming!" He popped his head out of the curtains as Melisue got to her feet. "We certainly wouldn't want to be late on such an auspicious occasion."

Melisue eluded Rachael Bright's eyes and scurried into the bedroom to dress. Within the hour they were on their way back to Montgomery.

"I have no choice," the preacher intoned self-righteously. "I must give a sermon against the sins of the flesh. Beth Ann and James Thomas must be exposed and punished."

Melisue's mouth set in a thin line. How could he condemn someone for a sin he so obviously wanted to commit himself? If she so much as looked like she might agree, he'd be in her bed without batting an eye.

"If you say one word about my sister from that pulpit, I'll never speak to you again, and I won't travel with you anymore, either." Melisue couldn't think of any worse threat on the spur of the moment, and from the dour look on the preacher's face, it seemed, neither could he. "After all, I'm a decent, God-fearing woman," she said self-righteously, "and don't you forget it."

Remembering the passion she had shared with Black Hawk the night before, Melisue held her breath and waited for God to strike her down. Not that she wasn't decent—in her own way she was—but in Black Hawk's arms everything changed, and she didn't fear anything.

Her body still ached from the rigors of their lovemaking. It had taken an hour of applying cold water to her lips to get the swelling down after the impassioned kisses Black Hawk had bestowed on her, kisses she had returned in kind.

But Black Hawk was gone, and she had cast her lot with this pudgy preacher. She could still feel Black Hawk's lean strength against her. It was impossible for her to bear another man's touch so soon after the ecstasy she had known.

"I'll marry you as soon as we find a man of God to perform the ceremony," the preacher vowed. He felt relatively safe in his promise. There was no other minister within a radius of a hundred miles, and he wasn't about to take Melisue beyond those boundaries to find one.

Melisue sniffed indignantly. Her eyes scanned the landscape. "What's that over there?" She pointed to a spiral of smoke in the distance.

"It looks like a campfire," the preacher mumbled as he urged the horses over the bumpy trail.

Melisue leaned out of the buggy and called to Rachael Bright, who was in the wagon a short way behind. "What's that smoke, Rachael Bright?"

Rachael Bright drew her spring wagon up beside the buggy. "It's a campfire. Probably belongs to Black Hawk. He always camps there when he's in the area."

Melisue settled back in the seat as they resumed their journey. So that was where he had taken her last night. It looked to be about halfway between the town and Rachael Bright's cabin. Try as she might to shut Black Hawk from her mind, her eyes strayed again and again to the smoke in the distance.

"And so, my friends, you can see that the wages of sin are death. And sins of the flesh are the worst of these. Sins of the flesh that separate husband from wife, sister from sister, and man from God. There is no place in God's plan for such sins!" He slammed his hand on the pulpit. "There is no place in this church for such sins! And now, in the sight of God and this congregation, I beg of all those who indulge in such sins to publicly repent!" His eyes scanned the astonished assembly. "Repent of your own free will, or you will be identified and cast out as the sinners you are! Repent now! Step forward, I say! Repent, or I shall call forth your names as they will be read on the day of atonement!"

Again he overlooked the congregation, but no one moved.

"Is there no repentance for living a life of sin and licentiousness?" Preacher Fullbright's eyes centered on James Thomas and Beth Ann and their guests. It would be interesting to see how their straitlaced houseguests took his revelation. The couple seemed like nice upstanding folks. The man, his graying hair lending an air of distinction, and the woman, with her sparkling eyes and merry smile. He could imagine the expression on their faces when they realized their hosts were sinners in every sense of the word. This was definitely the sermon to preach today. A memorable sermon on a memorable occasion.

Unable to stare the Montgomerys down, he turned his gaze to Melisue, who sat in front of the choir, a hymnal clutched piously in her gloved hands and an unearthly, beautiful smile on her face as she relived the night of love she had spent in Black Hawk's arms, oblivious of the preacher's accusations.

Chapter Twenty-one

"Very well, then!" Preacher Fullbright slammed his hands against the pulpit in exasperation. "As you have sown, so shall you reap!"

Again he glanced around the congregation. Every eye was upon him as the people waited for his next words. Several men squirmed uncomfortably in their seats, and he wondered about the circumstances under which they lived, but he had proof only of the sinful liaison between Beth Ann and James Thomas, and that would suffice to bring home the point of his sermon. He rose to his full height, towering like the wrath of God from the pulpit.

"James Thomas Montgomery and Beth Ann Cadwalder," he cried, his voice booming through the silent building, "I declare that you are living in sin without the sanction of marriage before God."

The silence was broken by a general intake of breath from the people who had gathered from near and far to take part in the church dedication. The next moment, the church was abuzz with whispers.

He looked at Melisue. Her eyes were so bright, her lips so full and rosy. The rise and fall of her breasts beneath the bodice of her dress took his breath away.

"Furthermore, since this couple has deigned to live in sin, deceiving this congregation and flaunting their adulterous liaison in the face of God, I hereby proclaim them unworthy of God's forgiveness and do declare that I will not perform a wedding ceremony between them until they have repented before God and this congregation and proved that they are sorry for their sinful ways."

Beth Ann quietly placed her hand over her husband's. She could feel the tension in him and knew he was ready to leap from his seat and throw the pompous little preacher from the pulpit. His eyes met hers, and she felt his body tense as he made ready to refute the man's words.

Beth Ann's heart ached as she saw the look of horror on Melisue's face.

As a result of their upbringing, Beth Ann understood her sister's consternation. Public denunciation and dishonor were tantamount to death.

Regardless of Melisue's sometimes outrageous behavior, the woman believed that as long as her indiscretions went undetected she could do as she pleased. Her self-indulgent character prohibited her from putting anyone before herself, but any scandal regarding her family honor affected Melisue. She was outraged that the preacher in whom she had put her trust would betray her by exposing her sister's transgressions.

While Beth Ann was disturbed by Preacher Fullbright's denunciation, she believed the truth would come out. But, please God, not through an altercation between James Thomas and the preacher in the church. Her attention was so focused on her husband that she didn't realize the man seated next to her had risen.

"Preacher Fullbright," he began, "and good people. Please be assured that Beth Ann and James Thomas are indeed married, legally and before God."

He would have gone on, but the voice from the pulpit drowned him out. "I declare any marriage to be null and void! There can be no union when there is no repentance of the sin. They must be chastised! Ostracized! Made to pay for their deceit! Their child must be branded with title of bastardy. Only then can their sin be forgiven!" He neglected to pause for breath during his tirade, and his face turned red with effort. "As circuit preacher I declare any ceremony void!" He clapped his mouth shut and glared at the tall man walking toward him.

The man lifted his hands to quiet the crowd. His voice, strong and true, rang out. "My friends, some of you know me. I am George Henry from Wyoming, an ordained bishop of the church. And as an honorable man of God I swear to you that Beth Ann and James Thomas Montgomery were united in marriage by myself, with my sister as one of the witnesses. The marriage is legally recorded and cannot be undone by this man's words or accusations." He raised his hands above the congregation. "What God has joined together, let no man put asunder."

The people rose as one, applauding the bishop's revelation as he returned to his seat.

Completely unnerved, Preacher Fullbright fumbled for something to say, but there was no way he could override a bishop's authority. "Now we will sing 'Rock of Ages,'" he croaked. It was a hymn everyone knew. He stepped away from the pulpit, anxious to make his escape while they sang, but he had reckoned without Melisue, who was frantically thumbing through the hymnal.

"What page?" she whispered as he passed her. She reached out and caught his arm, her voice carrying across the front rows. "You fat bastard, what page?" The congregation burst into song and the rest of her words were mercifully lost in the music.

* * *

Beth Ann clung to her husband's arm as they returned to their house with Bishop Henry and his sister, Caroline, who lovingly carried little Jason.

"I'm so glad we could be here to clear up Fullbright's accusations before the situation got out of hand," the bishop was saying. "It's terrible when a man of God becomes overzealous and allows himself to believe he *is* God."

Beth Ann nodded in agreement while her husband expressed his appreciation for the bishop's intervention. Their life since they had returned from Wyoming had been idyllic, and Beth Ann was happier than she had ever been in her life. She looked back toward the church, gleaming white in the sunlight, and wondered where Melisue would go now. The look on Melisue's face at church had portended no good for her relationship with Preacher Fullbright. She needn't have worried, for, within the hour, Melisue and the preacher arrived at the Montgomery house.

The preacher, still red-faced and sweating, shoved his way through the door. He was somewhat taken aback by the roomful of people. He had hoped to be able to badger Melisue's sister into confessing that the bishop was nothing more than a family friend, proving himself correct in his allegations and becoming a defender of the faith in Melisue's eyes. But the presence of the Montgomerys, Bishop Henry and his sister, and Rachael Bright and her husband, dampened his appetite for a confrontation.

"I assure you, I am what I profess to be," Bishop Henry said aloud, having predicted Preacher Fullbright's skepticism. "I'm sure that Mr. Fullbright will attest to my words, for we have met before."

The preacher was unable to hide his confusion. He looked at Melisue for support, but she had none to give. "I'm sorry," he finally managed, "but I don't seem to remember ever having met you."

"It was several years ago, before you started on your ministry," the bishop reminded him. "We met at a conclave for the clergy in Hannibal, Missouri."

The words hung in the air like a death threat, and the preacher turned from red to gray.

But Melisue was elated. She waltzed over to the bishop and took his arm. "Then, if you really are an ordained bishop, you're just the man we wanted to see." Her sugary smile took in everyone in the room. "Mr. Fullbright and I want to be married so that we can continue our ministry together as man and wife. His being the only circuit preacher in the area has been such a trial. It's impossible for a man to marry himself to the woman he loves. But now that you've come, there's no reason why the ceremony shouldn't take place here and now, in the presence of all those I love."

No one was taken more off guard than the preacher himself. His face now paled to a bluish-white, and he stared bug-eyed at the Bishop, unable to utter a word.

"I'm afraid that is impossible," Bishop Henry said solemnly.

"Of course it's not impossible." Melisue's voice was firm. "Beth Ann can be my matron of honor, and Rachael Bright, my bridesmaid. I'll wear my white dress," she said, smiling at the preacher. "You remember the one, don't you? You said I looked like one of God's angels the last time I wore it." A small frown creased her brow. "It would be more festive, though, if we could have the ceremony in the church." Her face brightened. "That's it! We'll have the ceremony in the church and celebrate our marriage right along with the rest of todays activities."

"Melisue, I don't think..." Beth Ann began.

"Now, don't worry about not having any nice clothes to wear. I think something of mine can be let out to fit you and Rachael Bright so you won't have to feel dowdy."

Bishop Henry cleared his throat and looked directly at the preacher. "As I was saying," he continued, "when I met Preacher Fullbright in Missouri, he was accompanied by his wife and children."

Melisue gasped. "That's just not true! What a horrible thing to say! How can you claim to be a man of God and stand there and defame the character of one of your colleagues?"

Sweat broke out on Preacher Fullbright's forehead and ran down into his shirt collar. "Melisue, I must speak to you privately." He took her arm and nudged her toward the door. "Excuse us, please," he called over his shoulder as the door shut behind them.

"If I wasn't a lady, I'd put my ear to the door and listen," Rachael Bright laughed.

"I'm no lady—I'll listen." Casey rocked on the back legs of the kitchen chair as if to get up before his wife stopped him.

"We should get our food together for the church picnic," Beth Ann reminded them, but she, too, strained her ears to hear the conversation beyond the door.

The food was nearly packed and the bishop and his sister had discreetly excused themselves to join the people at the church when Melisue came back into the room, alone.

"Where's the preacher?" Casey Stubbs asked sarcastically. "Did you kill him?"

Melisue gave a little gasp and darted for the bedroom.

"I hate him! I hate him!" she sobbed into the bright patchwork quilt. "How could he do this to me? He lied, and I believed him. He should be taken out and shot! They should never let him in a church again."

"There, there," Beth Ann said, patting Melisue's shoulder. "It's not the end of the world. There are plenty of men out there who would love to have a beautiful wife like you," she said comfortingly, silently thanking God that James Thomas wasn't one of them.

"There isn't a one of them that I'd give the time of day." Melisue wiped her tearstained face with a lacy handkerchief. "Why, the only man who's proposed to me for ever so long is Black Hawk, and even being married to him would be better than this."

Beth Ann was shocked at her sister's words. "I thought you didn't want to live like a squaw."

"I don't, but with Black Hawk I wouldn't have to." She got from the bed and made her way into the other room, where she sat down next to the window and stared out morosely.

"What do you mean, you wouldn't have to live like a squaw if you were married to Black Hawk?" Rachael Bright asked.

"Black Hawk has built a house. A big house. It has five or six bedrooms, and he has servants that see to his every need, and a woman to do his cooking. If I had married him I would have lived in comfort, even if I was out in the middle of nowhere."

"Black Hawk has a hogan," Casey whispered to his wife. "A big Indian lodge. The bedrooms she's talkin' about are bunks cut into the wall. And you have to stoop over on your hands and knees to get through the door." He started toward the fireplace. "She don't know what she's talking about."

"I do know what I'm talking about," Melisue declared. "Black Hawk told me all about it when he asked me to be his wife."

"And you said no because you were living high on the hog with the preacher," Casey said as he lifted the lid of the pot hanging above the fire and smacked his lips. "Don't worry about it," he advised. "You probably made Black Hawk a very happy man."

"That's not true," Melisue bristled. "We love each other." She felt a little flutter in her stomach that had nothing to do with the memory of their lovemaking. What if she carried his child?

"You love each other?" Casey dropped the lid into the fire. "I thought Indians was smarter than that. Must be some white blood in his veins somewheres."

"When he's with me, there's fire in his veins. He told me so."

"Fire in his veins and ashes in his head." Casey fished the lid out of the fire with a poker. "Nothin' worse than a lovesick Indian," he grunted as he deposited the lid in the dry sink and sat down, rocking the chair onto its back legs. "Besides, what about the preacher?"

Melisue bridled. "I sent him away with a bug in his ear. You can be assured of that." She watched the women bring out bowls and plates piled high with food. "Until I can make other arrangements, I'll go home with you and Rachael Bright. You have an empty bed."

Casey lost his balance. The chair came crashing down as the front legs hit the floor.

Melisue gave Casey her most alluring smile. "You'll like me once you get to know me. Most men do."

"I already know you well enough to know I don't like you," he grumbled as Rachael Bright handed him a basket of food and shoved him toward the door.

Melisue realized that she faced disgrace. Had the preacher married her she would have been able to hold her head up in public, but the way things stood, she would be a social outcast for the rest of her life. Even if she went back to her parents, there would be a great deal of explaining to do.

She knew Beth Ann did not want her. And James Thomas was most outspoken about not having her in his house. Somehow she would make them see how shabbily they were treating her.

"We're all family," Rachael Bright had said. How did the woman dare to include herself as a member of the Cadwalder family when she had colored blood in her veins? Melisue thought. And Beth Ann had just smiled as though it were all right! Their mother would never have allowed such words to be spoken in her presence. Why, Suzanna Cadwalder had practically sent Melisue away in disgrace when she had come home a bereaved widow after Reginald's funeral—and he had only been a gambler. And her father, the honorable Brandt Cadwalder, who had fought a stupid duel and caused them to move away from the beautiful, genteel life in New Orleans, barely acknowledged Rachael Bright as a lady's maid, let alone a member of his family.

Remembering those who had mistreated her in the past sent tears to Melisue's eyes. They should feel sorry they had wronged her so. Even Black Hawk! If he hadn't made love to her, she might have been able to forget him. The way it was, he slipped into her mind a hundred times a day.

His fierce, dark eyes, his hair, carrying the scent of woodsmoke, and his body, her chief delight through those hours of passion. And what if there was a child? A little half-breed to be raised at Fort Kearney, where being a half-breed was only a little worse than being a bastard. This child would carry the stigma of both. And Melisue would be its mother! Damn Black Hawk!

But, even as she damned him, she could almost smell the woodsmoke in his hair. It seemed to surround her, permeating her senses until she had to close her eyes to keep from crying. How she longed to feel his strong arms around her, protecting her from the harsh realities of the world. She coughed into her handkerchief, trying to control the sobs that built up in her throat.

She wanted Black Hawk! She wanted him now! She needed him more than she'd ever needed anyone in her life, and she wasn't going to go on without him, regardless of what anyone thought or said.

Jumping to her feet, she brushed past James Thomas and ran through the door. Casey was helping Rachael Bright into the buggy while his horse waited in front of the trading post.

Without a moment's hesitation, Melisue threw herself into the saddle, ruffles and hoops flying. She kicked the animal into a full gallop and disappeared into the trees.

"Come back here!" Casey shouted after her. "That crazy female stole my horse!"

"James Thomas, Casey, go after her," Beth Ann pleaded as she ran outside. "She's hysterical. She doesn't know what she's doing."

"That woman always knows what she's doing," Casey grumbled as he climbed into the buggy. "And it looks to me like she's going after Black Hawk." He whipped the horse into action, and they careened down the road, James Thomas following in their wake.

It was several weeks before Black Hawk and Melisue came back to Montgomery to retrieve her belongings. Although initially Beth Ann had had doubts about her sister's decision to run off with Black Hawk, the satisfaction in Melisue's eyes alleviated her worries.

"I expected to see you dressed in deerskins and beads," James Thomas said as Melisue arranged her hoop skirt on the seat of the wagon in which her belongings were packed.

Melisue took his words as a compliment. "I see no reason to change my way of life or my mode of dress simply because I'm living with Black Hawk. He likes the way I look."

Black Hawk smiled in agreement. He was proud of his woman and pleased that she had come to him. He was determined to make her happy, especially now that he knew she carried his child. The only cloud on their happiness was their inability to get a minister to marry them.

Preacher Fullbright had flatly refused, citing the Scriptures and spouting righteous indignation over the liaison between a white woman and an Indian. The man was an overzealous troublemaker, and Black Hawk would be glad to get back to his trading post, away from the preacher's influence and malicious tongue.

Black Hawk had worried about Beth Ann's reaction when she learned her sister was pregnant, but Beth Ann had shown no sign of disapproval, congratulating them both profusely and expressing excitement over becoming an auntie.

Black Hawk tied his horse to the rear of the wagon and sat down beside Melisue, taking the reins in his hands. "Are you riding with us for a ways?" he asked James Thomas.

"Not this time. I've got to meet Casey. I sent a message for him to come and get his horse. He should be here any time now."

"I'm sorry to have missed him," Melisue said, with all the proper courtesy of a Southern lady. It was a lie, but a polite one, so it didn't count, she assured herself. She didn't like Casey Stubbs and was well aware that the feeling was mutual. "Please tell him I appreciate his letting me borrow his horse."

"We would have brought it back sooner," Black Hawk explained, "but Melisue was...indisposed." Her quick look told him to say no more. While it might be all right for the Indians to discuss their women's pregnancies, he was fast learning that such things were not openly discussed in the white man's society.

"I'll give Casey your thanks," James Thomas assured them as they rattled off down the rutted road. Beth Ann held little Jason on her hip and waved her dish towel until they were out of sight.

She had hardly reached the front door when Rachael Bright and Casey pulled their wagon to a halt. "You just missed Melisue and Black Hawk," Beth Ann greeted them.

Casey lumbered down from the wagon and went off to the pasture where James Thomas kept the horses, and the women embraced.

"I thought I'd come along," Rachael Bright explained, "Casey wanted to ride his horse back home. By the way, what's going on at the church?"

Beth Ann's brow furrowed in thought. "Nothing that I know of," she said. "This isn't cleaning day, and there's no quilting bee this week."

"It's not women, Beth Ann," Rachael Bright told her. "It's a bunch of men. I could hear the shouting all the way to the road, but I couldn't make out what they were saying."

As if in verification of her words, a group of men and horses thundered down the road.

"What's happening?" Rachael Bright asked as the dust settled.

"I'm sure I don't know." Beth Ann ushered her friend into the house. "James Thomas didn't say anything about there being any problems. Though I must admit we were a bit worried when Preacher Fullbright came to town while Melisue and Black Hawk were here.''

"I shouldn't think that man would have the nerve to show his face after his denunciation of you and James Thomas at the church dedication," Rachael Bright protested. Before she could say more, the air was split by a woman's screams.

"Beth Ann! Beth Ann!" Melisue shrieked over the sound of the snorting horses and groaning wagon. "Get your gun and come quick! They've got Black Hawk down by the sawmill! They're going to hang him!"

Chapter Twenty-two

Beth Ann shoved the baby into Rachael Bright's arms. "Take care of Jason and go find Casey and James Thomas," she ordered as she ran out of the house, a loaded rifle in each hand. "Tell them to come to the clearing down past the sawmill, as fast as they can."

Melisue was already turning her wagon while her sister struggled to hold on to the seat and the guns at the same time. Tears streamed down Melisue's face as she stood and whipped the horses to greater efforts.

"What happened?" Beth Ann managed.

"A bunch of men came up and said there was a law against Indians taking white women. I told them I went of my own free will, but that damnable preacher twisted every word I said. I thought they were going to let us go, but then Fullbright said Black Hawk was a horse thief—and that's a hanging offense. I told them I was the one who took the horse and that we'd brought it back.

"Then one of the men said they should hang us both. Black Hawk jumped out of the wagon and hit him, but there were too many of them for him to fight. He yelled at me to get away, and I grabbed the reins and came after you."

Beth Ann could scarcely believe her ears. She had lived with these people and grown to love them and the ideals for which they stood. And now she was being told that these same people had been stampeded by a fast-talking, vindictive preacher into hanging an innocent man. It was a nightmare! It couldn't be true! But the terror in Melisue's face said more emphatically than any words that it was true, and somehow Beth Ann must find a way to keep these people from hanging Black Hawk.

She clutched the wagon seat and prayed that she could find a way to stop them, and she prayed even harder that James Thomas would come quickly, because as they burst into the clearing she saw that her sister's hysterical account was not exaggerated.

Black Hawk stood next to a horse, his hands tied behind his back. A hangman's noose dangled from a tree limb above his head. The men grabbed the horses as Melisue urged them on in an effort to get closer to Black Hawk. The wagon was still moving when Beth Ann stood up, gun in hand. "Let him go! Black Hawk's no horse thief. I can bear witness to that."

Preacher Fullbright's little eyes glared in malicious contempt. "It's not only a horse he stole," he expounded. "He's taken a good Christian woman and led her into a life of dishonor. He deserves to pay for his sins."

"You pompous fop! You're the one who tried to lead me into sin with your promises of marriage when you already had a wife." Melisue ignored the shock on the faces of the men as she screamed out her accusations.

"I am a man of God!" the preacher thundered as he sensed the change in the demeanor of the crowd. "Are you going to believe me, or a fallen woman?"

The men grumbled and shifted from foot to foot in indecision.

"This is a holy war," Fullbright yelled. "Sin must be wiped from the earth."

The men grabbed the struggling Black Hawk as Melisue jumped from the wagon and threw herself against him, desperation ringing in her voice. "Please don't take him from me! I won't let you take him from me!"

She slipped her arms around him and shoved a knife into his bound hands before the men could pull her away. Kicking and scratching, she fought them as they struggled to take her back to the wagon. "Beth Ann! Do something! Don't let them hang him!" she cried, well aware that as long as all eyes were on her, Black Hawk had a chance to free himself. But even her frantic efforts could hold off the inevitable for only so long.

"My husband and Casey Stubbs will be here in a few minutes," Beth Ann shouted. "They'll tell you that you're wrong, no matter what that weasel preacher says." She saw some of the men dump Melisue into the wagon while the rest hoisted Black Hawk onto a horse and dropped the noose over his head. "Stop this at once!" But they didn't stop, and desperation crept into her voice. She looked to Melisue for help and saw her sister struggling to free herself from the tangled yards of material from her skirts which rendered her helpless. There was no time to wait for Melisue to free herself. No time to wait for James Thomas. She put the gun against her shoulder and shouted above the noise of the crowd. "Stop! I'll shoot the next man that moves."

"Go ahead! Shoot!" Preacher Fullbright challenged. "When that gun fires, the horse will bolt and the Indian will die."

"And you'll die with him, because man of God or devil incarnate, this gun is aimed at you." Despite her brave words, Beth Ann knew she dared not fire the gun. But the men didn't know. They fell silent. Even the wind held its breath.

Before anyone dared move, Melisue managed to free herself enough to grab the second rifle from the seat of the wagon. For the first time in her life she was faced with a situation in which coyness and beauty would not get her what she wanted. There was no time to reason with these people and make them see things her way. There was no time to use her womanly wiles to change the mood of the crowd. She must act—or lose Black Hawk forever.

She drew a deep breath and cocked the rifle.

The horse shied nervously, but Black Hawk made no move.

Two women armed with guns were capable of doing a great deal of damage if they fired into the closely packed men. Especially two women who watched them with eyes as blue and hard as steel.

"Go ahead! Fire your weapon!" the preacher taunted.

Melisue ignored his words. Her eyes met those of her sister, who stood gallantly beside her, and she knew a moment of communion never shared before. Then Melisue's voice rang out, clear and strong.

"I would leave Black Hawk if I believed it would save his life. I would leave him if I didn't love him. There are a million reasons why I might leave him, but before God, I'll not let you take him from me."

She gripped the gun tightly against her shoulder. "I love you, Black Hawk." The words came through gritted teeth as she closed one eye and took aim.

Her words carried to the rise above the mill where James Thomas and Casey Stubbs stared in shock at the two women, guns against their shoulders, holding the men at bay.

Beth Ann's gun was pointed at the preacher, but Melisue aimed directly at Black Hawk.

"Holy Mother of God, she's gonna blow Black Hawk's head off!" Casey put heels to his horse and careened down the embankment as the sky exploded with the sound of a single gunshot.

They pulled to a halt, guns drawn, as a horse galloped off through the dust and smoke.

Casey closed his eyes, afraid to look. "Now you've done it!" He opened his eyes, thoroughly expecting the worst. To his amazement, a severed rope dangled uselessly from the tree.

"The Indian got away!" the preacher screamed. "Go after him!"

"Move and die!" Melisue grabbed the gun from her sister's hands. The men stopped in their tracks, still awed by Melisue's marksmanship. Casey and James Thomas walked through the crowd, collecting the weapons.

"Why did you take my gun?" Beth Ann whispered to her sister. "I can shoot, too."

"But you might not want to shoot the preacher," Melisue observed, "and it wouldn't bother me a bit."

"Where'd you learn to fire a gun like that?" Casey asked as he jerked the rope from the tree and came toward them, fingering the severed end.

"Well, you can't expect us to make love all the time," Melisue said bluntly. Casey's face reddened at the audacity of her answer. "Black Hawk taught me lots of things," Melisue added.

"I'll just bet he has." There was a twinkle of admiration in Casey's eyes. He turned to the crowd of men. Most of them were newcomers to the territory, rounded up by the preacher for his private vendetta against Melisue and the man she loved.

James Thomas stepped forward. "You men are new to the territory and don't know how things work. If you want to live here, you're going to have to learn. The first thing is that we don't dig into our neighbor's lives, their business, or their past. The second thing is that Fullbright is an immoral man who tried to seduce my sister-in-law and tarnish the reputation of my family.''

"But he said the Indian was a horse thief," a man said, defending himself.

"The horse is mine," Casey shouted, "and what I do with it is nobody's damn business."

"You mean the preacher lied?" the man asked.

"The preacher's very good at lying," Melisue affirmed, her eyes searching the horizon.

"Preachers ain't supposed to lie." The man shook his head. "Ought to tar and feather a preacher who lies."

"Do what you like, but get him out of Montgomery," James Thomas told them.

His words were lost on Melisue, for she saw Black Hawk riding toward them through the trees. Without a backward glance, she ran to him, and he pulled her onto the horse and into his arms.

"Did you hear?" she asked between kisses. "They're going to tar and feather the preacher."

"I heard you," he said, drawing her closer. "And I saw you, and I'm glad you're my woman."

"Oh, Black Hawk!" Melisue ran her hands over his face. "I was so afraid I was going to miss the rope, or hit you. Weren't you scared to death?"

"Not after I heard you say you love me."

Black Hawk said the words for Melisue's ears alone, but Casey overheard. "A couple of hours ago I'd have said being loved by Melisue was more frightening than either of your other options, but after the way she stood up for you I'm thinkin' I might have been a bit hasty in my judgment." He reached up and helped her from the horse as Black Hawk dismounted.

"I want to be sure and return this horse to its proper owner," Black Hawk said as he glanced over the crowd for some indication of ownership. His eyes met those of the minister.

Preacher Fullbright took one look at Black Hawk's hate-filled face and bolted up the hill, but the men followed, howling in hot pursuit. The clearing emptied quickly, although several men hung back to tell Black Hawk they were sorry for their part in the fiasco.

"Lot of good that would have done if they'd hung you," Melisue pointed out.

"You wouldn't have let them do that," Black Hawk assured her before turning to the others. "She slipped a knife into my hands and then shot through the hangman's rope. What a woman!" His eyes met Beth Ann's. "I want to thank you, too, Beth Ann. You stood up to the whole crowd to defend me. I didn't think you had much reason to like me all that well."

"Melisue loves you the same way I love James Thomas, and that's all the reason I needed."

Beth Ann snuggled into her husband's arms as Rachael Bright hurried toward them. "They're talking about tar and feathers for Preacher Fullbright up in town," she told them as she handed little Jason to his father.

Knowing Rachael Bright's outspoken opposition to any kind of violence, Casey asked, "What did you tell them?"

Rachael Bright shrugged. "I didn't tell them anything. I just gave them a pillow and came down here."

Everyone laughed as Black Hawk helped Melisue into their wagon.

"I still can't believe Melisue is such a good shot," Casey reiterated. "She hit that rope above Black Hawk's head like she'd been doin' it all her life. I thought sure she was going to blow his head clean off."

Black Hawk raised his eyebrow and lifted the singed hair on the top of his head. "She's still got some learning to do," he said, grinning.

"Well, take me home and teach me." Melisue leaned against him as he clucked to the horses and the wagon drew away. "Besides, that old gun just about broke my shoulder. I'm going to be all black-and-blue. You're just going to have to help me with everything, because I know I won't be able to move."

James Thomas started up the hill, his arm around his wife's shoulders. It was amazing how, for all her newly acquired achievements, Melisue never changed. She still wanted to be waited on and pampered while she sat back and tried to get people to do things her way.

"It's getting late," Beth Ann said. "We should have asked them to stay the night."

"I think they'd rather be alone," James Thomas replied.

"Are you sure they'll be all right?"

"I'm sure." He slipped his arms around her. "Like us, Black Hawk and Melisue will be fine as long as they have each other."

Beth Ann couldn't hide her doubts. "Melisue has always wanted so much from life," she said, resting her head against his shoulder, "and Black Hawk can give her so little in the way of luxuries."

"And what luxuries do *you* want from life," he asked gently.

"You, always you, only you . . . forever."

"So it is with me," he assured her, "and with Casey and Rachael Bright and with all those who love. If Melisue has found that kind of happiness with Black Hawk, she has everything she's been searching for. Just as I've found all I want in life with you." He repeated her words in a prayer of thanksgiving. "You, always you, only you . . . forever."

* * * * *

Harlequin® *Historical*

WARRIOR SERIES

The WARRIOR SERIES from author
Margaret Moore

It began with A WARRIOR'S HEART (HH #118, March 1992)—the
unforgettable story of Emryss Delanyea, a wounded Welsh
nobleman who returns from the crusades with all thoughts of
love put aside forever . . . until he meets the Lady Roanna.

Now, in A WARRIOR'S QUEST (HH #175, June 1993), healer
Fritha Kendrick teaches mercenary Urien Fitzroy to live by his
heart rather than his sword.

And, coming in early 1994, look for A WARRIOR'S PRIDE, the
third title of this medieval trilogy.

T E X A S

TEXAS HEART—A young woman is forced to journey west in search of her missing father.

TEXAS HEALER—A doctor returns home to rediscover a ghost from his past, the daughter of a Comanche chief.

And now, TEXAS HERO—A gunfighter teaches the local schoolteacher that not every fight can be won with a gun. **(HH #180, available in July.)**

Follow the lives of Jessie Conway and her brothers in this series from popular Harlequin Historical author Ruth Langan.

Relive the romance...
Harlequin and Silhouette are proud to present

by Request

A program of collections of three complete novels by the most requested authors with the most requested themes. Be sure to look for one volume each month with three complete novels by top name authors.

In June: **NINE MONTHS** Penny Jordan
                              Stella Cameron
                              Janice Kaiser

Three women pregnant and alone. But a lot can happen in nine months!

In July: **DADDY'S HOME**   Kristin James
                              Naomi Horton
                              Mary Lynn Baxter

Daddy's Home... and his presence is long overdue!

In August: **FORGOTTEN PAST**   Barbara Kaye
                              Pamela Browning
                              Nancy Martin

Do you dare to create a future if you've forgotten the past?

Available at your favorite retail outlet.

Harlequin is proud to present our best authors and their best books. Always the best for your reading pleasure!

Throughout 1993, Harlequin will bring you exciting books by some of the top names in contemporary romance!

In July
look for
The Ties That Bind by

JAYNE ANN KRENTZ

Shannon wanted him seven days a week....

Dark, compelling, mysterious Garth Sheridan was no mere boy next door—even if he did rent the cottage beside Shannon Raine's.

She was intrigued by the hard-nosed exec, but for Shannon it was all or nothing. Either break the undeniable bonds between them . . . or tear down the barriers surrounding Garth and discover the truth.

Don't miss **THE TIES THAT BIND** ...
wherever Harlequin books are sold.

THREE UNFORGETTABLE HEROINES
THREE AWARD-WINNING AUTHORS

Untamed

MAVERICK HEARTS

A unique collection of historical short stories that capture the spirit of America's last frontier.

HEATHER GRAHAM POZZESSERE—over 10 million copies of her books in print worldwide
Lonesome Rider—The story of an Eastern widow and the renegade half-breed who becomes her protector.

PATRICIA POTTER—an author whose books are consistently Waldenbooks bestsellers
Against the Wind—Two people, battered by heartache, prove that love can heal all.

JOAN JOHNSTON—award-winning Western historical author with 17 books to her credit
One Simple Wish—A woman with a past discovers that dreams really do come true.

Join us for an exciting journey West with
UNTAMED
Available in July, wherever Harlequin books are sold.

MAV93